KISS HER KILL HER

Lisa Dewar

iUniverse, Inc.
New York   Bloomington

Kiss Her, Kill Her

Copyright © 2010 Lisa Dewar

This is a work of fiction. All of the characters, names, incidents, organizations, and dialogue in this novel are either the products of the author's imagination or are used fictitiously.

iUniverse books may be ordered through booksellers or by contacting:

iUniverse
1663 Liberty Drive
Bloomington, IN 47403
www.iuniverse.com
1-800-Authors (1-800-288-4677)

Because of the dynamic nature of the Internet, any Web addresses or links contained in this book may have changed since publication and may no longer be valid. The views expressed in this work are solely those of the author and do not necessarily reflect the views of the publisher, and the publisher hereby disclaims any responsibility for them.

ISBN: 978-1-4502-5998-9 (pbk)
ISBN: 978-1-4502-5999-6 (cloth)
ISBN: 978-1-4502-6000-8 (ebk)

Library of Congress Control Number: 2010914030

Printed in the United States of America

iUniverse rev. date: 9/14/2010

For Wayne …
Thank you for believing

Before you hand me over
Before you read my sentence
I'd like to say a few words
Here in my own defense …
Some people struggle daily
They struggle with their conscience
Till the end
I have no guilt to haunt me
I feel no wrong intent

(Gowan, "A Criminal Mind")

PROLOGUE
July 13, 11:10 PM

TARRYN STOOD OVER THE WOMAN, TRYING HIS BEST
to keep focused. She was gagged, bound to a chair, and was struggling
against the restraints. Knowing that she was secured, he finally had a
moment to relax.

It had become far too difficult after the day's events to know what
to do next. He knew that he *had* to kill her. Not only was it in his
blood, but the entire day had also been spent working toward this
moment. He *wanted* to kill her. By taking her life, she would forever
be special—not only in his eyes and his mother's eyes, but also in the
eyes of the world.

He had learned so much about her over the past fifteen hours. She
felt like ... a part of his mind wanted to say that she had become a
friend, or perhaps a better term was a kindred spirit. Her life had been
hard, just like his own. After all that she had told him, he was amazed
that she was still walking the earth.

The monstrous part of his brain screamed that he owed it to her to
put an end to her misery. It was what she wanted—what she needed. He
knew that he had to do it. But something was holding him back.

Kiss her or kill her? His mind and body were tired—more tired than
they had ever been. He was desperate for guidance. He tilted his head
upward and stared at the stippled finish on the ceiling. When he moved
his head back toward his victim, the obvious path was crystal clear.

STEP 1–SELECTION
July 13, 7:35 AM

ONE

THE EARLY HEAT OF THE JULY MORNING WAS MAKING Tarryn Cooper Love lethargic. Wanting to get through the final part of his midnight to 8:00 am shift doing as little as possible, he pulled his car over into a strip mall parking lot and reclined his seat. Just a quick catnap would do the trick. The warmth of the sun through his window heated his leather seat and soothed his mind. As he relaxed his limbs and let his heavy eyelids fall, he reminisced about his last kill.

She had been an average girl—nothing spectacular in the looks department. Tarryn remembered the details of her curvaceous body, her crooked smile, her soulful laugh, and her throaty voice. She would never be on the pages of a magazine, and most men would probably pass her by for the bleach blonde with the melon-sized boobs at the other end of the bar, but she had something special. It was the "it" factor that he so often found himself drawn to, an unexplainable element that made her irresistible to him. He tried to wrap his mind around why he was attracted to certain women. Maybe it was the strength in them, the spark of *alive* that he wanted to extinguish.

Tarryn remembered the first time that he had met the curvy redhead. Fond memories of that day swirled playfully in his brain. He had picked her up just a few blocks from where he sat now. Tarryn mentally wandered through the day with a lazy gait. She called herself Crimson and told him that she wanted to be a dancer someday. She was coming out of a club at four o'clock in the morning, exhausted from a long night watering her customers down with more than their fair share of libations. She complained about the lecherous patrons who took the liberty of grabbing more than just their drink. Tarryn, of course, was sympathetic and a good listener, adding in appropriate comments to make her feel at ease.

She was all smiles, wiggles, and giggles, as he flirted with her through the rearview mirror. She was a simple kind of girl whose biggest challenge in life, pre–New York City, had been putting on warm bowling shoes and whose "Pappy" probably reminded her on a regular basis that if brains were dynamite, she wouldn't be able to blow her nose. Still, despite her mental shortcomings, she was eye-catching and available for the taking.

It didn't take long for him to realize that she wanted him. He wanted her too—though not in the same way. He dropped her off at her apartment. She had invited him in with the promise of good things to come. That choice had sealed her fate. His back tingled as he remembered the details of her final moments—the initial grin on her face in anticipation of a passionate embrace and then the terror washing over her when she realized she was going to die. It was a milestone kill, number thirty-six. It had been a thrill a second, and he had enjoyed the extreme sense of accomplishment as the light in her eyes had faded to black.

It seemed like an eternity since he had fed the hunger that was in him. It was already three months since he had met the wannabe dancer. The urge was there, but he knew that his success was contingent on controlling his compulsions. His next kill would officially secure him as *the* master of his craft. He didn't want to rush into it and make mistakes.

Tarryn was rolling the thoughts around in his mind, like a sweet, silky piece of chocolate on his tongue. Almost every moment was consumed with malicious thoughts nowadays. The next victim was more than just a kill—it was a success, an accomplishment that he had worked his whole life to achieve. He knew that there was certainly a number thirty-seven who would present herself when the time was right.

The cab radio interrupted his daydreams with a jolt.

"Thirteen-seventy-five?"

Tarryn, dragged back to reality, grabbed the radio, "Yep."

"Got a trip for you," the dispatcher replied. "One-seven-nine Terrace Grove. Name is Carmen."

"Got it. On my way." All of the creamy chocolate brain waves melted away.

Terrace Grove sat right in the center of the upscale neighborhood of Bellview Heights on the outskirts of New York City. It housed the rich, the famous, the corporate giants, and the Jewish lawyers; and it was funded mostly by old wealth. As the ancient money moguls were dying from health issues that even their substantial coffers could no longer fix, their massive estate homes were being sold off to the young up-and-comers. It was a neighborhood of large, established sugar maple trees that made a lush green canopy over the streets where the hired help kept the gardens free of weeds and the lawns were manicured so perfectly that most golf courses would be jealous.

Terrace Grove was pristine and not the kind of place where you typically saw a Yellow Cab driving around. Tarryn wasn't intimidated in the least by the wealth and power—he had killed the likes of them in the past—but he was acutely aware of the curious and somewhat suspicious glances of the neighbors as he passed through the monolithic stone archway belonging to his fare.

The driveway went back about a hundred yards and was flanked by colorful flower beds and tall, protective trees. The front façade of the house was huge, and the side walls seemed to go on forever. Tarryn estimated it to be at least ten thousand square feet. The woman standing at the front door was dwarfed by the impressive oak doors that looked too large to open. Tarryn guessed her to be in her midthirties based on her trendy pair of tight designer jeans, black stiletto heels, and a stylish retro T-shirt. Her face was flawless, with very little makeup, and her long auburn hair was tied in a thick ponytail. Tarryn guessed that she was either a second wife or a spoiled child of whoever owned the massive estate property. She certainly didn't look like a money mogul. She was far too pretty and young.

"Carmen?" he asked as she opened the back passenger door.

"Yes," she replied, leaning into the backseat. "I need to go to the animal shelter in Spruce Hill." She placed a midsized animal carrier into the cab and climbed in next to it.

"Hold on. I don't want any animals in my car. What are you doing?"

"He's in a carrier, and your dispatcher told me it would be all right. Just drive, okay? I don't have much time." The woman's eyes darted back and forth between her taxi driver and the house.

Tarryn was steaming. He was very particular about the inside of his car. At no point did he take on fares that included people *and* their dogs. The hair was a bitch to get out of the seats, and it could cost him a fare if the next customer had allergies. After fifteen years of driving for Yellow Cabs, Harold, the shit-ass dispatcher, knew all about his rules. He even refused to take guide dogs. *Fuck the human rights laws.* This was not going to work at all.

"Thirteen-seventy-five," Tarryn barked into his handset.

"Thirteen-seventy-five, go ahead," the voice came over the car radio.

"I'm at Terrace Grove, and this woman has a dog in my car."

"Actually, it's a cat," Carmen said quickly, "and he's in a carrier."

Tarryn shot an annoyed glance her way. "Correction, it's a cat. Either way, I don't take animals in my cab. You need to get another driver here," he spat the words into the microphone.

"Not an option. Sorry. I don't have anyone else close by," Harold, the shit-ass, replied.

"Look, I have money, and I will pay to get your car detailed after you drop me off. Just hurry. Please," Carmen said, waving a wad of green bills toward the front of the car.

Tarryn got a good look at her as he turned toward the back of the cab and thought better of his first reaction. His back had begun to itch, a sure sign that she was worthy of his special attention. Anytime that he heard a great woman singer, the hair on his neck stood up, and every time that he found a potential playmate, the scars on his back would itch. He didn't consciously will it to happen; it was merely his body, announcing that it was time to add on to his laundry list of victims. He glanced in the mirror at her worried face. She was very pretty, young enough that she got him excited sexually, and she had money. Perhaps this could be an opportunity instead of a liability.

The next kill was meant to be special as it marked a major milestone in his life. He wanted to make sure that the victim was fitting of the honor. She was a strong possibility, and his back had never steered him wrong in the past.

"Okay, I'll take her, but don't pull this again, Harold. We're going to Spruce Hill."

TWO

TARRYN LOVE COULD WALK AMONGST THE GREATEST of men, the smallest of men and feel comfortable with both. Perhaps it was his clean-cut appearance, or the fact that he was the spitting image of a young George Clooney. Maybe it was that he appeared well educated, or that he also had experience with people on the street. It probably wasn't one thing but a combination of things. Either way, he was always welcome in any social circle; a fact that he was more than willing to exploit.

He had been told that people perceived him as personable, and he was able to carry on titillating conversations with everyone who entered his cab, even the drunks—and there were more than a few of them. He read the newspapers each and every day from cover to cover to ensure that he was never short on topics of conversation. And his grooming habits were impeccable—perfectly ironed clothes, perfectly tousled hair, perfectly manicured nails, and a perfectly white smile.

He was proud of the fact that the persona he had perfected over the years had allowed him some freedoms that the typical selective killer could not have. He could pick his victims from anyone—some had been the very rich, some were very poor, and others were just your run-of-the-mill, middle-class schlumps. He could dazzle them with his wit, get their guard down with his charm, and ultimately lure them anywhere he wanted. After all, doesn't everyone expect that a killer would have some telltale sign of evil plastered on his face? No one was looking for a well-bred white guy who could pass for a movie star.

He had a few idiosyncrasies, but they were well hidden. One such oddity was his preference for the term "selective killer" over the title of "serial killer," as the latter always reminded him of the smiling pirate on the Captain Crunch box. That fact aside, to a casual observer he was everyone and no one.

It had become so simple to feed his hunger that he knew he would never be caught—although sometimes he wished that he would be. How else would anyone know of his extensive list of victims? He compared himself to the meathead that works out constantly to get a buff body and who can only show it to his wife. Isn't the accomplishment worth sharing with the rest of the world? He wasn't ready for retirement yet, nor was he ready to turn himself in to the police to get the recognition he so rightly deserved. For the time being, he was lounging in the knowledge that he was at the top of his game and was soon to be the most successful selective killer in the US—at least in his mother's eyes. And that was all that really mattered.

While he hadn't taken a life in months, the hunger had been building over the past two weeks. It was time to add to his resume again, but until now no one had jumped out as the perfect playmate. He looked in the mirror again. Carmen seemed like a very strong possibility. He had long ago stopped thinking of the victims as human beings. They were simply a means to an end, a chance to prove himself worthy. It was all consuming some days, occupying every free moment. Today the need felt like a screaming animal wanting to be released from its cage. It wouldn't be held back for much longer, and Tarryn knew he needed to nourish the primal part of himself soon.

He was, however, becoming more particular in his old age. In his late teens he had cared less about the victim and more about the act of killing. His tastes leaned more toward younger girls and a couple of teenage boys. At that time in his life, he was still perfecting his craft—learning the ropes, so to speak. The young ones put up less of a fight, especially when plied with booze and blow.

In his twenties, his hunger was focused on older women. Some would say that he was choosing older women to compensate for issues that he had in childhood. That couldn't have been further from the truth. It was just a time in his career where maturity and confidence were the most attractive traits in a victim.

Now in his midthirties, he was having a midlife crisis of sorts and wanted only pretty women with natural beauty. He was looking for the type of woman that he wanted to have sex with—although carnal acts were never part of his MO. It was all about the cat-and-mouse chase of gaining their trust and then savoring the ultimate betrayal—murder. In that moment the sun was brighter, the sky was bluer, and he was all powerful.

Tarryn glanced in his rearview mirror and surveyed the woman in the backseat. She was pretty enough, but her chest was a bit large for her frame. He was disappointed that it was becoming all too common for girls to go to the plastic surgeon as soon as possible so they could make themselves more in tune with movie star perfection. He preferred a more natural physique, but Carmen seemed to have the "it" factor that he always looked for. There was an energy about her that was interesting. His back was tingling with anticipation. He would evaluate the situation on the forty-five-minute drive to the Spruce Hill Animal Shelter.

As Tarryn maneuvered the cab back down the driveway, the howling began in the backseat. "What's wrong with your cat?"

"He doesn't like car rides. He'll settle down once we get on the freeway," Carmen snapped.

Tarryn watched as she cooed gently into the cage, poking her fingers through the front gate of the carrier to give the cat some comfort. His name was Sabre, based on the countless times that she said his name in the first five minutes of the drive. The howling continued even after the taxi entered the already blocked freeway. With car horns blaring and sirens wailing, Tarryn was reevaluating his thoughts on Carmen's fate. She would be covered in cat hair after this drive, and he was not an animal lover in the least. He found them to be filthy, vile creatures that were too needy to be of any real value. His mantra, taught to him by his mother, had been the same for many years—"I will only befriend those that can return my friendship equally." Consequently, a pet, which required feeding, grooming, and deposited its hair all over the house, did not fit the criteria. Neither had most people, women included, and Tarryn had purposely spent the majority of his life alone. Luckily, with his mother by his side, he had never felt the pangs of loneliness.

"Why are you taking him to the animal shelter? Is he sick?" Tarryn asked over top of the incessant noise.

"Why are you asking so many questions?"

"Are you British? Answering a question with a question? I'm just trying to make conversation to drown out Sabre. Sorry." He glanced in the mirror as he spoke. She didn't catch his gaze, her focus strictly on the cat.

"He's not sick. You don't have to worry about catching anything."

Tarryn wondered if he should push the subject further and decided against it. He needed to get to know the woman in the back of his car without the attitude if he was going to execute step two in the plan.

"Nice house you have. Bellview Heights is a beautiful area."

"It's my husband's house." Her faced muscles tensed as she said the word "husband."

Ahhh … Tarryn was excited. There was a pretty good chance that she was the second wife, and she was pissed at the husband. If he wanted her for his trophy, he could have her. He giggled to himself; she could be a trophy wife twice over. The conversation was not flowing as it typically did, but he liked a challenge. It made the final act in the play even more delicious.

Sabre had started to settle. The howling had moved from constant to intermittent, with the only ear-splitting sounds coming when Carmen stopped cooing and petting.

"Look, my name is Tarryn, and I'm sorry about earlier—you know, getting upset about the cat. It's just that I've had people turn me down in the past if they see any animal hair on the seats. Executive types can't go to meetings with hair on their thousand-dollar suits. And then there are allergies. It's a competitive world out there. I can't afford to lose fares. If it makes you feel any better, I have three cats myself. I don't know what I would do without them."

Carmen softened a little, her voice losing some of the razor-sharp edge, "Understood. You're just trying to make a living. Not to be rude, but I don't feel much like talking. Can we just forgo the chitchat?"

"No problem." He couldn't put his finger on it, but there was something about the woman that made him nervous. She had the "it" factor, but something else was smoldering underneath—there was something dark and dangerous about her … and yet something soft and yielding. He mulled it over, glancing at the side of her face whenever he could safely take his eyes from the traffic. She was definitely beautiful. Maybe she wasn't meant to be a victim but instead a lustful indulgence. He wished that his mother was with him so that he could ask; she would know what to do. Unfortunately that particular scenario was not possible, due to his lack of control so many years ago. *Kiss her, kill her, kiss her, kill her* —the options were endless.

The remainder of the drive was spent in relative silence, with the odd cry of despair coming from the orange mound of fur in the backseat. Carmen whispered softly almost the entire way, telling her feline companion that everything was going to be okay.

THREE

TARRYN PULLED UP IN FRONT OF THE ANIMAL SHELTER after what felt like the longest fifteen-mile drive of his life. Rush-hour traffic was brutal at the best of times in New York, and today was no exception. He had consigned himself to the fact that the woman in the back of his car was not going to fulfill his needs. Even in the forty-five minutes that they had been in contact, he knew very little about her, and she had barely glanced at him the entire ride. From experience, he knew that it was hard to gain someone's trust when you couldn't look them in the eye.

Tarryn desperately wanted to move to step two, but Carmen was proving to be a challenge in more ways than one. He knew there would be other opportunities with other people, but when you get the idea in your head that you are going to have a steak dinner, the cravings start to take over. He rubbed his hands over the small of his back and allowed the memories of prior kills to calm his nerves. He briefly heard his mother's voice in his head, "Pretty one. She could be thirty-seven."

"Pull up to the Incoming Animals door and wait outside."

Tarryn followed the signs to the side of the grey cinder-block building as instructed. He smiled at two women who walked blindly in front of his car, but they seemed to have their minds on other things and ignored his friendly gesture. In his mind's eye, he imagined slicing open their ungrateful throats; it made him feel better.

"I'll be back in about twenty minutes." Carmen didn't wait for an answer as she grabbed the cat carrier and walked quickly to the shelter.

Tarryn thought that he picked up a familiar vibe from her in that moment. She was commanding and strong. His mother had been commanding as well; and for some reason, his mother had liked to pet cats. Not own them, just pet them. She said it was soothing to the soul. He never understood that particular trait of her personality, but he adored her nonetheless.

He watched as Carmen disappeared into the depths of the shelter and debated which art form his thirty-seventh kill should take. He imagined holding Carmen's ponytail in his hands, tilting her face back for a kiss, and then cutting her throat. Maybe it would it be better if he strapped her down and used his specially designed electrical devices to fry her from the inside out. Or … strangulation with razor wire … beating her brains in with a hammer … gutting her with a fishing knife. More importantly—what would his mother want for the all-important moment?

He didn't like to think about his mother very often. The pain of losing her was almost too much to bear, even after so many years. He remembered the story she told of how she chose his name. It always seemed so magical and special when the words left her lips. In the two dozen or so times that she had told him the story, the scene was always the same—Tarryn curled up in her lap, with her warm arms wrapped around him.

It was 1970 and his mother was a young girl full of hope, living in Charlotte, North Carolina. She wanted to be a star but not in the movies or on television. She wanted to be a "shining, blinding, gleaming light on Broadway." She could sing a little, dance a little, and act a little—in her mind, she was the triple threat that everyone wanted to be. She gained some bit parts in local theater and decided to move to the Big Apple to finally show the world her many talents. It had been a hard road being an unknown in the big city, but on an audition, she had met a man that would be her saving grace.

She said that the man, a struggling actor himself, had kind eyes and a warm apartment. He gave her a place to stay until she got on her feet. He supported her emotional and physical needs and told her she was beautiful and talented—words that she had always longed to hear. He also showed her the world of drugs. They used almost every day. She said that they told themselves it was just to take the edge off the stress of looking for work. In time, it became all consuming, as drugs tend to do. Things changed once she got pregnant. Tarryn's father asked her to leave once the baby bump starting pushing at the waistline of her jeans. She said that despite the fact that she was preggers and unemployed, she had been excited. Even in the throes of her addictions, she had always dreamt of a child of her own. It was a chance for a new beginning and a welcome turn in the road.

Tarryn remembered the story fondly, even though she was admitting to excessive drug use—something she insisted that he avoid at all costs. When he was a child she never sugarcoated anything about her past—the drugs, the men, the failure to reach her lofty goals of Broadway stardom, or her interest in serial killers. From moment one in his memory, Tarryn felt grown-up and special. She had treated him like an adult, and he was proud that she thought so highly of him that she could be honest.

His mother had said that wanting to stand on her own two feet, she quit the drugs and got a real job. It wasn't much, but she was determined to make it work for her and her new baby. She started waitressing in a local coffee shop. She said the tips were good, and she got free meals during each shift. Things were apparently looking up.

In her final trimester, his mother was on a bus going home from the café where she worked and saw a public transit bench with an ad for a realtor named Tarryn. She said that at the precise moment she saw the bus bench, her water broke. It didn't matter if her child was a boy or a girl, Tarryn was going to be its name—Tarryn Cooper Love. She said it was a sign from above that he was destined for great things in his life.

Tarryn never knew his father's name nor did he care to ask. He supposed that most people would want to know their natural father, but he had decided as a young child, his mother was more than enough parent to make up for a missing man in his life. She was his everything and more. The total and unconditional love that he felt from her seemed only fitting of their surname. She had been a wonderful woman who showed him the ways of the world, and she was an endless source of knowledge on how to kill.

What method would she prefer for this victim? Poisoning?

Dismemberment? Drowning? His back was burning like it was on fire.

The warm thoughts of torturous murder and his mother were interrupted as the back door of the cab opened up, and Carmen slumped in the rear seat, minus the cat carrier. She looked so different from the woman that had left his car twenty minutes earlier. Her face was ashen and streaked with tears. Her makeup, what little she had on, was a dark puddle underneath her puffy eyes.

"Drive. Please just drive," she sobbed.

"Back home?" Tarryn was taken aback by the dramatic change in her personality. For the first time in recent memory, he was flustered.

"No. Just drive around, I don't care where."

Tarryn pulled the cab out of the parking lot and hit the road. Not sure of his destination, he kept to the side streets to avoid going down the freeway in a direction that would further upset the woman in the back.

"Is the cat okay?" he probed.

"He's going to have a new home. He'll be fine." Her voice cracked with sentiment.

Tarryn was shocked, not used to seeing such raw emotion. The fleeting contact that he had with women's feelings in the past fell neatly into two categories—lust and passion in those times when he was seducing them and unbridled fear in the moment before he took their lives. He prided himself on his even-keeled persona even when he was in the act of killing, but he wasn't prepared for the gurgling pile of flesh in his backseat. He stole the odd glance in his mirror, watching with curiosity as the strong feminine presence he picked up a little over an hour ago was reduced to a blubbering child. He was curious—why would she give up the cat to the shelter when she obviously cared very deeply for him? It wasn't adding up.

Having given himself the equivalent of a throbbing, mental hard-on while he had been waiting in the parking lot, he tried to picture her as she was when he picked her up. The challenge of gaining her trust was becoming a huge mountain of a task, and he was wondering if it was worth the effort. He fast-forwarded his brain to the moment that he would take her life, imagining the lustful power. He felt the welts on his back against the warm leather of his seat, and the thrill of anticipation coursed through his veins. He was willing to give it one more try.

"Are you all right? Can I do anything to help?" He passed a roll of paper towel over his shoulder, kept on hand to clean up any messes left behind by the night crawlers.

"I'm not okay, and you can't do anything," she screamed in between sobs. "Just keep driving."

Tarryn did as he was told for the next ten minutes, occasionally glancing in his mirror to see the state of affairs in the backseat. Carmen's retching sobs were becoming quieter as the time went on.

"I don't mean to pry, but why would you surrender your cat that you love so much? I don't understand. Are you sick? You look fine to me."

"Yes, I'm sick. Sick in the head for living my life like I have. Sick in the heart for everything I have done, and if you want to know the truth, he's better off without me. Everyone is." Carmen continued her angry rant with the tears still streaming down her face, "Why do you ask so many questions? What do you care? You'll get paid. In fact, here …" She threw a wad of cash into the front of the cab. "I don't want this fucking burden anymore."

Stunned by the outburst, Tarryn looked at the front passenger seat strewn with hundreds and fifties. *What the fuck? What just happened?* He mulled over the details of the past hour in his head and realized that Carmen wasn't just a woman in crisis over her cat; she was a woman about to take her own life. It was the only explanation that came close to making sense. The knowledge was confusing to him and electrifying all at once. She wanted to die. If he killed her, he would be doing her a favor. But why did she want to commit suicide? And why did *he* care about her motivation? He didn't need to gain her trust; he could just take her life. It was an interesting thought, but the betrayal of trust was the thrill behind everything that he did. It was all too much—sensory overload. His ego was talking loud and clear, *You're that good. You can bring her back from the brink and then kill her. Bundy didn't have that on his resume.*

Knowing that he wouldn't be able to savor the final act if she didn't trust him and want to live, he decided quickly on his next move. He thought of it as a precursory task to move him toward step two. Tarryn pulled off to the side of the road, gathered the mess of bills off the front

16

seat, and handed them back to his passenger. "Look, I don't know you, but it sounds to me like you could use a drink … or two. Wipe your eyes, and I'll take you to a bar I know. It's a little early for the more reputable joints, but this place serves beer in coffee cups until the legal drinking day starts. It's quiet and dark. No one will know that you've been crying, and you can collect your thoughts. You just went through a traumatic thing back there."

Carmen finally looked up at his reflection in the rearview mirror as she wiped the tendrils of mascara from her cheeks. He watched as she evaluated every corner of his image. He tried his best to look friendly and honest, his eyes emitting kindness and truth. He wanted to tell her that it wouldn't matter in a few hours anyway, the world would be gone, the pain would be gone, and the memories of her life would be gone. Tarryn knew that those words were best kept inside for the time being. He watched as Carmen sniffled and nodded at the worried face in the mirror.

After a quick call to dispatch to say that he had completed his trip to the animal shelter and was signing off for the day, they were on their way to a part of the city that Carmen had always been told to avoid.

FOUR

THE BAR, SAM'S SUDS, WAS EXACTLY AS TARRYN HAD promised—small, out of the way, and dark. It was located in a run-down strip mall on the outskirts of the Bronx. As they drove into the predominantly nonwhite section of the city, Tarryn wondered if the woman in the backseat was going to start getting nervous. She didn't look like the kind of girl who would be comfortable rubbing elbows with a rough-and-tumble crowd. As they pulled into the parking lot, he glanced into the mirror but didn't see any signs of distress that weren't cat related.

The adjoining businesses included a low-end liquor store with a flashing neon "Open" sign; a convenience store whose facade suggested that patrons would be best served to check the expiry date on the milk; and a Chinese food restaurant whose windows were so dirty that MSG and salmonella were sure to be present in every dish. It was the kind of place that was flanked by cars that, at best, were worth hundreds of dollars and whose main clientele consisted of people who were either out of work or trying to get themselves out of working. Tarryn didn't feel comfortable coming here after two in the afternoon as the patrons morphed into a much more unsavory bunch, but in the morning, it was the perfect place to get a beer.

He chose the location because of its many merits—it was out of the way, the area didn't have surveillance cameras, and if you paid with cash, no one cared who you were or what type of beverage was in your coffee cup. He pulled the cab up in front of the bar, watching for a reaction from his female passenger. She opened the car door and stepped over a broken bottle without a word or a sideways glance. It was the best that he could hope for under the circumstances.

Sam's was not the kind of place that women like Carmen were typically seen. She looked out of place in her designer clothes. Tarryn wondered how she would react to the smell of stale beer that had soaked into the ancient hardwood floors and the faint odor of the great unwashed. On the odd occasion that he had visited in the past, he thought that a more suitable name for the business would have been "Stinky's" to better depict the decor and the customers. Tarryn surveyed the small pub as they walked in the doorway. Only one other table was occupied. The man in his mid to late fifties was dressed in clothing that was just a step or two up from rags. With several days of growth on his face and unfocused, bloodshot eyes, Tarryn thought that was probably homeless or more likely a man just starting a long shift at the tavern to ward off the hangover demons from the night before. He wasn't going to be an issue.

Tarryn led Carmen to a booth in the back of the room. The leather on the seats was worn thin, and the chunky wooden slab of a table needed wiping. With a quick swipe of his arm, Tarryn had cleaned the table. Chivalry at its best.

The choices for beverages were fairly limited at that time of day, beer being the most sanitary option as it came from a sealed bottle. Tarryn went to the bar and got them both a drink. He sat opposite Carmen in the booth, sipped from the supersized coffee cup, and listened to the eighties soundtrack playing in the background, waiting for the liquor to loosen her tongue. It was twenty minutes and over a half a beer later, before she spoke a word.

"You must think I'm crazy, huh? Woman gets in your cab with a screaming cat then bawls uncontrollably and throws money at you."

"Naw, I get that all the time. Just part of a regular day's work." Tarryn smiled, turning the charm dial up to about six.

"I love that cat more than anything. He has seen me through countless days when I had no one else to talk to and nights when I thought I was going to lose my mind. He was a wonderful friend. You said you had cats at home, right?"

"Yep, three," he lied. "They are older now, in their teens. I don't ever want to think about when the day comes that I have to say good-bye. It'll be tough. Why'd you give him up?" Tarryn tried to match her vocal patterns, tempo, and vocabulary to keep her at ease.

"I can't take care of him anymore. They'll find him a new home. Probably one with a little girl who will brush him every day and pet his head." Carmen took a big swallow of her beer.

Noting that her beer was already getting low, Tarryn went to the bar to get her a refill. He didn't want her drunk—that defeated the purpose of getting her to trust him. Drinking made people do stupid things that they wouldn't normally do. Genuine trust was what he was after. The kind that he had with his mother, the kind that didn't require inebriation as fuel.

The second beer went down a little slower than the first, and Tarryn steered the conversation to more comfortable topics. He told her funny stories about recent fares—the wife who ripped her husband's toupee off and threw it out of the car window in a fit of rage; the young girl who explained to her five-year-old brother that a gynecologist was a mechanic for women; the older woman who, in a drunken stupor, made him go back to the bar where he picked her up because she realized that she had left her prosthetic arm behind. He joked about how relieved he was to get a call to her house instead of an old granny with a dirty diaper at the retirement home. She smiled at the appropriate times but didn't seem to be focused on what he was saying. Tarryn watched her face for any signs of a connection between the two of them but wasn't getting anything more than a blank stare.

After ten minutes of silence, Tarryn decided to take a risk and delve a little further into her mind. "Can I ask you a question? You don't have to answer if you don't want," he asked quietly, looking straight into her eyes. "Why are you going to kill yourself?"

"What gave you that idea?" she said nervously, looking down at her coffee cup.

"It seems like the only logical explanation."

"Well, you're wrong. You seemed like a decent guy. You offered to buy me a beer, and I agreed. There is nothing more to the story."

Tarryn looked at her face and knew that he had hit a nerve. "Look, you don't have to tell me what's going on. I understand that it's personal. But I might be able to help."

"You can't. I'm in way too deep, and everyone that has tried to help me winds up dead. Is that what you want to hear?" Carmen was agitated and looking like she might bolt out the door.

Tarryn wanted to reach across the table and kill her at that very moment, secure his thick hands around her throat, and dig his thumbs into her windpipe. "Hmm … all I know is that you're acting like a woman that is out of options. Would telling a total stranger really make things worse? Sounds to me like you've already hit rock bottom." He wondered what she meant by "Everyone who tries to help her ends up dead …" Alarm bells were chiming.

Carmen took a sip of her drink and let out a long, harried sigh. "Look, it's really complicated. I'm sure you don't want to hear the details. Just suffice to say that my life is no longer worth living, and I just gave away the only friend I have. I might look like a nice person, but I'm not, and I can't live with the memories of the life that I've lived."

"It can't be that bad. Anyone who could be so caring to animals certainly doesn't strike me as a devil in disguise."

"You have no idea." The tears started to flow again. "If you knew the truth, you wouldn't even sit here with me. I'm just a broken-down human being whose only redeeming quality is that I like animals. The rest is an unspeakable disaster. I've done things that you can't even imagine. Terrible, evil things."

An alarm went off in his brain once again … *Danger, watch your step* … but the growling hunger quickly drowned it out. "I've been told that I'm a pretty good listener—it's one of the required skills if you want to be a bartender or a cab driver. Do you want to talk about it?" Tarryn asked, dialing the internal charm meter up one more notch.

Carmen looked at him with a challenging, icy stare. "Why would I talk to you? You're a complete stranger, and you want me to confess my darkest sins to you? I'm not looking for a shrink right now. Psychobabble bullshit won't change a thing. And what makes you think that you would be qualified to hear my story, *Mr. Cab Driver*?" The sarcasm was rampant as she reminded him of his lowly status.

Tarryn took a deep breath. *Keep calm. Emotions are the enemy.*

If she only knew how smart and talented this "cab driver" was, her tone would change. "Well, first of all, I will probably be the last person on earth to hear your story based on what you just told me. Second, confession is good for the soul. And finally, everyone has secrets. I just might be harboring a few of my own, and that would make me uniquely qualified to hear your story." He wanted to walk the fine line between arrogance and confidence. Somehow that must have resonated with her because he felt a subtle change in her attitude.

Tarryn wondered if she would be sitting there if she knew *his* truth. Her face told him that he might have just gotten a toe in the door—not a whole foot but it was a start. He estimated one more beer and two coffees and she would be ready for step two. His back started to burn once again.

Carmen was looking so deeply into his eyes that he was sure she was reading his mind. He saw a subtle pain that was buried in her heart. He recognized it right away; he had seen the look many times when he looked at himself in the mirror.

Carmen thought for a few minutes. "You understand that I could be putting your life at risk, and you still want me to talk?" When Tarryn nodded, she spoke again, "Who the hell are you?"

"Just a guy who cares."

"Where do you want me to start?" she asked.

"Well, seeing as I have no idea what's going on, start at the beginning I guess. You know what it is and where it all began—you tell me."

He watched in silence as she decided where to begin. He wondered how detailed the story would be and how long it would take. He prayed that it was a short one. He hated to be out in public for too long with any of his victims.

Tarryn went to his happy place. *Strangulation was certainly a valid option.* He wanted to watch her face when she died. Would she show any signs of distress? Or would it be a relief?

FIVE

CARMEN STARTED TO TALK AGAIN AFTER THREE OR four minutes of mind-numbing silence. "To an outsider, it might look like the past ten years would hold all of the secrets. They were the most chaotic, and they were the years where I committed the most heinous acts. But now that I'm faced with starting my story somewhere, I guess I need to go back as far as I can possibly remember."

Tarryn's mind groaned. *As far back as she could remember? How fucking long was that going to take? Hurry it up, woman.* He needed to be patient ... means to an end ... means to an end.

"I was born in Canada. A place called High River, Alberta. Small town, right above Montana in case you don't know. Most people don't. Nice place in the summer, brutally cold in the winter. When I lived there, it was quaint and real ... no pretense of grandeur. The kind of place where you never locked your doors, and no one would honk their horns if you were tying up traffic. We weren't rich, but we were comfortable, and I had great friends. Great parents too ... not their fault, okay? I just want to make that clear."

"Sure," Tarryn replied. His excitement level was rising already. She had started to open up and trust. *Sorry, honey, but you're not going to commit suicide after all.*

"You know how some people can remember stuff from when they were really little, like two years old. Not me. My first memories start at about six. I think the beginning of that year was the best part of my entire life. My parents had a big birthday party planned for me with lots of family and friends. I guess I would have been considered popular back then. Mind you, in a small town, everyone is friends to a certain extent. You rely on the kindness of your neighbors to get you through when the snowdrifts are high and the farming is low.

"I can remember picking out the prettiest dress from the Sears catalog. It was white with pink flowers. I was excited, thinking how beautiful I would look on my birthday—how grown-up. I wanted to be as glamorous as my mom—she was a real knockout. She set up colored streamers and balloons all over the house. She baked a chocolate money cake. You know—the kind that has coins in each piece for the kids. You don't see that anymore—people would probably get sued now. Anyway, it was magical to me—all of the attention, the presents, the food. Uncle Ray was there, my favorite uncle. He wasn't really an uncle, just a guy who lived down the street and raised horses. I loved the horses, and I thought he was handsome.

"He gathered me up in his lap and told me how gorgeous I looked. He kissed me on the forehead, and I was so proud, so ecstatic that he noticed my pretty little dress. My mother smiled as she watched him stroking my ego. I felt so beautiful in that moment." Carmen drifted off into the past and left Tarryn sitting, staring at her face.

She was beautiful. Her face was angelic somehow, even with the swollen eyes and no makeup left to speak of. She was the kind of woman that his mother had been way back when, in the beginning.

"When I was a little girl, all I wanted was to be noticed. I remember how much my confidence went up after that birthday party. It was far too early for puberty, but it was an awakening, I guess. Every little girl wants to be attractive, and I was no different. Ray started paying extra attention to me. He would always offer up his lap as a place for me to sit. I can look back now and see that he was grooming me, as that type of man does with his prey."

He watched as the happy thoughts of a little girl's birthday changed to bad memories of the past. He had already anticipated what would come next in the story. It made him ill to think that someone would take advantage of a helpless child. He might have a lot of traits that society didn't approve of, but he was sickened by pedophiles.

"I think I know what comes next. You don't have to say the words if it'll be too hard."

Carmen snapped back to the present and gave him a half smile. "Sorry. No, it needs to be told if you want to understand who I am today and how I got to this point. Can you get me a coffee first?"

"Sit tight, I'll be right back."

Tarryn walked over to the bar and waited patiently while the bartender served a couple who had just walked in. He thought back to his childhood, trying to remember his first memory. It was similar in that he was about six or seven. His mother would work all day at the café down the street, and he would spend the day in the apartment next door. Betty, the neighbor, took him in, as well as several other kids in the apartment block, until their parents picked them up after work. He had good memories from her house—cartoons, grilled cheese sandwiches with tomato soup, and jelly beans. The red ones were his favorite. Each night when his mother collected him from Betty's, she would pick him up and hold him close. He would nuzzle in her hair, smelling the combination of fried food and hairspray. To Tarryn, that particular odor was comforting and homey. It was like smelling the sweetest flowers with sugar on top. Intoxicating.

They would climb the stairs to their apartment, and she would open up the takeout containers that she had brought home from work. Sometimes, it was just eggs and toast, other times it was a half a steak and mashed potatoes. What she brought home for dinner was always dependent on who ordered what in the café and who didn't want to finish their meals. On the odd occasion, an entire piece of pie—untouched— would make its way to their table. One of his first memories was a piece of cherry pie that seemed like it was as big as his entire head. Tarryn had gorged himself to the point of bursting, as his mother put *her* dinner of choice, cocaine, up her nose. She had once told him that she didn't use once she found out she "had a wiggly worm in her belly." He wasn't sure how long after he was born that she had continued to abstain, but by the time he was six, the drug use was back on track.

SIX

CARMEN WAS DEEP IN THOUGHT AGAIN WHEN HE
returned with the coffees. Tarryn knew that the longer they stayed in
Sam's Suds, the more risky the kill would be later. They had already
spent a considerable amount of time sitting in the back. Now was not
the time to start making mistakes and catch the attention of someone
who might be able to identify him later. She was nowhere near ready
for step two—he would have to be patient.

"As you guessed, Uncle Ray was not as nice of a man as he appeared
to be. I watched a television show about molesters recently. They have
an entire network now, where the men give each other tips on how
to manipulate their victims. There are even underground books and
Internet sites on how to get away with it. Sick bastards. Ray tested
the waters for a while. He made sure that I always sat on his lap, that
I always got big hugs, started stroking my leg. I was reveling in the
attention. I used to walk down the street a few times a week to go and
see the horses—he said I was always welcome. My parents were happy
to have someone who they trusted, to keep an eye out for their daughter.
It went on for quite a while before anything actually happened. By the
time it did, he had me convinced that I had asked for it—that I had
flirted with him over the years and that I was responsible for the entire
thing. He warned me not to tell anyone, said they wouldn't believe me
after all of the times I had teased him with the short dresses. I was so
ashamed. I knew it was wrong, but I loved the horses. I didn't want to

stop riding so I let it happen, over and over again." Carmen took a long drink of her coffee.

"You were a little child. You can't really believe that it was your fault. He's a sick, perverted bastard. Did you ever tell your parents?"

"No. He threatened to hurt them if I told. You're the first one to hear it. When you're a kid, you believe the idle threats. The disappointing thing is that he's still around, and he has grandchildren that are about that age now. I still don't know if anyone would believe me. It was so long ago." She paused and sipped her coffee. "I imagine that there's a statute of limitations on that kind of thing. I have no proof. It would be my word against his. Plus, I never wanted to tell my husband. He wouldn't understand."

"So you've harbored this guilt for all these years, and it's driving you to kill yourself?" Tarryn reached across the table and touched her hand; it looked so small next to his. "You've just told me, and I don't think badly of you. Screw your husband if he doesn't understand. You're a pretty woman, you can get another guy." Tarryn was beginning to think that this was going to be easier than originally anticipated.

Carmen pulled her hand away from his, smirked, and let out a long sigh. "No, I got over that particular hurdle many years ago. It gets worse—a lot worse. I just wanted you to understand where I came from. I've never told my story before and if you're going to be the only one to ever hear it, it might as well be complete." Her voice had an edge to it that told him he had crossed a line. *Two steps forward, one step back*, he mused.

"Sorry, I'll shut up now." He put his hands back on his side of the table. He liked it better when they were touching. Feeling her soft skin was like a preview of things to come.

"Thanks. The abuse went on until I was maybe thirteen. I lived a double life. I was the A student during the day and a loving daughter at night. I was molested in between. Uncle Ray moved away that year. I think he was getting afraid that he might be found out. I was getting more rebellious, and he was starting to lose interest in me. I was hitting puberty, and it was the young ones that he liked. It was a relief on the one hand but sad on the other. I was going to miss the horses, and part of me couldn't go back to being a regular kid. It was like I had outgrown my friends.

"From thirteen to fifteen my life steadily improved. I was getting more friends and started to have an interest in boys. It seemed like everything was going to turn around. I was settling down, and my parents promised to buy a horse for me if I aced my year-end exams. I was thrilled. I was reading everything I could on horses—how to care for them, what to feed them, how to train them. I picked out names—Chestnut for a boy and Princess for a girl. I can only describe it as idyllic. I convinced myself that Ray was just a speed bump in life that I had conquered. Then everything changed. I think back on that time and wish with all of my heart that I could go back and fix it. It was the first layer of guilt—the foundation of a life of crime."

SEVEN

THEY SAT IN SILENCE FOR A FEW MINUTES. TARRYN SPOKE first, "Are you going to tell me more?"

"You sure you want me to keep going? I would understand if you are bored with this. You don't know me, and it's not up to you to save my eternal soul," Carmen asked quietly.

"I'll listen to as much as you want to tell me." *Within reason*, he thought. *If you could feel my back right now, you'd know that I won't wait for long.*

Carmen was wringing the strap of her leather purse in her hands. "The next part is the hardest part to tell. There are a lot of things that I don't want to tell you. This one is the most difficult to say out loud. It's not the worst thing I've done by any means, but it's the one I'm most ashamed of." She paused as a tear fell on her cheek, and she took a deep breath before she spoke again. "The economy went for shit, and my dad lost his job. My parents sat me down and told me there was no money for the horse anymore. I was devastated. I had started to think of the horse as my salvation, a chance to move on from Ray and the past. They were telling me I couldn't have it. I was furious. I threw a fit. I cried, I screamed, and I told them that I wished they were dead. I went up in my room and sulked for three days.

"I can't imagine the stress that they were under back then. My dad was laid off, my Mom didn't have any marketable skills, having been a homemaker most of her life, and they were raising a daughter. I wish I had been more mature, but I was so caught up in my own world that it didn't matter. The last time I saw them, they were going into the city to have dinner with friends. I still wasn't speaking to them, and I remember grunting as they walked out the door. They were killed when a semi hit their car on the way home."

"I'm so sorry. That must have been awful." Tarryn didn't have to fake the sympathy, having lost a parent himself.

"The police came to the door and told me what had happened. The community gathered around me, as they always did in times of crisis, and I went numb. The guilt was more than I could bear, the pain was excruciating, and the weight on my soul was unbelievably heavy. I stayed with friends for a few nights while everyone figured out what to do with me. We had no immediate family in the country, so I was shipped off to LA to stay with my aunt.

"Shelia was a nice enough woman. She taught third grade and was dedicated to those kids. Luckily, she lived with a guy who was very understanding about having a fifteen-year-old girl come to live with them. I, on the other hand, was having a hard time fitting in. Everyone had this preconceived idea that Canadians were hicks and treated me like their retarded cousin from the frozen north. I was miserable twenty-four hours a day. Aunt Shelia tried to convince me that I should see a psychiatrist, but I was so afraid to tell anyone what I had said to my parents—those vile words that I had spat in their faces that day. I didn't want anyone to tell me that they knew I didn't mean it. I did mean it at the time. My heart was broken into a thousand pieces—no one could fix me. I refused the help—faking a smile, faking friendships at school, faking my life. Eventually, the talk of mental help wasn't brought up anymore. I guess I was suicidal back then too. Only back then, I didn't have the guts to follow through." Carmen's eyes wandered to the door as she spoke. Tarryn stopped himself from turning and looking at whatever interested her. He hoped it wasn't the cops.

"I was in full-blown puberty, so I had hormonal changes to deal with on top of a new school and the death of my parents. I couldn't get over the guilt from the way I treated them and the stress of starting over, so I started using drugs. They were easy to get, and I was accepted by the crowd of people that sold them. I was back to my double life again, and somehow it felt good. Normal is what you are most comfortable with, and to me, lies and deception were the cure for all that ailed me." Carmen stopped and swirled her now cold coffee in her cup. "I'm going to visit the washroom. Can you get us some refills?"

"Will do. You're coming back, right?" All of a sudden, Tarryn couldn't stand the thought that she might leave. Somehow their lives were connected. The drug use, the double life, the lies and deception. She was becoming more and more interesting all the time. This would be a kill to savor. She was talking about drowning in sorrow—maybe he could drown her in real life. It seemed fitting.

She showed him the slightest smile as she nodded and walked toward the dilapidated wood door marked with a picture of a crude high heel.

EIGHT

TARRYN WAITED PATIENTLY AND WONDERED WHAT HIS life would have been like had he lost his mother at the tender age of fifteen. Even now, he still relied on the wisdom she had given him before her passing—at fifteen she had just started the life lessons. Over the years, she had almost become two people in his mind—the one who nourished him and the one who was absent, even when occupying the same four walls.

The first of her personalities was the ultimate nurturer. She would whisper in his ear as she dropped him at school, reminding him how he was her "handsome boy." Even though they were poor, she made sure that no matter what, he always had food for dinner and saved some morsel of goodness for breakfast the next day. She would sit him on her lap and read stories about fascinating men who killed and eluded police. She was obsessed with everything to do with serial killers. She had an impressive collection of true crime novels that she got from the thrift store and would watch anything on television that had real-life murderers. It was "so amazingly impressive," she always told him, that those men were able to fulfill their dreams but keep the police in the dark. Every night he would curl up with her and learn more about their lives.

She was particularly enamored by Ted Bundy. To her, he was the "most delicious man." She continually gushed about his good looks, charm, and wit. She would discuss the details of each kill and talk about where he made his mistakes—not that she thought there were that many of them. With an estimated thirty-six victims under his belt, to her, he was the ultimate killing machine. When she spoke about Ted, her eyes sparkled to the point that Tarryn often wondered if a human face could possibly look more in love. Sometimes he would feel a tug of jealously, but he knew that Bundy was in jail, and he on the other hand, was right there with his mother. She might have had an infatuation with the charismatic killer, but he wasn't the one she tucked in every night.

On the odd occasion, she read the true crime stories of other killers. Tarryn was familiar with both the most famous and the more obscure cases. Each of their stories was permanently imprinted on his brain. *Repeat, repeat, repeat—until you know every detail by heart.* On many occasions he would sit with his mother and compare the killers, rating their skill, cunning, and body count. Every word from her mouth was a golden gospel.

According to his mother, Charles Manson was a coward because he had other people do his bidding. They were a sloppy group of amateurs that only executed seven people. John Wayne Gacy was a well-loved member of his community and threw parties for his family and friends. His mother respected the fact that he was so sneaky and able to dispose of the thirty-three bodies so readily—that took real skill, she always said. What she didn't like about Gacy was his penchant for raping and torturing boys—homosexuality in any form wasn't tolerated in their household. Jeffrey Dahmer was right up there with Gacy in her mind—smart—but the "butt bumping" and eating of human flesh sickened her. The list went on and on—David Berkowitz, Jack the Ripper, the Zodiac Killer, the Boston Strangler, Charles Cullen. Each killer's life was thoroughly dissected and rated against the man of all time—Ted Bundy.

From as far back as he could remember, those stories were the best entertainment Tarryn could imagine. He got to spend time with his mother, and the subject matter was fascinating. He rarely watched television unless there was a documentary on one of his idols. He loved to read about how the men selected their victims, lured them to the kill site, extinguished their lives, and disposed of the bodies. It seemed so glamorous, so exciting. The cat-and-mouse game of the kill was an obsession that rarely left his mind. In school he was an average student, certainly no A's on his report cards, but his mother, who was impressed with his photographic recall of Bundy and the others, let it slide.

He remembered a time when he was about twelve that he had been doing research in the library for weeks on end so that he could impress his mother with his knowledge of Ottis Toole. Mr. Toole was a little-known killer but was interesting due to the fact that he had the privilege of sharing a cell with Ted Bundy for a period of time in 1984. He carefully wrote all of the facts on sheets of paper and proudly carried them home. He didn't tell Ms. Betty, or anyone else, about the research. The passion for this type of information was something that he shared only with his mother. It was a special bond that he didn't want anyone else to discover.

There was always a fear that nagged at him, wondering if someone else would come along and steal the special time with her away. He was in constant panic that someone would have more knowledge than he did, and his mother would focus her attention elsewhere. It was imperative that, with the exception of Terrible Ted, he was the smartest and brightest star in his mother's eyes.

That night, when she finally came to pick him up at Betty's, he was almost bursting, wanting to show her what he had done. When he showed her his work, double-spaced neatly on letter-size paper and including photocopies of as many photographs as he could find, she picked him up off the floor and smothered him with kisses. So impressed by the effort that he had put into the project, she took him out for dinner that night to McDonald's. It was the first time that they had gone to a real restaurant, and he savored each and every moment of the experience; the colorful decor, the endless choices on the menu board, and the beautiful blonde girl who served them. The salty hamburger tasted so delicious that he thought his taste buds were going to explode with joy. His mother was beaming through dinner and gave him an extra big hug that night. In looking back, it was probably one of the few times that she ate dinner with him instead of using cocaine as her nourishment. Tarryn was ecstatic.

That night was the first time that the dark thoughts had started to encroach on his childish brain. A well-executed murder was certainly something that his mother valued. If his mother had reacted so favorably toward his research, he could probably make her over-the-moon ecstatic if he could perform an actual kill. He wondered what it might be like to take a life. He thought that one day he might even try it himself.

NINE

CARMEN SAT BACK DOWN AT THE TABLE AND THE
memory of McDonald's slipped away. She gave him a weak smile but
looked exhausted and seemed to be aging by the hour. Tarryn thought
that he was starting to break her down—just a while longer. His energy
moved from curiosity to kill mode and back. He wanted to hear the
rest of the story, but the urge to take her life was growing stronger.
His back was prickling with anticipation. Would she cry out when she
realized she was going to die? Or would she be in too much shock to
make a sound?

"So you were doing drugs? Tell me about that part of your life,"
Tarryn asked, knowing the depths to which addicts would go for their
prize. He knew from personal experience, that no matter what your vice,
drugs, booze, gambling, or even murder, if you wanted it bad enough,
you would be capable of things that you thought were impossible.

Carmen shrugged her shoulders and started speaking, "The teenage
years are a bit of a blur actually. Lots of parties, lots of drinking and
drugs. I felt like an empty shell of a human being and was trying to fill
the gaping holes with other substances. It was a horrible time in my life.
I didn't know it, but things were about to get a lot worse.

"I think I was seventeen. I was still living with my aunt. She had
never cared for a child before, let alone an out-of-control, drugged-up
teenager. I can't imagine what that must have been like. More guilt for
me. Anyway, I started selling drugs downtown to keep my habit alive.

There are lots of crazy people that live in downtown LA, but remarkably, there are some nice ones too. I felt like I fit in. The drugs can make even the good ones go nuts after a while. It was a balancing act—trying to have friends but keeping my distance from the pack.

"I was pretty successful at dealing. I was smart enough to spot a cop a mile away. I had a reputable dealer who sold to me, so the product was pure. I never ripped anyone off, and I'm pleased to say that I never got arrested. I look back on that part of my life, and it's amazing that I'm alive. I could tell you stories that would curl your toes. Not a nice place to be, believe me. It's not a time that I'm proud of ... not that I can say I'm proud of any part of my life to date. I tell you so that you know how I got roped in to the really bad stuff."

"You don't sell drugs anymore, I take it?" Tarryn asked, images of his mother danced in his head—her rolled-up dollar bill in her nose and a crack pipe always within arm's reach.

"No, that part was over a long time ago. I was just a kid. The streets are a hell of a lot meaner now than they used to be. The Asian gangs have no respect for life and kill at random. It's a bit too dangerous for that kind of work nowadays."

Tarryn felt a tingling in his brain with that comment. The Asian gangs had nothing on him—they were uncontrolled killers, he was a master. It was exciting to think that he was already well on his way to being trusted by her—she had already admitted to being abused and selling drugs. Sure, it was a slow and grueling process, but when she finally realized who he was, he knew that the shock on her face was going to be pure ecstasy.

"How did you get out of that scene? Look at me calling it a scene, like some seventies freak. Sorry, but I don't know much about the drug world—sheltered life. What made you leave?"

Carmen smiled at his clumsy attempt at street speak. "Lots of girls were selling themselves on the street, but something in me just couldn't do it. There was this Lebanese guy, Fadi, who owned a convenience store on the block where I sold my wares. He was a good customer and seemed like a nice guy. When you are on the street selling drugs, you need a safe haven in case anything bad goes down. You know—cops or a deal gone wrong. He was it for me, and he was always willing to chat when sales were slow.

"Fadi had a back room where we could go and get high. It was a filthy hole with an old, ripped couch and an old color television. Some of my friends would go with him to the back room to watch porn and give him blow jobs. They told me that he asked about me and if I liked to party—they said he was harmless and it was easy money. I kept him at bay for quite a while—trying to keep a good customer. He wasn't ugly or anything, but somehow knowing that my parents were in heaven watching, wouldn't let me cross that line. It was one thing to sell drugs and another to sell your body. That sounds crazy, doesn't it? I was willing to break the law but only in certain areas."

Tarryn didn't think it was crazy at all. He knew from personal experience that sometimes you broke one law, but your salvation was in the fact that you didn't act on another lustful thought. "Believe it or not, I get it—100 percent."

Carmen continued, "Things were okay for a few months, and then he starting getting more persistent. One night it was freezing cold, so cold that even the puke on the sidewalk was frozen. It was some freak weather anomaly for LA. I went inside his store to warm up. The street was relatively quiet, and Fadi was high. He kept touching my hair and asking for special favors in the back. Thinking that I could handle it, I stayed inside but kept pushing his hand away. I should have just gone home, but I was high as well, and I didn't want to face my aunt. Anyway, his reputation on the street wasn't violent, so I wasn't worried.

"He went into the back to use a little more. I have no idea what he took, but when he came out front, he grabbed me and slammed my head up against the wall. His eyes were wild, and he kept asking me why I wouldn't suck his cock as he choked the life from my body. I was petrified. I couldn't breathe, and all I kept thinking was that I wished I had made some better choices in my life. After a minute or so, he moved his hands to get a better grip on my neck, which gave me a chance to scream. It caught the attention of a guy across the street. The stranger outside just stood there and stared. I was being held up by my neck against a wall, and the guy just walked away. I guess that he didn't want to get involved. Maybe he was scared of what might happen to him if he did, or maybe, he just looked at me as a disposable street urchin. I realized at that moment that I needed to get out. I talked Fadi out of strangling me, by telling him that I would go to the back "just this once." We went to the back, and he undid his pants. I did the only thing I could think of—I took his nasty dick in my mouth and bit down as hard as I could. When he was reeling from the pain, I ran like hell.

"I remember how fast my heart was pounding. I had no idea what to do next. I had two options at that point, I could get my dealer to teach Fadi a lesson, or I could change my life. I took the money that I owed the dealer and walked away. I never went back."

"No one ever came looking for you? Isn't that what normally happens when you try to leave organized crime?" The mental image of someone else's hands on Carmen's throat was disturbing and exciting. He had hoped that he would be the only one with that honor.

Carmen shook her head. "They weren't that organized as far as criminals go. It was a long time ago. Like I said, things are different on the streets now. I was on the bottom end of the totem pole, and one less kid on the street made no difference to them—there would always be another to take my place. The money wasn't enough for them to come after me, though I wouldn't want to run into anyone from that side of the tracks ever again. The ones that haven't fried their brains can have long memories. Most of them wouldn't think twice about sticking a knife in my chest if the opportunity presented itself, and they were stoned enough. But they don't venture outside of their territory much, so I'm not worried."

Tarryn was amazed at how easily she said the words—they would kill her *if* they could remember to do so. It was interesting how little it bothered the seemingly well-bred woman sitting in front of him. He was starting to realize that there was a lot more to her than met the eye.

"I went back home to my alter ego—the good Carmen. Well, let's be clear here, I wasn't an angel. I still had major issues, but I started to try again. I wanted to make an effort to mend the relationship with what was left of my family. It was supremely difficult. I had matured so much in my time on the street. In the short time that I spent downtown, I had seen people beaten, cut up, and shot. I had seen people putting needles into their eyes because they had no veins left anywhere else. I had changed so much that I couldn't relate—not to my aunt or anyone else. I wanted a fresh start and everything about LA reminded me of death and pain. I moved out when I was eighteen and came to New York."

"Did you have a job? How did you make ends meet?" Tarryn was trying to keep the conversation moving. The violence was intriguing, and the drugs were sickening, but she had him fully engaged in the story. If it got better from here, and he anticipated that it would, it was going to be a hell of a day. Normally he would be asleep by now, after a long shift of driving, but he felt awake and alert and wanted to hear more. He was winning her over, and the payoff was going to be huge.

"I figured that I was going to do some modeling. You know, tame stuff, maybe lingerie or something. I didn't have any skills to speak of, and my best assets were these," Carmen said as she cupped her large round breasts and thrust them in his direction. "I had a bit of money that I had saved from the dealing days, and I took a bus from LA to New York. It was several buses actually, and it wasn't a fun ride. The people that take buses fall into two categories—those that are broke, like I was, and those that are nuts. I'm guessing the mix to be about fifty-fifty. I knew lots of psychotic people when I was working on the street, but buses and bus stations seem to be like a magnet for predators and anyone that is one brick short of a load. I had countless men who were willing to pay for favors in the public washroom and others that just wanted me to work for them, doing much the same thing on the street. There was even one guy that claimed he was speaking with God and that God wanted me to draw a cross on his forehead with my lipstick. Really weird stuff can happen in a bus station. Anyway, I can see how young girls get roped in to that crap. I was lucky that I had some street smarts, and I made it to the Big Apple without too many issues."

Tarryn made a mental note that the bus station sounded like an opportune place to hunt in the future. Carmen continued, but now her story was more about the telling than the listening. Her eyes were glassy as she recounted the next chapter of her life. If Tarryn was present, Carmen didn't seem to care; it was just a confession to the universe.

Tarryn's thoughts drifted once again to his mother. She had started to get that same glassy stare after one too many lines of "dinner." He remembered how hard he tried to keep her interest, bringing home book after book of true crime stories. He just wanted to keep her attention focused on him, and her obsession with Ted Bundy was the easiest way to fuel the fire. It had worked for a while, but then things had started to change. Tarryn, enjoying his memories less and less, purposely focused his attention on Carmen again. He thought about the possibility of electrocution and decided that he would let the thought fester in his mind for a bit before making a final decision.

Carmen continued, "I stayed at a cheap hotel for the first week. It was a dump that was crawling with smack heads, low-end prostitutes, and roaches. The walls were paper-thin, and each floor only had one communal bathroom. The postage stamp-sized room hadn't seen a cleaning lady in months, and the toilet had a layer of black fuzz on it that had its own ecosystem. I slept in my clothes and went to the local gas station for sponge baths. I kept thinking that it was a means to an end, just until I could get my first paying job.

"I went to every modeling agency that I could find in the phone book. At first, I contacted the ones that had the big splashy ads, then it was the ones that had small ads, then the ones that just had their name and a phone number. I heard that my ears were too far apart, that my upper lip needed work, that my eyes had uneven pigment. No one was interested. I was frustrated and losing hope.

"New York is different than L.A. When I dreamt about the city, I fantasized that it would be red-carpet-glamorous and exciting. In my mind it was where the beautiful people congregated and partied. Broadway, Times Square, museums, restaurants—they sounded perfect. It seemed like a great place to start a new life. The reality was a slap in the face. You'll never see photographs of the stinking underbelly in a tourism brochure. I guess that's true of every big city, but my fresh start turned into a stale, rotting nightmare. I was eighteen years old, and I wasn't even remotely attractive enough to work as a model according to the interviews I had. I was staying in a flea-bitten hotel, and the only thing I knew how to do was deal dope. It wasn't a pretty picture.

"That's when I met him. It was the beginning of the end, I guess. It's why I'm sitting here with you right now. I saw the stars in his eyes, and he was my salvation. I wish I had never gone into that coffee shop. I want to go back and shake the living shit out of my eighteen-year-old self and tell her not to fall in love. I want to tell her that he is pure evil, and once you make a deal with the devil, the only way out is to die."

TEN

TARRYN THOUGHT ABOUT THE FIRST TIME HE HAD FELT the tug of love in his heart. He had been fourteen when his hormones started to fire up. The girl of his dreams sat next to him in English class, and her smile lit up the room. Sandra, or Sandy to her friends, was the epitome of a perfect woman in his mind. Not only was she beautiful, with her lemon-pie-filling hair and glowing green eyes, but she was also athletic and smart and witty and funny and polite and popular and ... the list went on and on.

All day, every day, was spent hoping that she would talk to him in between classes. He started to try harder in school in an effort to catch her attention. His grades transformed themselves from Cs to Bs. He started to watch her badminton practice at lunch instead of doing research for his mother in the library. If his heart was a pendulum going back and forth from his studies with his mother and spending time with Sandy, that year, it had moved so far to the Sandy side that he lost sight of his mother's wishes altogether.

On the final day of school, knowing that it was now or never, he had finally gotten up the nerve to ask her out. It was a day that he could remember in such detail, that it could have happened yesterday. It was chilly outside, not the toe-numbing cold like New York can sometimes be, but just cold enough that everyone was dressed properly for the elements. Sandy had forgotten her coat. She was wearing jeans so tight that he was able to admire every inch of her below the waist. Her pink sweater was thin, and her nipples were hard from the dropping mercury. He was mesmerized. With sweaty palms and a stutter in his voice, he asked her if she might want to go to the movies with him.

She looked at him for what seemed like an eternity before the words left her lips—"Sure, give me a call."

Tarryn had almost crapped his pants. He repeat the conversation over and over in his head on the walk home, almost sure that he had heard her wrong, that she had actually said, "Not a chance, loser."

Tarryn knew that his natural good looks and indifferent personality were what kept him on the outer edge of the in crowd. They accepted him and treated him well, but he was careful to show them only a small portion of his true self. What they saw was a fabrication—one that he would perfect as he grew older and wiser. His wardrobe was always from thrift stores, but somehow that just made him cooler to the other kids. The night after he had arranged the date with Sandy, he reviewed his reflection in the mirror, his face was clear, his hair was trimmed, his smile was strong but his clothes … his teenage mind had all of a sudden become self-conscious about the way he dressed but knew that asking his mother for money for new clothes *and* a movie would be crossing a line.

He remembered preparing to ask his mother for date-money. What would she do? He hadn't even told her that he liked Sandy. Things had changed in their house that year. His mother was becoming more brooding about Ted Bundy, sending him letters on an almost daily basis. She was sure that the "nasty-ass-commie-prison-guards" were intercepting them and stopping her from contacting her one true love. She had become unpredictable, and the thought of asking her for cash was equally as panic inducing as asking Sandy for a date.

That night after dinner, he gathered up the nerve to ask for the money. It was the first time in his life that he had asked his mother for anything more than her love, and it was uncomfortable and awkward. His timing turned out to be particularly good that day, the tips had been flowing, and the cocaine level in her blood was at a manageable level. She too had said yes.

Tarryn remembered that day as being one of the best in his life. He was going to have his first date with the girl of his dreams, and his mother had agreed to give him the money to pay for it. He slept like a baby. But as it is with all good things, they come to an end. The next morning his mother had changed her mind about the money, and they had fought. It was the first time that she had yelled at him, and what she said wasn't pleasant. The words would be forever ingrained in his mind like the commandments were inscribe in stone—"You'll regret getting involved with this girl. Mark my words, Tarryn. You don't know women like I do. I wish I didn't give you that money, but you need to learn the lesson one day and now is as good a time as any. Don't you come cryin' to me when it ends bad. Ted Bundy wouldn't be cryin' to his momma—keep that in mind."

At the time, he had no idea what his mother meant by those words, but it wouldn't take long to find out. Much like the story that Carmen was telling, one of the key turning points in his life revolved around love.

ELEVEN

TARRYN WENT AND GOT YET ANOTHER ROUND OF COFFEE
and glanced around the dingy bar taking note of who might be potential
witnesses to the long hours he was spending with Carmen. It was after
eleven o'clock in the morning, and New York laws said it was officially
legal to sell liquor—Sam's would start to get busier from here on out.
The bartender was occupied, chatting up a local working girl at the end
of the bar, and barely glanced his way when he asked for another round
of the black tar they called coffee. As his weathered hands poured their
drinks, Tarryn noticed his graying temples and a wedding ring on his
left hand. He shook his head as he watched the barkeep return to the
young girl.

Sam's had a maximum seating capacity of about thirty, and now
two other tables were taken. The older man that he had seen earlier sat
in one booth and looked to have already had his fill of liquor. His eyes
could barely focus anymore, and he didn't look like he would remember
how he got home, let alone a cabbie and his girl drinking coffee in
the corner. At the other table, situated just a few feet away from their
booth, a very large dark-skinned woman was holding hands with her
much smaller male companion, slurring her words as she professed
her undying love. There was nobody to worry about right now, but he
wished that he had taken the seat facing the door, instead of his current
position facing the back wall.

While spending this much time with Carmen in public was not

an ideal situation, at least they were in a place where everyone kept to themselves. Tarryn had always noticed that the blue-collar crowd didn't care much who walked in the room, just a quick glance to cover your back was sufficient. In the world of high society, things were much different. A new person entering a room needed to be evaluated, dissected, and rated on their appearance and stature. Were they important enough to keep tabs on during the night? It was just a big game of lies and deceit.

"So you met someone in New York?" Tarryn asked, wanting to keep the conversation moving once he returned to the table. His back reacted to the sight and smell of his prey.

"I suppose this is where the real story starts, but I wanted you to know where I came from. That part was important, even if it was just for me to remember. I guess part of me wants to use the abuse, the drugs, and the trip to New York as an excuse." Carmen sighed. "But there really is no excuse for what I did in my life. I had the ability at every crossroad to take the right path. I chose the life that I've lived and the only one to blame is myself, though meeting Simon certainly didn't help.

"Anyway, as I was saying, I was in New York and couldn't get a modeling job due to the placement of my ears, the pigment in my eyes, et cetera. I was running out of money and had to do something to get more cash. I saw a "Help Wanted" sign in a café close to the hotel where I was staying and went in to apply. Somehow it just seemed fitting that I take a job as a waitress. It was a great place to meet other like-minded people that were struggling to break into the biz, and the tips gave me instant money. The Good Earth Café was spotless—pretty flowered curtains, sparkling white tables, and looked to have a decent clientele. Most were local businessmen from the corporate towers down the street. I was sitting at the counter, filling out an application when a man sat down beside me. He was young, clean-cut, handsome, and smelled like a combination of chocolate and oranges. I've never smelled anything like it before. I wanted to lean in and take a big whiff of his neck. It was crazy.

"The waitress automatically brought him a black coffee and a bagel. I was impressed that such a high-end businessman would frequent the place where I was potentially going to work. I finished the application, stealing a few glances in his direction, and threw him one of my best smiles as I left. I was totally infatuated with the idea of him. I had no idea what his name was, what he did for a living, where he lived, or if he was married. Up to that point, everyone I had encountered of the male species was out of control crazies, molesters, and drug addicts. He looked like everything that was right with the big city—a smart and successful businessman that was attractive and interesting. That night I started to make up a story about his life. Who I wanted him to be.

"In my fantasies, his name was Aiden, he was twenty-five years old and had a Harvard degree in business. He was off-the-charts smart and had a knack for financing high-end real estate deals. He lived in a big house in a fancy New York suburb with an indoor pool and servants. He was single because he had never found anyone who was down-to-earth enough, and he hated the plastic personalities of the typical New York models. He loved to hike on the weekends, threw fantastic parties that were catered by the best of the best, and was a loving son who called his parents at least once a week, no matter where he was. Oh yeah, he also had his own corporate jet and a dog named Charger who had his own special doggy seat on the plane."

"Holy shit. You have a very active imagination," Tarryn laughed out loud. "I have never heard such an elaborate story made up about a total stranger. You even gave his dog a name and a special seat on the airplane. Maybe instead of a model, you should have been a writer."

Carmen smiled a little, realizing how absurd it must sound. "Maybe you're right. I found out later that the reality was nothing at all like my fantasy. He was the devil in disguise," she said as the dark shadows returned to her face.

TWELVE

TARRYN'S MIND WANDERED BACK TO SEXY SANDY. HE had called her, twenty dollars in his pocket, and set a time for their date. Despite his mother's warnings, he was excited about the possibilities that could arise. Should he hold her hand in the movie? Should he put his arm around her? What would she smell like sitting just a few inches away from him? What would she be wearing? Would it be cold out? Would the hardness of her nipples be visible again? Would they kiss at the end of the night?

He was so filled with nervous energy that every moment of every day was agonizingly slow. They had agreed to see the movie *Alien*. It looked action packed but also slightly scary. Would she want him to hold her when she got scared? Would she want to leave and go somewhere quiet? What would he do with her if they were alone?

Tarryn just wanted to get to know her better. No hanky-panky—he wasn't experienced in that sort of thing and didn't want to look like an amateur. But what if she was expecting him to perform some sort of sexual act? He was beginning to get scared. His mother had warned him that women were trouble. In fact, she had told him that he would learn a lesson as a result of the date. Was she trying to tell him that Sandy was going to laugh at him because of his lack of sexual expertise? Knowing that his mother was less than thrilled with the situation, he didn't think it wise to go back and ask for clarification on the point.

He thought he could impress Sandy with his charm, but the

butterflies circled in his stomach every time he thought of the other things that might be expected of him. He couldn't screw it up. He wasn't going to let the only girl he ever liked slip away because he wasn't mature enough.

Tarryn remembered mulling over his options in his mind. He finally narrowed it down to three—cancel the date with Sandy, ask one of his friends for advice on how to please a woman, which was equally as bad as option one, or get some experience in the next couple of days before the date. After a heated debate between the best possible solutions, options one and three, he landed on option three.

There was another girl in school that his buddies had told him "spread like butter" if you supplied the booze. She had a reputation for sleeping with anyone and everyone who asked her for the privilege. Tarryn didn't waste any time and met up with Marnie the next day. He got someone to bootleg a six-pack of beer for him at the local liquor store. It reduced his popcorn and soda money for the date with Sandy, but he knew it would be a worthwhile investment in case Sandy wanted more than just a kiss. After downing three beers in her parents' basement, Marnie was kissing him on the mouth and rubbing his crotch. It was one of the strangest experiences in his life.

Tarryn remembered hating the feel of her chapped lips and the smell of her cigarette-stained breath, and yet on another level, enjoying the friction in his pants. Things were heating up and as he put his hand on her breast, Marnie moaned. He thought he must be doing something right so he took off her clothes and finally his own. She stared at his erect penis, smiled, and leapt on top of him. She rode up and down like a cowboy riding a bronco. He watched with amazement as her faced contorted into a look of pleasure. Why would she give herself to a total stranger so quickly? *Nasty, dirty slut.* He forgot about the feelings in his groin and started to get angry. Angry that this was what was might be expected of him. Angry that he had let this dirty whore climb on top of him. Angry that Sandy had made him do it. It was disgusting, and he wanted it to end. His erection came to an abrupt stop. Marnie looked down and laughed, asking him if he was chemically neutered from the beer.

The rage welled up in him. *The dirty bitch was laughing?* He grabbed Marnie by the shoulders and threw her hard to the other side of the room. She landed with a sickening thud against the wall. He looked over at her and for a split second thought that that she might need killing. Deciding that she had served his purposes already, he turned away. Without saying a word, he pulled his pants back on and left, still pulling his T-shirt over his shoulders as he exited the house. The whole disgusting event was done. He had his experience and was ready for Sandy.

That night he couldn't get home and showered quick enough. He had rubbed his skin raw. No matter what he did, he still felt the wetness of Marnie sliding up and down his penis. It made him nauseous.

It was the next day when Sandy called to cancel their date that he realized his mistake. Marnie had told the story to two of her friends, who told two friends and on down the line. He was heartbroken. He had let the tramp do things to him, not because he liked it, but because he wanted to be perfect for Sandy. And she repaid his sacrifice by dumping him? He was angry and relieved at the same time.

His mother was right, it was a valuable lesson that he would never forget. He vowed never to let anyone have that same control and power over him again.

He thought of Carmen and vowed not to let her gain the upper hand, no matter how much he wanted to get to know her. She was a means to an end—period.

THIRTEEN

TRYING TO FORGET THE MEMORY OF MARNIE AND SANDY, Tarryn tuned back in to Carmen's story. "As you probably guessed, I got the job. All of a sudden I was the one behind the counter, and the "Help Wanted" sign had temporarily disappeared to the storage room. It was a good place to be a waitress. Ed, the owner, was a stand-up guy. He reminded me of my dad—balding and a bit overweight but happy. And he always had a kind word for everyone. He told me that he hired me because he thought I looked like a steel rose, pretty but with a tough interior. On my first day of work he watched me like a hawk, micromanaging every single move. He wanted coffee poured in a certain way, the ketchup bottles were never, ever to be topped up so that the bottom portion was old and rancid, the water glasses had to be free of marks, and the cutlery had to be spotless.

"He ran a tough ship, but the food was homey, and his little café did a roaring business at lunch. The clientele was a mixture of regulars from the neighborhood and the corporate suits from the high-rise towers. The part I admired about him most was how he interacted with people. It didn't matter if they came in dressed to the nines or if they were in track pants, everyone was treated equally. He always stressed that money was money, no matter whose pocket it came from. I liked that. I liked him.

"Ed let up on me after the first few days. I was so grateful to have a job that I put every bit of energy into every shift. The customers were nice, and the tips were decent. It was about a week later that I was late for a shift. As soon as I walked in the door, I could see how pissed off Ed was. He was a stickler for being on time. In fact, he wanted everyone there fifteen minutes early for each shift so that the staff knew the daily specials and were ready to go when they clocked in. Ed took me aside and reminded me about the rules of the job. It felt like I was being scolded by a parent. I broke down in tears and told him why I was late. The roach-infested hotel had one more surprise that I hadn't expected—the owner of the place was a pervert who liked to break into my room and play with my underwear. It sounds crazy, but I caught him in my room when I came home from work the day before. Actually, I didn't know it was him at the time. I just saw a leg coming into my place through the window. I had no idea who it belonged to, but I wasn't about to let anyone in. I grabbed a kitchen knife and stabbed hard. There was a yell, and the leg disappeared into the night. I called the cops. They weren't particularly quick to respond, and when they did, their best recommendation was that I move. It was the next day when I left for work that I noticed the owner at the front desk limping. He couldn't make eye contact with me. It looked like I got him good." Carmen paused for a moment and smiled, a dark, disturbing grin.

"Anyway I hadn't been able to sleep. It took me hours to get the window and door barricaded to the point that I felt safe. I told Ed the story, standing in the back of the kitchen, with endless tears dropping on his spotless white floor. I was ashamed to admit where I was staying and was afraid of getting fired. I lied about my address on the application and thought for sure that the lie alone would be enough to get me booted out. I remember Ed staring at me, not saying a word and shaking his head. All I could think about was that if I lost the job, I would never be able to get a decent place. In the minute of silence as he stared at me, I was sure that I was going to end up doing special favors for guys like Fadi, to get enough money to go back to LA. All of my dreams of a fresh start were about to be crushed.

"To my surprise, Ed didn't fire me. He put his arm around my back like my father used to do and offered me a room above the café. I was so grateful. It was a small apartment, just one room with a tiny shower and a microwave. He kept it for nights when traffic was tied up, and he didn't want to deal with the hour and half-drive home. He took three hundred a month off my pay, which was absurdly cheap even for a hole-in-the-wall space in the city. That one gesture made us bonded somehow. I worked my ass off at that job, if only to repay his kindness.

"I couldn't grab my bags quick enough from the roach-infested den I had been living in. When Ed offered me the apartment, it was looking like a sign from above. I thought that maybe my parents were watching and lending a helping hand. It was so perfect that my first night above the café, I just sat and cried."

"Sounds like he was a wonderful man," Tarryn said, wondering if Ed would be the catalyst to bring Carmen back from the brink. He was obviously someone that she cared about and respected. He filed that tidbit of information away for use later, if the situation required it.

"He was the best man I ever met, other than my father. He ended up like a surrogate parent to me. He watched out for me and treated me like I was one of his own. It was maybe three weeks after I started that Simon, the guy I fantasized was named Aiden, walked back through the doors of the café. I had actually forgotten about him, but when he sat at the counter, my heart was fluttering and I could barely speak. I asked him if he wanted a coffee and bagel, and he asked if I was a mind reader. I think I muttered something about Janice, the other waitress, telling me what he ate. I couldn't admit that I had made up an entire life story for him based on the last time he had ordered that particular meal.

"Ed was working in the back and smiled at me as I took the man his breakfast. He knew that I was head over heels. He gave me a wink, which made me a bit more relaxed. I played it cool and got through the service without spilling on my handsome stranger or messing up the orders of our other customers. Ed took me aside at closing and said just one thing, "He's just a man like any other, and you are a beautiful young woman. He'll be back again."

"I dreamt of him over and over again that night. I imagined that I was his wife and how wonderful my life would be. It seems so ridiculous now. At the time, I would have climbed the highest mountain to have that man. You've heard the saying 'Be careful what you wish for'—I should have listened."

FOURTEEN

TARRYN THOUGHT THE SAME THING ABOUT HIS EARLY years. If he had only listened to his mother way back when. If he hadn't wanted the date with Sandy so badly, he wouldn't have needed Marnie's expertise. If he had only listened to his mother, he wouldn't have felt so dirty and disgusting. He had been angry with himself for not heeding the warnings.

Humiliated and downtrodden, he decided not to return to school the following year. He couldn't bear the thought of facing Sandy, Marnie, or the countless others that would hear the story over the summer months. He knew that he would be the brunt of countless jokes about his wobbling warhead.

1989 was also the year where his mother had started to fall from the loving woman that he adored into the dark pit of depression. Ted Bundy, the love of her life had been executed on January 24. Her hopes of meeting him, holding him, and perhaps even marrying him were crushed as the two thousand volts of electricity coursed through his body. His mother was sure that his final words "I'd like you to give my love to my family and friends" were ultimately meant for her. She cried for days on end, grasping a picture of Bundy in her hand. She was using crack almost exclusively at that point, and the frequency was accelerating—excusing it as the only way to dull the pain of losing her one and only love.

Having just turned fifteen, Tarryn was more than capable of earning a living and helping out with the bills at home. He got a job with a local roofing company who were so desperate for help that they were willing to train. With a fake ID in hand, he was on the crew. He told his mother his plans, and she was happy. Tarryn knew it was the kind of self-centered happy that she was starting to show more often. If he got a job, he could pay the rent and buy some food—her tip money would become more disposable for the things that she wanted for herself. She could mourn the passing of her precious Ted without the burden of a regular shift at work.

Tarryn's relationship with her had become strained after the whole date incident. He never told her what happened; he had been warned that real men don't cry. She didn't want to hear it, and he didn't want to tell.

He desperately wanted to get back in her favor. He didn't feel like he fit anywhere with anyone. With school over and starting a new job, he was longing for the days when they would spend hours together watching television or reading books. The roofing crew that he worked on was always looking at him with accusing eyes. He thought that they could see inside his mind and knew about his inability to perform. He just wanted to feel loved and comforted again, just like the old times.

It was increasingly difficult to impress his mother with new facts about Ted Bundy; she knew them all, and there hadn't been any new killers surfacing that they could discuss for quite a while. He knew that if she remained on the destructive path she was on, that he would lose her forever. It was time for drastic measures. It was time for change.

FIFTEEN

CARMEN HAD BEEN TALKING FOR ABOUT TWENTY minutes, and he hadn't been listening. Tarryn hoped that he hadn't missed any key points that he would need later as ammunition. Talking to Carmen was bringing back memories that he had buried deep within the catacombs of his brain. It was time to focus on the situation at hand. *Screw the past—the memories didn't serve a purpose.* If he lived his life by analyzing his history, it was the equivalent of driving a car by looking only through the rearview mirror. The welts on his back began to tingle, reminding him that soon he would take another life—in that one moment, none of his past issues would matter.

"Simon was charming and was everything that I could have wanted in a husband. Okay, so he didn't have a private jet, a dog named Charger, or a house with a pool. What he did have was a great job doing cyber investigative work for a big computer company, and he was single. He wooed me with flowers and candlelit dinners. He didn't care about my imperfect pigment or my misaligned ears. He was interested in my day and respectful of Ed. Simon had wonderful friends and came from a strong family background. He loved me for who I was. It was all I could do to keep from blurting out how much I adored him every time I saw his face. I was so young and stupid. You would think that I would have developed a pretty tough skin after all that I had been through to that point, but when it came to emotions, I was still a schoolgirl at heart. All I really wanted was to be loved.

"When Simon finally asked me to marry him a year later, he burst into the café with a violinist at his side and got down on one knee. Ed was in the back, grinning from ear to ear. He had asked Ed for his permission—it was a sweet touch. I was crying so much with joy that I could barely whisper the word "yes." It was a whirlwind fairy-tale romance. I felt like a million bucks.

"My past experience hadn't really prepared me for the next part of my life. I had never lived with a man before, and I certainly never had a bank account with money in it. I moved into his condo and left the café. It was a bittersweet experience. Ed held on to me for a long time as I handed back the key to the apartment and the café. Simon told me that my only job for the next six months was to plan our wedding. I had full control over the venue, the dress, the food, the flowers, and the cake. All of it would be about me. I was overwhelmed but really excited. I hired a wedding planner and started spending up a storm. Simon would come home at night and shower me with affection and compliment the choices that I had made. I had never felt so wonderful, safe, and secure. It was like the entire heavens were focused on my happiness. Business was booming for Simon. He was working long hours, but he was getting bonuses like crazy. It couldn't have been better.

"Six months later, we had the ceremony at the café to commemorate where we met. I just wanted something small. I didn't have any family to speak of, just my aunt in LA, Ed and the other waitress, Janice. Simon's parents flew in from Spain, and a couple of his friends from work showed up. It was intimate and beautiful. I wore a Vera Wang dress, which cost more than most cars and held the most beautiful bouquet of white lilies. I only knew three of the one hundred and fifty guests that attended the reception. Most were friends and must-invite business contacts of Simon's.

"Ed offered to cater the party, but trying not to hurt his feelings, I told him that he deserved a night off. The reception was planned and catered by Colin Cowie, decorator to the stars, and the entire room was filled with burgundy silk and the most beautiful candlelit centerpieces. Colin cost an arm and a leg, but to call the reception stunningly beautiful would be woefully inadequate.

"We honeymooned on the island of St. Thomas in the Virgin Islands. It was magical with its tropical scenery and white sand beaches.

We rented a catamaran and sailed to small quaint islands during the day, lunched on fresh seafood and made love every night. I couldn't have asked for anything more perfect. Simon treated me like royalty, and I was more than willing to move into the role of a princess."

"It sounds wonderful. So what happened? It doesn't sound to me like a life that you would want to get away from." Tarryn stopped mid thought and decided that it was now or never for step two in the kill. They had been at Sam's long enough, he had to move her somewhere else. "Hold on a sec before you get started. All of that talk of fresh seafood is making me hungry. So I guess I have a question—if it was your last meal on earth, what would it be?" It was a gutsy move, testing the waters to see if she was still in suicide mode, or if he had worked his charm and moved her back from the ledge.

Carmen's eyes clouded over again, and she stared into her empty coffee cup. "I guess even death row inmates get a last meal. I wouldn't mind a steak. Do you know anywhere that they serve steak in the dark?"

"Believe it or not, I do," he answered, an alligator-sized grin on the inside but keeping his outer facade in check. She was coming around, and Tarryn's excitement was growing by the second. He had officially eliminated the thought of gutting her with the fish knife ... too much undigested food was going to be inside her belly.

STEP 2–SEDUCTION
12:30 PM

SIXTEEN

SEDUCTION IS LIKE A DANCE. IF TARRYN COULD LEAD his partner's steps with a gentle guiding hand at the perfect tempo, he would achieve perfection. If he missed a step or moved too quickly, he knew he would fail.

Tarryn's pulse was accelerating rapidly as he opened the front passenger door for Carmen. He perused her long legs as she positioned herself in the seat and was impressed with his selection of woman. She was pretty, and the profile of her face was intriguingly wholesome as he closed the door. She was a perfect playmate for the day. He tried to calm himself as he walked to the back of the car. Mistakes get made when you lose control of your emotions, and talking to Carmen had brought up a few that he had wanted to leave behind.

He took a deep breath before he got into the driver's seat and smiled at her with the charm meter fully engaged. "It's a bit of a drive, but I know a little place just outside the city called the Stagecoach. It fits the criteria of a fantastic steak, and it's dark as well. Sound okay?"

"Sure. I'm good with that," she replied quietly.

Needing to get his nervous system calmed down, Tarryn remembered his first kill and reminded himself of the mistakes that he had made. He wouldn't let that happen again.

After working for the roofing company for three years and trying desperately to bring his mother back from the edge of drug-induced insanity, he was angry. She was the only woman in the world that he could trust and the only one who had ever accepted him for who he really was. Watching her wither away was tearing at his soul, and every day when he got home from work, she would be in a haze of intoxication. Knowing that the bills were taken care of, she had done exactly what he had feared—spent all of her tips and her meager wages on drugs. First it was manageable and she was still able to hold down her job, but after his eighteenth birthday, things had accelerated to the point that she could no longer work.

He wasn't sure how she was getting money for her habit now that she was no longer employed by the restaurant, and he didn't want to ask. The only thing that concerned him was getting her attention focused on something new. He had wracked his brain with so many different solutions, but most thoughts led to the same conclusion—she would have to leave for a detox facility. His wages from roofing barely covered the bills, and rehab was expensive. Plus, he wasn't willing to give her up—not even for a single day. He had to give her a reason to live, a reason to reconnect with him. Even at eighteen years old, he desperately needed the acceptance and love that she, and only she, had ever shown him.

When he looked back, Tarryn knew that by the time he was eighteen, the thoughts of attempting a kill had been festering for over five years. At first it was a little annoyance, like a mosquito buzzing in his mind. Then the tiny mosquito turned into a beetle, scuttling around his brain. Then by eighteen, the beetle had grown into a full-sized condor, soaring into every corner of his skull on a daily basis. He wondered if maybe saving his mother was just an excuse to fulfill the fantasy.

He picked out his first victim at a party. She was younger by a couple of years and was loaded to the gills with booze and other unknown toxic substances. Tarryn reminded himself of the subtleties of a successful killer—calm, thoughtful movements and measures. After years of study he thought it would be easy. It wasn't.

Even after countless reviews of the masters, he was still nervous. While he had spent years sifting through the details of other murders, he wanted to be unique and not a copycat of someone else. His mother would never be impressed by a facsimile of Ted Bundy; he needed to be better. While he had many ideas on what form his art would take, it was his first time, and it takes practice to be perfect. His first kill was far from it.

The girl he picked out glanced at him several times during the night. She was a waif of a person, with a small waist and long blond hair. They were never introduced, nor did he want to be. He smiled and winked a couple of times but kept himself at a safe distance where she wouldn't be able to talk to him. He wanted to be seen as a mystery to her—a sexy, interesting, mystery. He kept his eye on her movements throughout the evening, but not a word was spoken between them until midnight. Most of the other partiers were well on their way and were all engaged in their own conversations.

He watched as she went to the bathroom and followed her up the stairs to the second floor. He waited patiently outside as he listened to the tinkling sounds as she emptied her bladder. When she emerged, he smiled his best smile and kissed her hard on the lips. When the brief embraced ended, he whispered in her ear, telling her to meet him on the beach in ten minutes. Without another word, he turned and walked into the bathroom. His heart was pounding, and the steel of the hunting knife in his pocket felt cold through the fabric of his jeans.

He thought of the relaxation techniques that he had learned in drama class—slow breaths in from the nose and out through the mouth, thoughts of the beach, the smile on his mother's face. After reducing his stress to a manageable level, he left the washroom and said good-bye to his host. He didn't see the girl anywhere and hoped that she had done as she was told. He walked through the back passageway of trees and shrubs and found her sitting on a rock by the shoreline.

She was a pretty girl. He kissed her hard again, smiled, and grabbed her hand. He led her farther down the beach to a more secluded area. He whispered how beautiful she was and let his hands wander over her chest, just as he had done with Marnie. The experience paid off as she stuck her tongue into his mouth. Tarryn felt aroused in a brand-new way. She started to take off her clothes to allow him an opportunity to get better acquainted. He unbuckled his pants, and she looked at him with a glassy, lustful gaze. With a quick glance around the beach he pulled out the knife and started stabbing.

First he sliced her neck to eliminate unwanted screams, and then he continued over the rest of her body. He had originally planned to hit her heart with the second blow, but he hit a rib instead. The knife stuck in bone, and he had to pull hard to get it to release. As he yanked with all his might to remove it, he watched as the young girl's eyes registered what was happening. It was an incredible rush surveying the damage that he had done not only to her physical being but also to her mind as well. After several more messy insertions, she was dead. The entire thing had spanned less than a minute.

Covered in blood and drenched in sweat, his heart pounding like a bass drum, he stripped down to his underwear. There was a lot more blood than he had anticipated. He put his soiled clothes and the knife into a plastic bag that he had brought with him and calmly walked back up to his car. He was paranoid that someone would see him practically naked in the street, but he managed to skirt the neighboring houses and streetlights until he reached his car. He changed into a second set of clothes that he kept in the backseat and drove away, never exceeding the speed limit and obeying all of the traffic signs and lights.

He could scarcely believe what he had just done. He had just taken a life. Killed a girl. Holy shit—just like Bundy, Manson, Berkowitz, Dahmer, and the rest—he was officially a murderer. The realization felt a bit peculiar, but it felt kind of nice in its own strange way.

It wasn't until he got home, destroyed the knife and his blood-stained clothes that he allowed himself to enjoy what he had just accomplished. He had done it—his premiere kill. Tarryn felt something that he had never felt—an intoxicating mixture of lust, dizzying happiness, and godlike power. He wanted to tell his mother, to scream it from the highest rooftop, to take out a newspaper ad, telling everyone what he had done. It was his calling, his passion, his raison d'être, and he finally understood his mother's addiction to drugs. He wanted to kill again, right away. Now. That very moment. It was the beginning of something so exciting that he could barely contain himself.

He stayed up all night and the following day, watching the rolling news channel, waiting for the story to break. His heart was pounding every time a new story hit the screen. He waited and waited, hoping to see the proof that he had actually done it. *Just show the words* "Girl killed on beach—no suspects." He analyzed each step of the kill, trying to keep an arm's length perspective. His mistakes—he should have hidden the spare set of clothes in the bushes ahead of time. He was lucky that no one had come by as he was streaking back to his car. He should have been more careful about the location—the open beach, even a deserted beach, was too risky. He didn't like the method of this kill either. Stabbing was messy, and he could run the risk of hitting a rib again. He probably could have just cut her throat, maybe a bit deeper, and let her bleed out. It would have been equally effective. Maybe not as quick but certainly it would have sufficed.

The areas where he got an A—he had kept calm through the entire process, he had charmed the girl easily without drawing attention to his interest in her, he had isolated her from the crowd quickly, he had planned to have a bag for his soiled clothes, and he had disposed of his clothes and the knife in a container of acid that he had purchased two weeks before. Many things to be proud of and just a few areas for improvement.

Tarryn wanted to be specialized in his craft but was reluctant to use the same technique over and over again. It might be a signature move to stab his victims, but it was also a telltale clue for the police. There were so many options for next time that his head was spinning with excitement. When exhaustive sleep finally came, he was a bundle of nerves, wondering if his first kill would be his last. Would he get caught? Did he leave trace evidence behind? Were the mistakes that he made too many? Another part of his brain was already planning his next kill. One was good, but more was better.

SEVENTEEN

"WHAT ARE YOU THINKING ABOUT? YOU'RE REALLY quiet," Carmen asked.

"Oh shit, I'm sorry. I was just thinking about something you said earlier—how love can change your life."

"I guess I should say sorry. I haven't even asked about your life. I know you have cats, but are you married? Kids?"

"No, neither. I haven't found anyone that could compete with my mom's cooking. She spoiled me. Maybe someday I'll find the right woman."

"I'm sure you will. You're a kind man."

"It's still another twenty minutes or so to the restaurant. I'd love to hear some more of your story. You had a great honeymoon. What happened after that?" Tarryn remembered where she had left off.

"Yeah, it was a good time. I can't imagine a more beautiful place on earth. When we got back to New York, I was so excited about my new life. In St. Thomas, Simon had mentioned that he might want to start up his own business when we got back. He said that an old buddy had contacted him just before the wedding and that the two of them wanted to set up a business catering to corporations and their HR departments. He asked if I would be interested in helping out. You know, setting up the office, helping with administration-type duties. I was thrilled. Not only was I married to Simon, who I thought was the man of my dreams, but we were also going to have our own business. I was going to be a legitimate part of society. Not a drug dealer, not a waste of skin to be left in the street—a business owner.

"Simon's old buddy turned out to be a Hungarian man named Gustov. Everyone called him Gus. He was thick around the belly and had an accent to match. When I asked where the two of them had met, Simon said it was during a business conference ten years prior. Gus was the kind of man that made my skin crawl. Don't get me wrong, he was well groomed, polite, and funny, but there was something that kept nagging at me. At the time, I just ignored the tugging in the back of my mind, but I wish I would have listened. The experts say that there is a part of your brain that is very old in its way of thinking. It evaluates every image, every word, every nuance of day-to-day life and makes decisions for us that we aren't aware of. They call it the reptilian part of your brain, and it makes one of two choices—fight or flight. Every time I saw Gus, that part of my brain was screaming to run away.

"It took about six months for the business to be set up and legalized. We called it Phototecnics. Simon and Gus each owned 40 percent of the business, and I was a 20 percent partner. For taxes purposes, Simon told me—it was really about control. In the beginning, I was just the office decorator and receptionist. That was all I was qualified to do. I worked with the contractors to set up the office space and answered the phones while Simon finished out his days at his old job. The phones didn't ring much back then. No one knew who we were or what we did. It was a relief when Simon finally came to the office full-time. I was bored to tears and needed some human contact."

"Sorry to interrupt, but what is it exactly that Phototecnics did? Or does?"

"Organizations hire us to find out about how their employees react to certain situations. We conduct discreet tests so that the company can test their staff, or potential staff, prior to being promoted or hired. The employees don't even know that we are involved. We test them with simple things like giving them too much change at a cash register. Do they return it or keep it? We set up racial discrimination outside of the workplace to see how they respond to prejudice. We test them with situations like drug and alcohol usage, infidelity, childrearing. Every trial is preplanned by our team and executed in a way that the subject doesn't know that they're being tested. Even the organizations that hire us aren't sure when or where the experiments are going to take place. They are quick and easy assessments that show an individual's character and morals. For many high-profile organizations, putting a person into a senior position requires more than just a review of their résumé. It might be the public face of their organization or perhaps a position that deals with a high level of confidential information. Either way, if the company feels that it warrants a more thorough look into their personality, they hire us. Make sense?" Carmen had explained the core company business so many times that she almost believed it to be true.

"What if one of these people didn't get their promotion, wouldn't they be upset and want some revenge?" Tarryn was intrigued by the concept.

"No one would possibly know that we were involved. These people see us in social situations only and can't tie us to their workplace. Would you suspect the guy who sells you a newspaper in the morning of being responsible for you being turned down for a promotion?"

"No, I don't suppose I would. Are there a lot of people that needed that type of service? Are you busy?"

"That's a bit of a loaded question. Are we successful? Yes. Are we busy? Yes. Am I involved? Yes. And I'm in way over my head."

EIGHTEEN

UNDERSTANDING SOCIAL BEHAVIOR WAS SOMETHING that Tarryn had perfected over the years. After the first kill, he and everyone else at the party were questioned by the police. His victim's name, he found out during questioning, was Hanna Goldman. She had been sixteen years young, a synchronized swimmer, and was loved by everyone, including her doting parents. Tarryn had been seen leaving around the same time as Hanna, as were about ten others, and was questioned by police.

Tarryn had studied well over the years. He and his mother had spent hours discussing the subtle signals that people give off when they are lying. He had practiced telling lies in the bathroom mirror to eliminate the ticks, fidgeting, blinking, and stuttering that were synonymous with untruths. The police interrogation was a breeze. As he had no connection to Hanna through friends and wasn't seen talking to her at the party, he was quickly dismissed as a suspect. It seemed that he had done things right.

His mother, however, wasn't interested in hearing about the murder of a young girl on the news. He tried to pique her interest by comparing the killer's work to that of Bundy, but she wouldn't budge. Her mind was set—Teddy was the best, and no one else could compare. She reminded him that Bundy had thirty-six confirmed kills, and so far this new person had one. It wasn't worth the effort to "learn about some cheese-eating high school boy who probably got angry when his girlfriend refused to put out" and on top of that, she reminded him that she was in mourning.

Every day in the following weeks, Tarryn wanted to kill again. It was a feeling like no other, and he was addicted to the thrill. He felt no remorse for what he had done. It was no different than swatting a mosquito from his arm. Everyone who he passed during the day was a potential playmate for his next adventure. Who would he choose next? The girl that served him coffee at Dunkin' Donuts? The young-gun dope smoker that he passed on his way to work every morning? The woman who worked in the administration office at the roofing company? It was mind-boggling how many possibilities were at his fingertips.

Tarryn wanted desperately to put kill number two under his belt. Perhaps a second murder would get his mother to take notice. Being cautious and calm was the main concern. Human nature was to make mistakes in the heat of battle. He couldn't afford any errors. Every move from here on out would have to be calculated and sure.

The years of investigation into the other masters of the trade had given him the building blocks that he needed to establish a methodology for success. He developed what he considered to be the five critical steps for an accomplished selective killer. Step one was Selection—picking the perfect target was key. If he picked the same type of person time after time, he would be easy to catch. Every kill had to be different in some way—blondes, redheads, brunettes, girls, boys, women, different ages, different social classes, different ethnicities—there could never be an established pattern.

Step two, or Seduction, was important in that the victim had to trust you. This was probably equally as important as Selection, as the seduction of each person would need to be handled in a way that was meaningful for their personality type. He would have to have multiple plans in place to confidently coerce someone to believe he was a good guy. Bundy used the same story over and over again to lure his victims. Tarryn wanted to be unique.

Isolation was step three, for obvious reasons. He preferred not to kill in his home, but outdoors brought its own set of problems. Every time had to be somewhere different, but always locations that had been thoroughly investigated ahead of time. His options were fairly limited while he still lived with his mother.

Step four was the best in Tarryn's mind—Betrayal—the actual murder itself. To keep suspicions low, he wanted to perfect several types of killing methods. Stabbing was messy, as he had found out with his first murder, but it was personal and up close, and he enjoyed the intimacy of it. Strangulation had the same appeal, as did suffocation. Death by gunshot was quick and held less interest, but in a pinch it would suffice to mix things up. Poisoning was one that he wanted to play with. It didn't have the impact on someone's face that the others did, but Tarryn was working on the idea of an injection, which would give him a few minutes of time with the victim before it killed. Electrocution, beating, burning, and drowning were others that were flitting around in his mind. So many choices. He wanted to keep each kill fresh and interesting. Knowing that his mother would only be fascinated once he had several kills under his belt, he knew that there would be many opportunities for experimentation.

Step five was the most cumbersome as he had to dispose of the bodies. He knew that depending on where the actual kill took place, movement of the body might be difficult. He didn't want to burn the corpses or dissolve them in acid. He wanted someone to find each and every victim. He would have an impressive list when he finally showed his mother what he had done. He wanted to mark each body so that the police would know it was the same killer but not in a way that would allow them to profile him and catch him before he was done.

From his research he understood that he would inevitably leave some sort of trace evidence at each location. However, he had never been arrested, and luckily neither his DNA nor fingerprints were in the system. It took a few days of careful deliberation, but he finally devised the perfect method to tag his victims. It was quick and simple. He was so proud that he wanted to burst into his mother's room and tell her the whole plan. She would be impressed with his cunning.

The rest was easy, all he had to do was start clipping information out of the paper and get her to watch the news. He hoped that with the next two kills, he could pique her interest enough to start her on the slow road to recovery. Tarryn was excited to get them over with as quickly as possible.

In the meantime, he wanted a physical reminder of the events on the beach. He understood why many serial killers collected trophies from their victims—it kept the memories alive until the next extermination. This was also a high-risk maneuver. Jeffrey Dahmer was almost caught by his father when he kept a severed head in his bedroom. Tarryn's trophies would need to take on another form.

Not having thought of that particular detail when he was planning his first murder, another mistake made by a rookie, Tarryn decided on something more personal for each of his conquests. He fashioned a metal wire into the shape of HG3/92—Hanna Goldman March 1992. The piece was only about an inch long by a half-inch high. Big enough that the letters were well formed but small enough that it wouldn't be too large for its intended location.

With a blowtorch, he heated the homemade metal brand until it was white hot. Tarryn put a towel in his mouth to eliminate any accidental noise that might come from his mouth and pushed the hot wire against the top right of his back. The pain was excruciating. He left it on his flesh for as long as he could stand, which was probably only a minute but felt like an hour. The smell was horrendous, and the charred flesh attached itself around the number two as he removed the branding iron from his back. This would forever be the final piece of step five—the Branding. It would signify the end of the task and the disposal of the flesh.

He looked at his handiwork in the mirror over his dresser and winced when he saw the burning red welt. He smiled through the pain because he knew it was worth it. He would forever be marked with Hanna's memory. There would be no telltale collection of items to tie him to his victims. And, unlike Ted Bundy, who never admitted all of his accomplishments, Tarryn would have a permanent parchment on which he would tell his story.

NINETEEN

"TELL ME MORE ABOUT THE BUSINESS. I'M STILL HAVING a hard time figuring out what's so bad. Loving husband and a successful company—sounds like a dream come true for most people." Tarryn glanced over at her but turned back to watch the traffic on the freeway. He wanted to watch her facial expressions, but getting them to their destination in one piece was more important.

"At the beginning it was exciting. After Simon started marketing our services full time, things started to pick up. I was just playing the part of receptionist, but the calls were coming in from all over the country. We were the only ones to offer that particular type of service, and we were discreet. Employers could be sure that we would get the information that they wanted without jeopardizing their company image. As an example, theoretical of course, if word got out that Microsoft was using our services, it would ruin the entire concept. No one who was working there would feel safe from the prying eyes of the company. No one would act naturally, and the company could be viewed as crossing a moral line. We were meticulous with our records. Even our staff had no idea who the customer was. The only information that we provided to our Plants, the staff conducting the experiments, was a picture of the person in question and their first name. Everything else was secured.

"We had some high-profile customers at the beginning. Names you would recognize but that I won't divulge. Fortune 500 companies, oil and gas, manufacturers, government, politicians, law offices, accounting moguls, law enforcement—the list was the who's who of the corporate world."

"How much did they pay for the service? I assume it was expensive if you could buy that huge house I picked you up from today." Tarryn was thinking that he was definitely in the wrong business. Social experimentation was obviously the way to go.

"It depends on what the customer wanted. The deeper into a person's life we needed to go, the more money it cost. Typically the higher up in the organization that the employee was moving, the more investigation that needed to be completed. Most customers were paying anywhere from ten to a hundred thousand dollars. We had one customer that paid two hundred thousand for a complete review. We pulled out all of the stops for that one, and it took an entire year of investigation. The person in question turned out to be clean on all fronts and was promoted to a very high-ranking political position. Let's just say that you can rest assured that our country is safe in his hands," Carmen said proudly.

Tarryn wondered if she was even aware of where they were or where she was going. Carmen continued as she stared out of the windshield, "Like I was saying earlier, everything was going well. We had a full-time staff of twenty that were top-notch Plants, and we used contractors in different cities to supplement the core group. The customers were happy with the results we got for them, and my marriage was perfect. Then two things happened that would forever change my life."

Tarryn noticed that telling her story was getting easier with every word. She was remembering the good times as well as the bad. He expected that the worst was yet to come, and things looked like they were about to get juicy when they pulled up in front of his house. He could barely contain the bloodlust. Being so close to a potential kill zone made him excited.

TWENTY

"I THOUGHT WE WERE GOING TO A RESTAURANT?"
Carmen was not impressed by the venue.

"Sorry, I just want to go and get changed. I also want to change cars.
I hate driving around in this uniform and the bright-yellow banana car.
You can wait outside if you want. I'll just be a minute." Tarryn smiled
his most genuine smile and watched her face for signs of stress. The
sirens were going off in her brain, and it showed.

"I'll wait here," Carmen said, her brows scrunched together.

"Sure, I'll be quick. I promise." Tarryn cursed at himself for moving
too quickly. He would have to change clothes fast and prepare his house
for her return later in the night. The small two-bedroom house was
long and narrow, but it served his purposes. He did his best to keep the
front face clean and tidy, with a few annuals planted in the spring for
color. The neighborhood was older, and the ancient widows that lived
on either side were more interested in watching television than watching
the comings and goings on the street. The oversized single garage out
back was falling down so he kept his cars on the road. The garage was
only used when he needed privacy for certain tasks. Directly across the
street was a small park, but with the aging population of the street, it
was no longer used, which also worked in his favor. Tarryn was proud
of his little piece of real estate, though few had ever seen it, including
his mother.

He opened the front door and glanced back at Carmen sitting in the cab. She was an interesting specimen for sure. Her strength to get where she was now was unbelievable. Sexual abuse, her parents dying, the drugs, moving to New York—it was all so much for a young girl. It explained Ed's summation of her as the Steel Rose. She was beautiful and tough all in one. She reminded him of his mother at the beginning, before the crack cocaine had ravaged her spirit. Carmen was showing herself as a fitting person for today's special honor. Despite how she started the day, her death would not be in vain—after all, she would forever stand out in the history books.

He stepped inside and ran up to the second floor to change. He would only have a couple of minutes to complete the preparations before he risked losing her to the streets. He chose a simple pair of jeans and a loose-fitting golf shirt. Casual but approachable. He could no longer wear any tight-fitting shirts for fear that someone might notice the welts on his back. They were visible if anyone cared to look closely.

Next, he went back down to the main level and chilled a bottle of white wine. She could have one glass to relax before the end of her life. As he looked back, he knew that the first few kills were clumsy in some respects, and Tarryn prided himself on being more caring after years of perfecting the act. If it were him in the same situation, a final glass of wine would be a generous offering.

Finally, he walked down another set of stairs to the basement. The heavy door at the base of the stairs was locked with an electronic keypad. He placed his hand on the scanner, and the door unlatched with a loud snap. The second that he touched the scanner, his back began to itch. It happened every time he entered the room and didn't end until he had fulfilled his fantasy. The anticipation could be overwhelming at times.

He pushed the door inward to reveal what appeared to be a high-tech rumpus room, complete with classically built black leather couches, a plush throw rug, a big screen television, and stereo equipment. The abstract artwork on the walls was custom made for him by a local artist and depicted women in all types of poses. To the naked eye, they were just blobs and blotches of paint on a canvas, but to Tarryn they were a warning for anyone who entered that they were going to be next— though even if they could decipher the images, it would be too late.

He touched the power button on the face of the stereo, and the whirring sound of a generator kicked in. It ran some very special equipment, in addition to the stereo, which he hoped to be able to use later. It would, at minimum, give him options on how Carmen would spend her final moments.

Looking around the room for a final inspection, Tarryn dimmed the lights and felt pleased with the result. When Carmen finally entered his lair, she would be relaxed and would be able to enjoy the comfortable atmosphere that he created for his most special victims. It was rare that he actually brought anyone home with him. Anyone who was invited into the inner sanctum was typically a case where he wanted to savor the final moments without interruption. Carmen would be, by far, the most special visitor that he had ever had.

TWENTY-ONE

TARRYN LOCKED UP THE HOUSE ONCE MORE AND WAS relieved that Carmen was still in the cab. He pointed to a dark blue Ford Mustang across the street and waved his hands as a gesture for her to get in. She was still looking apprehensive as she shut the cab door behind her and walked across to the other vehicle.

"Thanks for being patient. I feel much better now." Tarryn smiled at her as he spoke.

"Look, I'm just not sure if I want lunch after all. I think I'll just go for a walk and go home. Thanks for the invitation, but I'm not hungry anymore," Carmen said with an anxious tone.

"Whoa, hang on a second here. I didn't mean to scare you by taking you to my house. I really want to hear the rest of your story. If I don't get to hear the end, it'll be lost forever based on your plans. Plus I promised you a last meal. If you went to the grave with an empty stomach, God might strike me down for not taking care of you. That's not a chance I'm willing to take. The restaurant is fifteen minutes from here. Okay?" Tarryn's eyes darted around the street. If he was quick, he could grab her and drag her into the house right now. The generator wouldn't be ready, but he knew other equally interesting methods to finish the job at hand. *Too risky—be patient.*

He felt Carmen evaluating him again. He pulled his eyebrows down low on the sides to hopefully convey a concerned puppy dog. She opened the passenger door to the Mustang. The puppy dog look, another of his specialties, had worked again.

"Thanks for sparing me the wrath of God. I still have a full head of hair, and I'm not willing to get it scorched off just yet." He smiled with the charm meter fully engaged.

As he dropped himself into the driver's seat, Tarryn noticed that Carmen was absentmindedly tugging at the bottom of her purse. He wondered what secrets were hidden in the folds of the brown leather. He knew from past experience that a woman's purse could sometimes hold the most valuable of items; things that when kept close, provided comfort and ease. It could also hold knives, small guns, pepper spray, and other noxious objects. He would have to keep an eye on the purse at all times as things progressed.

"So before I so rudely interrupted your story to get changed, you were saying that everything was going perfectly and then two things happened. What were they?"

"Actually, I think that it's my turn to ask a question or two. I was sitting outside waiting for you, and I realized that I've been doing a lot of talking and you haven't told me anything about yourself. Now I'm driving to a restaurant that is God-knows-where, with a man who could be a rapist. The whole thing is a bit surreal to me." Carmen was agitated.

"I guarantee you that I am not a rapist. The thought of anyone taking another person in that way is disgusting to me," Tarryn didn't have to try to look genuine, it was the truth. "What would you like to know about me? I wasn't trying to be sneaky. I just didn't want to interrupt your story."

"Where were you born? Do you have any brothers or sisters? You talked about your mother before. Does she live around here? How long have you lived in your house? How long have you been driving a cab?" Carmen was firing questions at him at a rapid pace.

"Hold on. Slow down. I'll give you the *Reader's Digest* version before we get to the restaurant, and you can decide if you need more detail from there. Okay?"

"Okay."

Tarryn contemplated the consequences of telling *all* of the truth, *some* of the truth, or fabricating a completely new life history. How much reality he injected correlated directly to how confident he was that he would be able to move to the Isolation stage of his plan. He turned the corner off his street and onto the main road. He was feeling confident but how much so? Fifty percent? Seventy-five percent? Ninety percent? There never was 100 percent certainty that each kill would work exactly as planned. Unforeseen circumstances could foul up even the best-laid plans. It hadn't happened to date, but there was always a first for everything.

He started telling his story based on an 80 percent success rate. His confidence running high, he told of growing up in New York, his schooling, his mother's drug addiction, the café where she worked, Betty the neighbor, his job as a roofer, choosing to drive a cab, the details of purchasing the house and the length of time that he lived there.

"Did your Mom die from the drug abuse? You haven't mentioned what happened to her." Carmen looked more relaxed now that he was so forthcoming with the details of his life.

"She died a long time ago from an overdose of heroin. It wasn't pretty, but it made me even more determined to make her proud of me. I work hard every day to live up to her expectations for my life. I still have a hard time thinking about her. She really was my everything." Tarryn knew that the statements were only 80 percent true, just like the rest of his story, but it would keep Carmen satisfied for the time being.

He stole a quick glance at her face and wondered if suffocation would be a suitable ending to her life. A strong possibility.

TWENTY-TWO

THE STAGECOACH RESTAURANT WAS ONLY SLIGHTLY more upscale than Sam's Suds. On the plus side, it was dark and quiet but on the downside, it was not much cleaner than the earlier drinking hole. The walls were covered with dusty pictures of the Wild West and contrasted by the modern televisions hung in each corner of the room. The waitress was in her late sixties and looked as though she had tanned much of her life. Her skin was a thick, leathery coating over her gaunt frame. Her eyes had long ago lost the bright light of youth, and her support hose did little to cover up the thick varicose veins exposed under her black skirt.

"Just the two-o-ya?" she snarled as she grabbed two menus from the side of the bar and handed them to Tarryn. "Pick any table you want. We're slow today. Just holler when you're ready to order." She turned on her low-heeled black shoes and went back to drinking her coffee at a table near the front of the restaurant. Tarryn watched as she started fingering through the local newspaper mere moments after she had left them.

As expected, there were very few tables that were occupied. Tarryn had spent a considerable amount of time during his travels in the cab looking for locations just like this one, good food but not the high-end price or exposure. "Despite the charming personality of our hostess, this place has fantastic food. I've eaten here a few times," Tarryn assured Carmen, who was looking more than a little apprehensive about taking even one more step toward a table. "It's one of those gems that only the locals know about, and our lovely hostess apparently wants to keep it that way."

Carmen didn't say a word but gave him a look that could only be described as downtrodden. It was obvious that she had given up on her life, and this was just par for the course. Tarryn couldn't risk moving her again. "Look, I know that it's not the Ritz, but it's quiet and we can talk without interruption. The food is good, and the bathrooms are clean. You willing to give me a chance on this?"

"Yeah, I suppose," Carmen replied.

Once again, he felt like he had taken a major step backward. "Where would you like to sit, m'lady?" Tarryn gestured with a sweep of his arm.

Carmen chose a table in the middle of the restaurant and perused the menu for several long minutes in silence. Tarryn was pleased that *this time* he had secured a seat facing the door. It made him much more comfortable being able to watch who was coming and going at all times. He flagged down the battle-ax of a waitress, and they ordered two hearty fourteen-ounce strip loins with baked potatoes, asparagus, and the signature beef stew to start. The surly server brought them each a glass of water and a pitcher of sweetened iced tea. The tea was soothing with a hint of honey on Tarryn's tongue. It was a refreshing treat that wouldn't compromise Carmen's ability to make decisions.

"Are you ready to tell me about the two things that changed your life? I'd really like to hear," Tarryn probed.

"Yeah, I guess I should finish. As I was saying, my life with Simon was about as perfect as I could ever have imagined. The money was rolling in from our big customers, and word of mouth in certain high-end circles was getting us more and more revenue. We started upping our prices because of the high demand. I spent my days answering phones and taking messages, but I didn't really have a hand in the business end like I had hoped. Simon and Gus were the ones that hired the Plants and arranged for the corporate tests to take place. Gus was more of a silent partner I suppose. At least I didn't see him all that often. He had a physical office in our building, but it was more for show than anything else. He rarely spent any time behind his desk, and when he did, I wanted to be somewhere else.

"I told Simon that Gus gave me the creeps. He dismissed it, saying that I just didn't know him, and he would grow on me. He wanted me to make a special effort to find a common area that we could talk about and connect on. The unfortunate thing is that I found it—Gus liked women. Gus was obsessed with Internet porn, which was why he didn't spend much time in the office. He preferred to work from home where he could view a certain type of Web site in private. I found out by accident. I wandered into his office to bring him a coffee, my version of an olive branch, and caught him with his pants down and his hands full, so to speak. I was mortified. He just looked up at me, smiled, and continued with his … um … situation, without missing a beat.

"I didn't know if I should tell Simon. I didn't want to create problems in the office. I was ashamed that I had walked in unannounced. I told myself that I should have knocked a little louder, cleared my throat as I walked in, something, anything, to have avoided the situation. I broke down and told Simon what happened that night after work. It was our first fight. He giggled and told me that boys will be boys, and I should just be thankful that he didn't have anyone in there with him. He reminded me that Gus was a 40 percent owner of the company, and sometimes you have to make allowances for people who have certain tendencies.

"It wasn't the reaction I had expected from my new husband. I wanted Simon to talk to Gus and tell him that what he was doing was not appropriate behavior for the office. I wanted him to tell Gus that he was disgusted that he would do such lewd things when his wife was just outside the door. Most of all, I wanted him to tell Gus to keep his piece in his pants. He didn't do any of those things. I started to think that I was just being old-fashioned, that I was really the one with the problem. At that point in time, Simon was the air I breathed. Instead of jeopardizing my marriage, the partnership, and the business that Simon was so proud of, I turned tail and never mentioned it again.

"It was a turning point of sorts. It was a red flag that things weren't as perfect as I originally believed, although I didn't see it at the time. More importantly, it was a sign that Gus was every bit as sleazy as my instincts told me and more. I think it was about a week later when I saw him again. I was expecting that he might be a bit sheepish after our last encounter. Instead, he had the bravado of a bull in heat, with his puffed-out chest and sly wink as he walked passed by my desk.

"I couldn't stand it and told Simon that the work in the office was getting to be too much for me, and I thought it was time to get a professional secretary and accountant. He agreed quickly—too quickly. I imagine that Gus had already suggested the same. It was two weeks later that I left the day-to-day operations of the business and the same time that Gus convinced my husband to sell our souls to the devil."

TWENTY-THREE

THE CONVERSATION WAS STALLED AS THE BEEF STEW arrived at the table. The battle-ax waitress was short on personality, but somehow she made up for it with efficiency and speed. Tarryn wasn't quite ready to stop the story at that particular point and was disappointed when Carmen focused her energy on the thick flavorful broth instead of on him. Knowing that it was her last meal, he decided he would make allowances.

He was amazed that hearing Carmen's experiences were once again bringing back the memories of his own life. She was being so honest about her entire past that he felt guilty that he had not been as open with her about his own experiences. He had relayed some of the key points, of course omitting the special interest area that he and his mother shared—the killings and the impressive strategies that he had developed over the years. She didn't know it, but she was about to find all of those items out firsthand.

He wondered if she would be impressed to know how many people he had killed. She was so close to the documentation of his lengthy career. It was all there permanently impregnated into his back. There were so many scars, that to the average person, it might just look like a jumble of numbers and letters. To a police officer however, it would be pay dirt. A detailed confession to twenty years of murders.

The second and third kills had come quickly after the first. At the time, Tarryn realized now, he was like an out-of-control drunk who was just desperate for the next drop of alcohol to hit his tongue. He made some terrible mistakes on the next two murders, so much so that in looking back, he was amazed that he hadn't been caught. Luckily his mother was there to critique and assist.

His second kill was a teenage boy. Tarryn wanted to change his pattern, as previously planned, so he purposely picked a different gender. The boy, Grant Hallan, was sixteen and a star football player. He was trying to score drugs in Central Park when he met Tarryn. He said that the pressure from his parents and school was too much, and he needed a break. With a promise of some cocaine and two hot girls, Tarryn had lured him into the bushes and bashed his head in with a rock. This time, he had already stashed some clean clothes in the area and had hidden an appropriate-sized rock in a secluded part of the pathway. He marked the dead boy's forehead with a large number two in black felt-tip marker. There would be no mistaking that there was a killer on the loose once the numbered corpses started to pile up.

Kill number three was another young boy in his teenage years. Tarryn had lured him in much the same way but took him for a drive in his car to the supposed site of an outdoor bonfire party. The seventeen-year-old kid, Chad Bellows, had gone willingly and excitedly, looking forward to the night. Tarryn was still trying to tell as much of the truth as he could to each victim, just in case his lying skills weren't perfected. In the case of Chad Bellows, he had told the truth about the bonfire, but the part he omitted was that Chad was the kindling for the flames. Tarryn cut his head off and marked it with a three before setting the rest of his body in flames.

With their initials and dates firmly implanted in his back, Tarryn thought that he would have felt better, but he realized that while he was fulfilling his destiny, it was leaving him feeling empty. The second and third kills were not as good as the first. Something had changed. It didn't take him long to deduce that killing boys didn't give him the same thrill as killing females. His mother wouldn't have approved of that type of behavior; it was too close to the homosexual tendencies that she despised. He made a vow to be more selective about his prey from that point forward. With three kills under his belt, it would hopefully be enough to get his mother back engaged in conversation. Tarryn wanted to get her opinion on his handiwork. She was after all, the connoisseur of serial killers, and she would be the best one to help him refine his craft. She hadn't let him down.

"Good stew," Carmen commented.

Tarryn had no idea how long he had been firmly planted in the past. Sometimes he found it hard to get himself back to reality when he was thinking about his mother. He missed her dearly.

"See, I told you this place wasn't as bad as it looked. Just wait until you try the steak." Tarryn pursed his lips and held his hand up to his mouth. "Magnifico," he said, with a thrown kissing motion.

Carmen giggled, just a little, at his chef impersonation. "So I was telling you about Gus. I was back to being bored. Without the day-to-day interactions with customers on the business front, there wasn't much to do. I was Suzy Homemaker, and I was dying a slow death. So I decided to start a small business of my own. Simon was fully supportive of the venture. I wanted to open a pet store. I always loved animals and thought it would be a great way to spend the day. Simon and I had been trying to have a baby, but things just weren't working out. He was becoming more agitated and anxious, and sex was starting to go by the wayside in favor of building the business and sleep. The store would be my baby until the time that we were blessed with the real thing. I leased a little store front in a busy strip mall and called the business Whiskers and Paws.

"It wasn't long until I had a good clientele, but I wasn't making enough to get the company in the black. The revenues from Phototecnics were supplementing my other venture. I felt like an imposter and a complete failure. Some little piece of me kept tugging at my brain, saying that I wasn't capable of doing anything on my own. I was just an ex-druggie with no business savvy, and the world was going to realize it soon enough.

"I was starting to get depressed all over again. So I turned to the one person who had always been there for me no matter what. Our relationship wasn't as strong as it had been when I was working for him, but Ed and I still kept in touch. The corporate world that Simon was in didn't mesh well with Ed's blue-collar ramblings. I found his stories endearing, but Simon had drawn a line on how much time he wanted to spend with Ed outside of the cafe. When I showed up at Good Earth, I was greeted with open arms and open hearts—just like I had been there every day. The customers were happy to see me, Janice was happy to see me, and Ed was over the moon. I felt like I was home again.

"I sat with Ed and chatted all day one Saturday. It was probably killing him not to be shouting out orders to the staff and harassing the customers, but he took the time to hear me out and listen to my problems. At the end of several hours and a few pots of coffee, he reminded me that my issues were ones that most people would be happy to have—great husband who has a successful business, a pet store, where it didn't matter if I made money, and the possibility of a baby when the timing was right. To Ed, it was just a matter of feeling happy, and the happiness would come. Dream it and you will receive it.

"I left there feeling on top of the world. I don't think that Ed's advice was particularly poignant or that anything he said changed in my situation. It was just the atmosphere that brought my spirits up. That undeniable feeling of home. I guess seeing Ed also helped me feel connected to my parents. He was the next best thing to being able to ask them for advice." Carmen stopped as the main course arrived at the table. "Let's eat and we can talk more afterward. The smell of that charred beef is making me drool."

Hurry up with the damn story. Kill her, kill her, kill her. The juices running from his steak reminded him of the reason for the meal.

TWENTY-FOUR

THE STEAKS WERE DONE PERFECTLY, MEDIUM RARE as requested, the potatoes were creamy, and the asparagus fresh and flavorful. The conversation changed over dinner to discussions more fitting a nice meal. Tarryn talked about the books he was reading—Patterson's latest was a page-turner. Carmen mentioned the antics of Sabre the feline with fond regard—according to her stories he had "cattitude." The downtime in the discussion served two purposes in Tarryn's mind—one, it gave him a chance to gather his thoughts; and two, it was critical in the seduction step of his plan. He wanted her to feel comfortable enough to continue the story, but more importantly, he wanted Carmen to fall for him. It wouldn't be love, it never was, but a minimum of lust was required.

The conversation was easy. No awkward moments of silence, no long gazes out the window, wishing she was somewhere else. Tarryn was feeling very confident that he had moved her past the suicidal thoughts that she had when they first met. His mother's voice flashed in his mind for the second time in the day, "She's a beauty—thirty-six and counting." He tried to hold on to the thought and the memory of her voice, but it was gone as quickly as it had arrived. He didn't have a photograph of his mother and spent at least a half hour of every day purposefully remembering the details of her face and her voice. He knew that once those thoughts were erased, she too would be gone.

This was by far the most intimate interaction that he had ever had with a woman. Typically, the conversation was limited and consisted of the well-practiced lies that he told them to move them through the process. Tarryn wondered why this particular woman had been brought into his life. Why did it seem that every portion of her story reminded him of his own journey in some way?

Even her last installment in the tale had reminded him of the day when he asked his mother for advice about the kills. He wanted so desperately to impress her, but before he could, he needed to ensure that the kills he had done were worthy of her critical eye.

After the third murder, word was out that there was a monster on the loose in New York City. The telltale sign of the black number on the victims' heads was enough to convince the authorities that the bodies weren't just part of the over two thousand homicides that took place every year. This was the real deal. There was a serial killer on the streets, and police had no leads. The newspapers and television broadcasts were all speculating on where the killer would strike next and while victims two and three had been found, presumably there was another body somewhere with a black number one emblazoned on its forehead.

Tarryn remembered the first time he had talked to his mother about his handiwork. They were watching the news, and as usual she was high on God-knows-what.

"Wow, looks like there's a new kid on the block. Three kills already in just a few weeks. The guy's pretty brave to do that many so quickly." Tarryn waited for her to respond with bated breath.

"Interesting, I guess. Probably some faggot getting his thrills. The guy will get caught. He's already making mistakes," she said with a tone of boredom.

"Really? Why would you say that? No leads so far. The cops are chasing their tails, looking for suspects. Plus I don't think it's a faggot. No sexual contact with either of the last two victims," Tarryn replied. He was hurt that she thought he was a homo. He should have marked the girl as well. It was far too late for that. Mistake noted.

"The guy is obviously trying to get a headcount. Why else mark the victims with numbers. The press is calling him the Numbers Killer. If that's his goal, he's bound to make a mistake. He'll get sloppy just to get the numbers up. Ted didn't worry about the numbers, he was controlled.

This guy isn't. Too many kills in the same area too quickly. He'll get caught," she noted matter-of-factly.

"Yeah, good point, Mom." Tarryn was upset that she was so hopelessly negative but was curious what pearls of advice might come from her lips.

"Plus," she added, "I still think he's an amateur. He's taking kids who are high. Every victim so far had drugs or alcohol in their systems when they died. He's not capable of seducing his victims. Ted was particularly good at that. He convinced every single one of them to help him in some way, carry something, pick something up. Whatever he wanted, he got those girls to do it without drugs. Now that's impressive. This guy still needs work."

Her smug attitude felt like a cheese grater tearing at his heart. He was trying. Sure, he was still early in his career, but he thought he would have received some word of praise for his accomplishments, just a little nugget of interest from his mother. She was right in her assessment, of course. He needed to branch out to areas outside of New York, and he needed to establish a more random pattern, just like Bundy had done. The upside was that she was talking to him again, just a little glimpse that he had started his mother back on the road to recovery. A few more strategic kills, and she would be his again.

The roofing job was too restrictive. Nine to five was great if you had a family at home, but for his chosen extracurricular activities, predictability meant jail. He quit his job the next day and applied to be a taxi driver for Yellow Cab. Shift work gave him the flexibility that he needed to expand his horizons and make his mother proud.

TWENTY-FIVE

CARMEN WAS OFF IN HER OWN WORLD AGAIN. THE conversation had lapsed as the two of them sat, digesting their dinners and their thoughts. She broke the silence after five minutes of cerebral rest.

"You know, when I was a kid, back before my parents' accident, I dreamed that I would be a princess. I wanted to live in a castle with billowing pink curtains and a big four-poster bed. I wanted an entire stable of perfectly white horses and servants that would bring me whatever I needed. I can't remember ever having a logical thought in my head about a career or a real job in my whole life. Most kids have some kind of dream—doctor, lawyer, vet, whatever. But I had nothing. I just let the world dictate who and what I was going to be. I wasn't the director of the play, I was just an actress, playing the role that someone wrote for me."

Tarryn contemplated what the correct response would be and was surprised that the answer came so easily. "You did what you had to do based on your life's experience. You can't look back and try to change where you've been. You can only live in the moment. It's all that any of us have." He touched her hand briefly. "This is it. Right here. Right now. We were brought together for a reason. I think that it's destiny somehow. You need to tell your story, and I need to hear it."

Tarryn's back was itching as his predatory instinct reared its head again. In that one moment, Tarryn felt that he had been more honest with her than he had been with any other woman he seduced. He needed to hear more. He was no different than she was, living a life that had been predestined from the day he was born. Part of him wanted to know what would drive her to suicide so he could save her, but another part of his brain was screaming that if she was going to be "the one" he wanted to know that she was worthy of such an honor. After all, this was a momentous occasion—he was about to surpass Bundy's record. *Kiss her, kill her, kiss her, kill her.*

"All I wanted was to succeed at something … anything. Ed helped me realize that I had already come so far from when he first met me, that scummy hotel, living with the street filth. I was feeling better and threw myself wholeheartedly into the business again. It didn't matter about the bottom line, as long as I was happy, everything was right with the world. Simon and I were still so in love. The incident with Gus was stored in the furthest depths of my memory, and we were back on track.

"It was about a year later that I found out how far *off* the track things had gotten since I left the business. I noticed little changes in Simon. He wasn't as attentive as he normally was. At first, I just chalked it up to the fact that he was so busy. I tried to talk to him, but he just smiled and told me he was thinking about expanding the business. It was supposedly taking up a lot of his energy. When I tried to get the details, he was reluctant to share information. He told me not to worry and that I should focus on the retail store. I could see the anguish burning in his soul. I wanted to help him, but he just pushed me away every time I tried. I started to get suspicious that he was having an affair. I asked him, and he denied that there was anything wrong. This went on for months before I finally had enough. I didn't care about anything but our marriage. The store, the business, they could all disappear. I just wanted my husband back, the man that I fell in love with and whose baby I someday hoped to bear.

"Simon and Gus went on a business trip. It was the first time that we had been apart, even for a night, since our wedding day. I was devastated at first, my imagination running wild with infidelity, drugs, too much booze. I didn't know what had changed Simon, but as I told you before, my brain was on a roller coaster of crazy thoughts. Then I realized that this was the opportunity that I was looking for. I went to Phototecnics one night after the office had closed and started my investigation. If

Simon was having an affair, I was sure that I would find the proof in his office.

"I had no idea what I was looking for. Maybe a phone number or a pair of women's panties—it was an emotional decision that was, at best, a half-baked plan. I was so afraid of getting caught, and my heart was thumping so loudly that I thought my chest was going to burst. I started in Simon's office. He had a picture of the two of us in St. Thomas on his desk, and I immediately felt guilty for being so suspicious. We looked so incredibly happy. How could I possibly accuse the man I loved of any wrongdoing? My heart told me I was wrong, but my head told me to keep looking. His desk drawers yielded little more than a pack of Tic Tacs and the usual pens, pads of paper, and business cards. His file cabinets were locked, and I didn't have a key. I didn't want to break in to the cabinet. While I had lots of experience on the street, breaking and entering was not one of my strengths. I sat down in front of his computer and hoped that I knew him as well as I thought I did. It took me three tries to get the password right—Caramello—his nickname for me. He said I was as sweet as a Caramello. Carmen drifted off into the past again.

Tarryn was getting impatient. What had she found? *What was the big fucking secret?* Dinner was over, and he wanted to get her out of the restaurant. His intellectual side was telling him to be patient, but the animal inside of him was roaring like a lion. The frustration was building at a rapid pace.

"Did you find anything?" Tarryn asked with his kindest, sincerest tone. He was afraid that the thin veneer of normal society that he painted on in these situations was going to crack and betray his true intentions. For a split second, he wondered what his true intentions were … *kiss her, kill her, kiss her, kill her.*

"What I found were a bunch of e-mails that didn't make sense. They were in some kind of code. The words were English, but the sentences were gobbly goop—"The blond lama took a train to the twenty yellow spoons." What the hell did that mean? There were maybe thirty e-mails like that from e-mail addresses that I had never heard of … ones that ended in .uk, .pl, .dh, .de, .fm. I wrote a few of them down so that I could look at them later. To this day, I still can't figure out the code even though I know what the e-mails are about. I shut Simon's computer down and went into Gus's office. That was what almost got me killed."

"Can I get you folks anything else?" The waitress was gathering up the soiled plates and looking impatient while she waited for an answer. Tarryn shot her a nasty look for the interruption.

Tarryn looked at Carmen and shrugged his shoulders. "You want a dessert or coffee? They make a mean apple pie."

Carmen seemed oblivious to what the waitress was asking. "Sure, whatever," she replied.

Tarryn cursed himself for offering. *It wasn't a damn date. She was a victim—number thirty-seven.*

With the waitress off to get coffee and pie, Carmen rushed to finish the current installment of her life. "Anyway, I went in to Gus's office. It was one of those moments that I was almost sure that he was sitting at the desk with his pecker in his hand. I had that strong of a memory. I gagged just from the smell in the office. It smelled like him—the chair, the desk, the curtains. They stunk like his cologne, and the entire room just felt greasy. I had to remind myself over and over again that he wasn't in the city. It was the first time in months that I had gone back in his office, and I felt dirty for having walked through the door. I rummaged through the papers on his desk but didn't find anything of interest. I was going through the bottom desk drawer when I heard the key in the front office lock. I panicked. How was I going to explain that I was in Gus's office in the middle of the night? If my heart was pounding before, it was doing double duty all of a sudden. A voice that I didn't recognize asked if anyone was in. I was frozen in place. The footsteps came closer to Gus's office door, and I did the only thing I could think of—I ducked underneath the desk and hid.

"That's when my life changed. That exact moment. The moment that I found out the mess that my husband and Gus had gotten us into. That's the moment that leads up to where I am right now—sitting in a restaurant with a total stranger, spilling my guts about my life. Waiting to finish the story so that I can finish my miserable life." The tears were streaming down her face again, her body was tense, and her voice rose above normal speaking volume. And then, the waitress showed up with their pie.

Tarryn remarked to himself that the withered old woman had the worst timing of anyone he knew. Her constant interruptions were going to make him lose his mind. He was not only going to give her a crappy tip, but he was also going to put her on the list of potential victims for the future. She didn't fit the criteria of his special selections at this point, but she deserved to die, and not in a pleasant way. He might need a quick hit to keep him happy down the road. The battle-ax with the bad timing would be top of his list.

As she placed the coffee cups and pie on the table, she looked at Carmen in an unusual way. Tarryn wondered how much of the last few sentences she had heard. He needed to change the subject again to lighten up the conversation. He needed Carmen to giggle a few times before the waitress started to remember them too clearly.

When the waitress wandered off, Tarryn worked his magic. "Wow, this sounds like it's getting pretty serious."

"It is about to," Carmen said with a whisper.

"Can we make a deal? How about we finish our coffee and pie and then we can continue on? I really wanted you to enjoy this meal. You're starting to get upset. Don't get me wrong, I want to hear the rest, but I want you to enjoy the pie too. Deal?" Tarryn's charm meter was up to about eight. It wouldn't go any higher until they left the restaurant. That was when he was going to need to pull out all the stops.

"Deal." Carmen managed a half smile.

TWENTY-SIX

THE MINDLESS BANTER CONTINUED WHILE THEY ATE. Tarryn was coffeed out, but he sipped it anyway. It was beginning to taste bitter, as coffee often does later in the day. Carmen probed more about his life. High school sports? Favorite movies? Best television shows? It was all casual conversation and memories of the fabricated Tarryn, the real one kept at bay to allow the public persona his time in the spotlight. He kept his truth percentage at the 80 percent he had mentally agreed to, every once in a while catching his mouth divulging more than his mind would normally allow.

"You talk very fondly of your mother. She must have been a great woman," Carmen commented, putting a forkful of the sweet apple and flaky crust into her mouth.

"Yep, she was the greatest. I didn't really appreciate that until just recently. She was the only woman to truly understand me. I haven't found anyone else that even came close. I'm just disappointed that she isn't here today. I think she would have liked you."

Tarryn wondered if, in fact, his mother would have liked Carmen. At minimum she would have been proud today. Today he would break the record that had been dangled in front of him like a golden carrot for so many years. Would it be enough? How many would be enough? Bundy had publicly admitted to thirty-six victims. Where there more that he kept secret? He had used information to stay two executions, giving out tidbits of knowledge about particular kills. Even on the day he was executed, he wanted to tell more, but the executioner still flipped the switch. His bargaining power was exhausted.

The freedom that being a cab driver gave him was wonderful. Kills could happen at any time during the day or night. The cab gave him the ability to check out new kill sites and meet many new victims of all shapes, sizes, and races. Potential victims seemed to present themselves on a daily basis.

Heeding his mother's advice, he didn't murder anyone in the vicinity for six months after number three. His thoughts were consumed twenty-four hours a day with exacting a flawless execution in every single aspect of the kill. As his confidence started to build, there had only been two aborted attempts with victims. He was getting better all the time and was trying to perfect Seduction without the use of toxic substances.

Victims four, five, and six were all women that were taken in Massachusetts over a six-month period—one by strangulation, one with an injection of liquid drain cleaner, and one was stabbed. Unlike his first attempt at stabbing, he reviewed a few medical journals at the library first to understand exactly where to place the blade. The result was a much cleaner kill zone, and the blade hadn't caught on a rib once.

After number six, Tarryn had also realized that branding the initials of his victims into his flesh was more challenging on certain areas of his back. He rigged up a sliding wooden box where he could secure the brand in place at the level he required and a dual mirror system to ensure that the hot metal found just the right home on his back. It made for much easier documentation.

Victims seven, eight, nine, and ten were from New Jersey. The youngest girl was sixteen, and the oldest was forty. Each one had a special place in his heart, but Tarryn was particularly happy with the older woman. She was strong as an ox and was dripping with diamonds. He watched her eyes intently as she took her last breath. At first they were as brilliant as the diamond necklace that she had around her neck and then the next moment, dull as a piece of coal. There was something special about that woman; she was everything that he had ever hoped his mother would be. He hated the woman for having the life that he wanted for his own. He hated her for holding on to her wealth and not sharing it with the likes of his family. He hated his mother for not being more like his victim, and he hated himself for thinking negative thoughts about the only woman that ever cared for him.

It was the start of a new era of his career. For the next eight years he wanted to kill that rich bitch again and again and again.

"How hard was it to learn the city when you started driving cab? I think the constant blaring of horns and sirens would drive me bonkers, not to mention all of the people that cross against the lights downtown. How do you keep sane?" Carmen asked.

When Tarryn looked up to respond, he saw something that he wasn't expecting—a uniformed police officer was talking to the waitress at the hostess station. He felt his heart skip a beat as he watched the interaction between the two.

"Hello?" Carmen tried to get his attention.

Tarryn looked at Carmen again. "Sorry, I got distracted. You were asking about driving in the city? It …" Tarryn looked toward the front of the restaurant again and noticed that both the police officer and the waitress were looking in their direction. *Damn, did she overhear Carmen talking about offing herself and called the cops?* He needed to get a grip. And fast. "It was difficult at first, but you start to learn all of the shortcuts when you do it eight hours a day."

He glanced at the hostess station again. The police officer was gone. *Where the hell did he go?* Tarryn had never had any issues with the cops. Ever. He wasn't about to start today. It was arguably the biggest day of his entire career, and he had already invested so much time in Carmen. He wouldn't let it all fall apart.

"Hey, I was just thinking, do you want to go and take a walk in the park? I'm kinda full, and you can tell me about what you found under Gus's desk." Tarryn glanced over at the door again. No sign of the cop.

"You know, I think I might like that." Carmen seemed to be falling for his charm. Maybe he would be okay after all.

TWENTY-SEVEN

TARRYN SIGNALED TO THE WAITRESS TO LET HER KNOW to bring their bill. She smiled a half smile that he found unnerving. He felt like she was boring into his mind and uncovering his plans for Carmen. The foundation for his house of cards was starting to crumble. The thoughts in his head were swirling, like water going down a sewer grate in a torrential storm. Where was the cop? What was the waitress thinking? How was Carmen feeling? Where do we go next? His mind was whirling.

The waitress put the bill on the table and stared at Carmen. "You okay, honey?"

Tarryn felt his armpits moisten and the moisture leave his mouth. *Damn it, what was she going to say?*

Carmen looked at Tarryn and then returned the waitress's gaze, "Yep, I'm fine." She looked back at Tarryn and smiled.

The waitress, still looking apprehensive, turned and left the table without another word, returning to her corner and her open newspaper.

Tarryn hadn't realized that he had been holding his breath since the waitress had brought the bill. The pent-up air left him in a long whoosh. He knew that no matter what happened past this point, Carmen was his and his alone. There wasn't anyone, including the boys in blue that could change her fate. She was officially victim thirty-seven, his highest accomplishment and the highest honor he could bestow on another human being.

Tarryn glanced at his watch and spoke with a newfound confidence, "Let's get out of here. It's almost three o'clock, and I don't think we want to be wandering in this neighborhood after dark. Plus there's something I want to show you if you'll let me." He took some cash from his pocket and put it on the table, waiting for Carmen's response, but already anticipating the answer.

"I have no idea why, but something in me tells me that it's okay to go with you. You're a nice man, Tarryn."

"Like I said before, I want to hear the rest of the story. You can tell me as we walk. The place I want to take you is just a few blocks from here."

Carmen smiled as they got up from the table. Tarryn smiled back, not knowing what was waiting for him outside. He was all too eager to move forward, his back twitching like a kid on a dance floor trying to look cool. He opened the door for Carmen and went out into the warm afternoon air.

TWENTY-EIGHT

ALL OF THE ANTICIPATION AND EXCITEMENT LEFT HIS
body as he turned toward the stall where he had parked the Mustang.
The cop that was in the restaurant earlier was now blocking their exit
with his cruiser. This prompted an adrenaline rush that almost knocked
him to his knees. *He had been meticulous for so many years, why was this
happening now? He should have dragged Carmen into the house when he
had the chance. She would have been dead by now, and he would have
been sleeping.*

Figuring that a good offense is your best defense, Tarryn walked
directly over to the police officer. "Evening, Officer. Is something
wrong?"

"Are you the owner of this Mustang?" he replied with an icy
formality.

"Yes, I am."

"Your name is Tarryn Cooper Love. Correct?"

"Yes, sir." Tarryn glanced at Carmen who was looking more and
more nervous every moment.

"I'll need to see some ID please."

Tarryn took his driver's license from his wallet and showed it to the
police officer. He looked it over, verifying what he had learned from
running the Mustang's license plate.

The cop turned to face Carmen and asked, "And your name?"

"Carmen Halder," she replied softly.

The cop asked to see her ID, and she fumbled in her purse to find it. Tarryn wanted to peek inside while she was searching but decided against arousing further suspicion. She handed over her ID, and the cop looked it over.

"Are we in some kind of trouble?" Carmen asked as he passed her back her driver's license.

"No, ma'am. But the waitress inside was concerned about your safety. She was worried that Mr. Love might be trouble for you." The cop watched carefully as she answered.

"Oh my God. I didn't know that having a few tears in a restaurant would cause a five-alarm emergency. I was just telling Tarryn a story … a sad story. I'm fine." Carmen stood solidly in front of him and spoke with an authoritative tone. Tarryn was amazed yet again by her strength and poise. *Kiss her, kiss her.*

The cop eyed her up and returned Tarryn's driver's license. "Have a good night." He returned to the cruiser and drove off.

Tarryn stood in silence behind his car and watched the cruiser as it disappeared into the city streets. He mused that this was turning out to be the most bizarre day. Was it a sign that he should abort the kill? Or was his mother somehow guiding him from above and just warning him to be careful—to get the girl out of sight as soon as possible? He had been out in public with her since eight o'clock that morning. Between the cab ride to the shelter, the hours spent at Sam's, the drive back to his house, and now a late lunch at the restaurant, he had been with her for seven hours. Time was flying by, and while he was closer than ever to getting her back to his house, she was starting to draw unwanted attention. In addition, he was tired and hadn't slept in what felt like forever.

"That was strange. You okay?" Carmen asked.

Fumbling for a lie, Tarryn replied, "Yeah, sorry. I've just never even had so much as a parking ticket before, and that whole experience was a bit unnerving. I guess I've always been nervous around authority figures—goes back to school days when you were taught to respect all of your elders and anyone in a uniform. Somehow I always feel guilty even when I've done nothing wrong."

"That's funny—I've always felt the same way." She mumbled under her breath, "When I finish telling my story, you might wish that the cop was back."

He looked at her wondering if *she* might want the cop back if she could read his mind. Luckily she couldn't. "All of us have things that we're not proud of in our past. I'm not afraid of what you might tell me."

TWENTY-NINE

"I WANTED TO SHOW YOU A PARK NOT FAR FROM HERE. It's quiet, and there are a few friendly pigeons that frequent the pond. You up for a short walk? We can leave the car here and come back and get it later." Tarryn started two steps in the direction of the park, hoping she would agree and follow.

"Sure."

After a few feet, Tarryn prodded for some more of the story. "So when you left off, you were under Gus's desk, and there was someone else in the office. Then what?"

Carmen sighed, "Yes, I guess that's where I stopped, didn't I? I was under the desk, and a man's voice was asking if anyone was in the office. I figured out later that it was the building's security guard. He saw the light under the door and wanted to make sure that nothing sinister was going on. Anyway, I was curled up under the corner by the file drawer and noticed a paper sticking out of the side. I could hear the security guard moving around in the office. His steps went from reception to Simon's office, to the coffee room and back to Gus's office. My heart was pounding. I look back on that moment and wonder why I was so afraid—I had a right to be there. I was one of the owners of the company. I'm not sure why I hid. I just didn't want anyone, mostly Simon, to know that I was in the office unannounced. I should have noticed that big red flag too, but I chose to ignore it, like so many others before and after.

"Once the coast was clear from the security guard, I tugged on the paper and pulled it free. It was a picture of a woman. She was clothed but was obviously trying to look sexy. Her details were written below. Her name was Katlana, she was five-foot-seven, blond hair down to her shoulders, her measurements were 38-26-36, she spoke English, and was in good health according to the report. Initially, I thought that maybe it was part of Gus's porn collection, and she was an Internet sensation or a phone sex beauty. Then I noticed the phone number at the bottom of the page. It was Gus's cell phone. I had paid the bills for so many months that I knew it off by heart.

"I was shocked and upset. Was Gus involved in Internet porn? Or worse, was Gus involved in prostitution? About a million different thoughts went through my mind. Was Simon involved? Was our company involved? I wanted to know what the hell was going on. Simon had to be involved somehow. The strange e-mails in his inbox and his lack of interest in our marriage were enough to convince me that he had his hands in something dirty. I just wasn't sure of the specifics." Carmen let out a big sigh, "I was so upset. My whole life had just turned upside down. Simon was my life, my everything. He was the air that I breathed. I was his wife for fuck's sake, and it was apparent that he was keeping a pretty big secret from me. Just when you think that you know someone, they throw you a curve ball that changes your entire existence. I didn't have the details but my intuition was screaming that I was in trouble—big trouble. It was right."

Tarryn had been leading her toward the park, and they had finally arrived. "Holy shit. Was he selling girls on the street? I thought your company did social experimentation for corporations. That's a pretty big leap from harmless ethics tests to prostitution." He led her toward an empty bench, in a secluded area by the pond.

"That's what I thought. I kept thinking that there must be a mistake. I must have misinterpreted what I saw somehow. And if I did in fact get the premise right, that Simon must not be a willing participant. Gus must be either doing whatever it was without Simon's knowledge, or he was blackmailing Simon to keep quiet. Either way, I didn't know what I was going to do next." A brown pigeon came over to them to investigate if they had a free meal to share. Her thoughts interrupted, Carmen reached into her purse. Tarryn tensed as he watched her pull out a granola bar. She unwrapped it and broke it into small pieces. "We should have brought some bread from the restaurant. I don't think that granola bars are on the list of approved pigeon food." She shrugged. "I guess it'll do."

Kiss her, kill her, kiss her, kill her. Touch her face and hold her close. Put a plastic bag over her head and watch her eyes bug out when she can't breathe. His mind was playing tricks again.

THIRTY

TARRYN WATCHED AS CARMEN GENTLY HAND-FED THE small bird and thought about something she had just said, "Simon was the air she breathed." That was exactly how he felt about his mother. There was nothing more important to him that her well-being—both physical and mental. It was only after his tenth kill that he felt like she was beginning to heal in both respects.

The Numbers Killer was constantly in the news, and the public was warned to be alert at all times and weary of strangers. The FBI profilers estimated that the killer was a white man in his midthirties, well-educated, friendly, and lived on his own. They suspected that he might be a truck driver or bus driver given the wide kill zone.

Tarryn was flattered, his ego growing large with the praise. They had guessed him to be far too old. At the time of his tenth kill he was only twenty-one. That proved that he had achieved a level of experience typically found in a much older man. And he was still living in the small apartment with his mother, driving cab five days a week. Another kudo thrown his way. The police didn't expect that a killer of that magnitude could keep the secret from someone they lived with. While he and his mother spoke often of the kills, she still wasn't aware that her son was the most wanted man in America.

After the fifth kill, she was mildly interested in the news again. After six and seven, she had started to take notes after each newscast, jotting down the little details that she thought were good and bad.

After eight and nine, she had an entire manila folder that contained all of the newspaper articles and Internet speculation on the potential mastermind. And by kill number ten, she had become a full-fledged junkie for the Numbers Killer.

Tarryn noted that his mother had reduced her intake of crack by about half and spent hours on end researching the crime scenes, trying to get insight into the new kid on the block. She was pleased that Tarryn had saved all of the clippings from the first kill forward—even when she hadn't been interested. She thanked him many times, noting that at the beginning, she was "partly out of her head and skeptical that the new guy was going to be worthwhile tracking."

She was on the mend, and Tarryn was thrilled. He wanted so much to tell her all of the details of what he had done. But to her, the mystery was as enticing as finding out the truth. He wanted to wait until he had amassed enough experience that she would be proud. It wasn't time yet. It was only the beginning.

It was a learning experience every time they discussed the cases. Of course, she compared him to her idol, Ted. But it was nice that she could critique his work honestly, without the worry of insulting her son. If he told her the truth, her tongue might not be as loose and harsh. Without those conversations he wouldn't have gotten as good as he was today.

His time with her was as intoxicating as it had been when he was a young child curled up in her lap. He listened intently to every word as she speculated on what the Numbers Killer might do next. Only now, she wasn't talking about Dahmer or Gacy or Manson—she was talking about *him* and *his* merits as a killer.

Yes, she had been the air that he breathed, every day until the day that she left him. On that day, he hadn't treated her like the lady that she was. That day was the only regret in his entire life.

THIRTY-ONE

"YOU DRIFTED OFF FOR A FEW MINUTES. IS EVERYTHING all right? Am I boring you?" Carmen asked as she fed the last few crumbs of granola bar to another hungry pigeon.

Tarryn gently touched her arm. "Never. I have never met anyone like you before. Somehow, our lives are meant to be intertwined. You say a lot of things that take me back in my own life. I was thinking about my mother again. I haven't thought about her much lately. I try not to. She was everything to me, and it hurts too much to know that she's gone. You aren't boring me in the least. What happened next, did you confront Simon? Did you find out the truth?"

Tarryn promised himself that he would no longer reminisce about his prior kills or his mother. It was jeopardizing everything, and he was deviating from a proven methodology that had been successful thirty-six times in the past. Today was not the day for distractions.

"I snuck out of the office building, hoping that I wouldn't catch the eye of the security guard again. I was lucky and made it out of the back door unnoticed. I tucked the paper in to my purse and went home. Simon wasn't going to be back for another day, so I had ample time to think about what to do next. Initially, I decided that the best thing to do was to be honest and tell him the truth—I had been worried because he was acting strangely, I went to the office to see if I could find out the source of his stress, and I accidentally stumbled onto some strange things that made me believe he was involved in something illegal. Then of course, having more than twenty-four hours to decide, threw that idea out the window. My second thought had been to act like nothing had happened, drop subtle hints about Gus being involved in something odd, and watch for his reaction.

"Funny enough, when he finally came home, I did neither. I was a blubbering mess by the time he walked through the door. He had barely taken his coat off when I screamed and yelled like a lunatic, accusing him of being a pimp, a cheater, and a liar. Needless to say, it wasn't the well-thought-out plan that I had hoped for. His reaction wasn't what I expected either. He didn't deny the allegations. He just grabbed me and gave me a big hug. He let me weep on his shoulder for a good ten minutes before he walked me over to the couch and told me a story that I could barely believe."

"He didn't deny anything? I assume that he was guilty as charged?" Tarryn was amazed that Simon would have been so forthcoming with the truth. When his mother had finally figured out who the Numbers Killer was, Tarryn's first instinct was to deny the entire thing. *Crap, he was back in the past again.* Time to focus.

The tears started to well in her eyes again as she spoke, "It was much worse than I originally thought. I was married to a monster. He and Gus were bringing women over from the former Soviet Union and selling them to the highest bidder. They were essentially trafficking women to wealthy U.S. citizens."

"What? Are you joking? How the hell did they get away with that?" Even for Tarryn, soon to be the top selective killer of all time, the story seemed incredible.

"I have a basic idea of what happened, but that's only the tip of the iceberg. It gets a lot worse. I think back to that day, and I was just as shocked as you. My husband had just admitted to me that he was doing something so illegal and immoral that it made my stomach churn. I sat silently in a stupor, and he told me how it all began."

THIRTY-TWO

"PHOTOTECHNICS HAD BEEN ASKED TO DO SOME WORK for a corporation out of Houston. We didn't have any Plants in the city, but the customer was offering such a large amount of money for the job that we took it anyway, figuring that we could find some locals to do our bidding. The person that we were investigating was a bigwig in an oil company and was being groomed for the CEO's position. The new role would give him access to billions of dollars, and he would be the front face for one of the largest oil producers in the world. He was white, and there were concerns that he might have an issue with African Americans. The corporation also wanted his background checked to make sure that there weren't any skeletons that would jump out at an inopportune time.

"Simon had told me about it when we were first approached. It was over a year after that fateful day that I found the paper under Gus's desk. When Simon told me that Gus was going to fly to Tampa to do some of the legwork himself, I was happy. The job paid a hundred grand, and I was thankful that Simon could stay home. It was the last I heard of the project and the last time that I thought about it.

"I didn't understand how a client in Houston could be the catalyst for the big pile of shit that we were in, but as Simon kept talking, it all became pretty clear. When Gus went to Texas, the first part of the experiment went off without a hitch. Over a two-week period, the person in question was tested on three occasions with African Americans in different social and business situations."

"What do you mean—tested?" Tarryn was interested to discover what lengths Phototecnics took to clear their subjects.

"The man was put into a social situation where our Plants were using racial slurs. He objected to the use of them and walked away from the conversation. In another situation, he was given the opportunity to jump ahead in a line in front of a black man, and again he passed. He showed integrity and obviously didn't think of himself as superior. And finally, his children were tested by a Plant to see what they had been taught by their parents. Prejudice is taught at home after all. They also passed with flying colors."

"Just those few things were enough? They paid a hundred grand? That seems pretty minor to me."

"That was just the beginning. Based on the few scenarios I just told you, it was probable that the gentleman was not a bigot and could handle a business situation with African Americans. The bigger part of the investigation was surrounding his background. That's where Gus found the dirt that would be my undoing. Gus, posing as an Internet repair person, wangled his way in to the man's home and gave himself access to the man's computer. He could connect remotely at any time. I was mortified. At no point had we ever done anything illegal during the course of any investigation. Gus had crossed a line that I wasn't comfortable with. It's funny that I was so upset about that one incident given what came next, but I was so angry and I hated Gus. In my mind, Gus was the enemy, and Simon was an unwilling partner in the crimes."

"You wanted to believe. I understand. We all want to believe that our family members are beautiful and pure. No one wants to think that someone they love would purposely hurt them." His mother's face flashed momentarily in to his brain.

"Simon kept telling the story, and I realized that he was in just as deep as Gus. I also found out that I was involved too—I owned 20 percent. Anyway, Gus was watching this guy's Internet usage every day and started to notice some strange messages. I assume that they were similar to the ones that I saw on Simon's computer that day in the office. Apparently, Gus was like me at the beginning and couldn't figure out what they meant. He suspected that the oil and gas executive had a girl on the side, but he needed proof. Gus started following the man twenty-four hours a day. He tailed him to work, to restaurants, and back home. Nothing seemed out of place for the first two or three days. Then on the fourth day, the man went to an industrial warehouse and spent three hours inside, opening the bay door three times. Once to drive his Lexus in, another to let in a black sedan, and finally to let both the sedan and his tan Lexus out.

"Gus watched from across the street, curious as to what was happening but not wanting to blow his cover. The two vehicles went in different directions, and having to choose one to follow, he picked the sedan. He followed from a safe distance as the car weaved through the city to the west side, where it finally stopped outside a modest middle-class home. Two people got out. The bear of a man that was driving supposedly went around and opened the rear passenger door for a leggy blonde, who was maybe twenty-five years old. The driver rang the bell and exchanged the woman for a brown envelope with the owner of the property. The sedan drove off. Gus lost track of the car about two miles later at a light.

"At that point, Gus was still confused as to what was happening but knew that the oil company was going to get their money's worth once he figured it out. He ran the plates on the sedan and checked out the name of the company who rented the warehouse. Both were dead ends. Both were registered to a fictitious company, which according to the landlord, was in the shipping industry. Gus kept up the twenty-four-hour surveillance for the next two weeks, sleeping in his car close by to the suspect's home. Nothing out of the ordinary happened, and he set his sights back on the warehouse. After scoping out the property, without any results, he broke in to look around. The warehouse was just an empty shell. No desks, computers, tables, chairs—nothing. Gus went back to surveillance, and a week later it paid off. The suspect did the same trip to the warehouse, same black sedan left as did the suspect's Lexus. Gus followed the sedan again, this time to the south side of the city to a more upscale neighborhood. The driver was the same huge man, but now the woman was a brunette."

"Hang on here. You're telling me that Gus figured out that the oil and gas executive was trafficking women?" Tarryn asked.

"I don't think that Gus really knew what was going on, but being the consummate investigator that he was, he wanted to find out. The other thing that you need to know—Gus was cheap and impatient. He had already spent a month in Houston, and he wasn't interested in spending anymore of our profits on hotel rooms or restaurant meals. He wanted to clear up the mystery of the warehouse and the women, as quickly as possible. Simon explained that Gus basically drove the exec off the road one day, and pretending to be a good neighbor offering a ride, kidnapped the man, and took him to the warehouse for some privacy. Simon said that Gus talked to the guy for a while, and the exec admitted to being part of a human trafficking ring. Knowing what I know now, I assume that the "talking" involved a gun or worse. I can't imagine a guy giving up the details of an illegal enterprise to a complete stranger, without some kind of motivation."

"Gus sounds like a real asshole," Tarryn remarked, his face turned into a scowl for effect. There was a part of him that was quite interested in Gus's techniques, but it wasn't time to ask.

"Yeah, he was a real piece of work."

"Was? Did something happen to him?" Tarryn asked.

"Yep, once again, one of the reasons why I am, where I am today. I'll get to it soon, but you need to understand the next piece of my story first," Carmen replied as she stared out over the park.

Tarryn just nodded as she continued. "Gus wanted the details of the trafficking circle, and the executive gave them up, I assume with some prodding by Gus. The exec and a partner in the former Soviet Union brought young women to the US to be assistants, maids, and nannies for wealthy men. The women were brought in as tourists, given new identities, and sold to their new "owners." Simon told me that they were so desperate to get out of their own countries that the legalities of the situation didn't matter to them. They were, according to Simon, willing participants in the whole thing." Carmen paused as a bird came up looking for a handout. "My mind was reeling. The whole thing was so surreal. How was it possible that the man I loved with every ounce of my heart could be involved in this mess? I so much wanted to believe that it was a victimless crime, but the sane part of my brain knew that the whole thing was just plain wrong."

"I assume that Gus and Simon took over the trafficking ring?"

Tarryn asked as he glanced at his watch—3:45—it was time to move again. He had to get Carmen to his house before someone noticed them together.

"To make a long story short, yes. Gus threatened to expose the exec and ruin his career. The man willingly gave up his contacts and helped to do introductions. As I understand it, Gus came back to New York and gave the oil company a clean report on the man. He had what he wanted, the contacts that would make him a very rich man. The girls sold for ten grand a piece. The operation was fairly small when Gus discovered it, maybe three girls a month. But he had bigger plans—much bigger."

Tarryn took her hand and looked deep in to Carmen's eyes. "Wow, that's quite a story. I guess I still don't understand why you want to die over it. None of this is your fault, you didn't even know it was happening."

Carmen smiled weakly. "True. But when I said that Gus was no longer around—I had everything to do with that."

Tarryn was starting to feel frustrated. Her damn story was interesting, but they need to get going. But if he rushed her, he would lose the prize. He had already invested too much time—he had to move on.

Tarryn put on his best shocked face. "You get more interesting by the minute. I have been with you for ...," he let go of her hand and looked at his watch again, "a grand total of eight hours now, and I am just starting to scratch the surface of your life." He turned on the charm again and touched her knee with the tips of three fingers. "Can we finish talking at my place? I can get you a glass of wine and we can keep chatting. I hope by now you know that I'm a nice guy who wants to help. No funny stuff, I promise." Tarryn waited patiently for her reply. If she agreed, he could move to the next step in his plan, if she said no, he was running out of time and might have to abort. He was on his second wind and didn't know how many more there would be before he hit the wall and required sleep.

Carmen looked out again at the pond for what felt like an eternity before she faced him and spoke, "I think I would like that."

Tarryn's back tingled, reminding him of the world of excitement that was on the horizon. *Kill her, kill her, kill her.*

STEP 3–ISOLATION
4:00 PM

THIRTY-THREE

AS THEY WALKED BACK TO THE CAR, STILL PARKED AT THE restaurant, Carmen didn't speak more than a few words. It gave Tarryn time to think about the next step in his plan. His eyes were scratchy, and his mind was beginning to lose its sharp edge. She obviously trusted him now, but did she have the will to live? Tarryn wondered if he had taken her that far yet. She wasn't finished telling the story, and he knew that there could be any number of memories that might set her back down the dark path of suicide.

He thought about how hard it must have been to hear that her husband had changed from the loving man she married into a criminal. After all that she had been through in her life, she deserved better than to get tied up with a piece of shit like him. Tarryn giggled in his mind, as he realized how absurd that thought was … he felt badly that Carmen had met Simon? Perhaps the better sentiment should have been that he felt sorry that she had gotten into his taxi this morning. However, he reasoned, had she not met Simon, she wouldn't have wanted to commit suicide and therefore would not have gotten in the cab in the first place. Yes, Simon was the culprit. Or, he mused, maybe it was Uncle Ray, the child molester. Had she not met him, then she wouldn't have been so maladjusted as a child and could have handled her parents' death better. Or maybe they wouldn't have died at all. She had started her story there, so maybe he was the catalyst. There were so many opportunities to lay blame if you were looking. Every single choice in a person's life takes them down a new path. It was complicated, that was a given.

When he finally decided to hang up his hat in the game, he wondered what the media would have to say about his life. Where would they try to place the blame? Probably on his mother, after all she had been the sole adult influence in his life. Would the news reporters eventually dig up the details of his adolescence and even find out about his first love? Would someone try to connect his outburst with Marnie as the first signs of trouble? Or maybe the non date with Sandy as to why he disliked women? They would speculate of course; everyone wanted to have a concrete reason, an understanding of what drives people to do certain heinous acts.

He supposed that they would be right if they drew a line between the killings and his mother. But it angered him to think that they would blame her parenting skills for the events that had taken place over the past two decades. She had always been the perfect parent in his eyes. Initially, he had started killing because he loved her so much and wanted to save her life. Now, it was the memory of his mother's love that drove him to complete the task. Today was it—the day had finally arrived.

It was hard to admit it, but after the first dozen kills, he had actually thought about stopping. It was tiring to continually think of new and inventive ways to murder someone. He took a brief hiatus after victim twelve, but after just eight months of retirement, the press, and his mother were hungry for more. Reluctantly, he started killing again, but the next kill was just as sloppy as his first. He had screwed up majorly on kill thirteen and marked it as twelve. The newscasters and reporters had had a field day with that. They actually joked that the Numbers Killer could only count to twelve. Even his mother had a chuckle over the amateurish mistake.

Victim number fourteen was taken within two weeks of the wrongly marked thirteen. It was much sooner than he originally planned, but he had to save face. He didn't wait for the welts on his back to itch; he just grabbed the easiest woman, desperate to reclaim the respect that he deserved. When the mutilated body was found, the media changed their tune. In fact they speculated that the Numbers Killer might have an issue with the number thirteen and therefore might have religious ties. His mother and the rest of the world stopped laughing, and Tarryn was able to relax back into his regular routine again.

THIRTY-FOUR

TARRYN OPENED THE DOOR OF THE MUSTANG FOR Carmen and looked around nervously in the parking lot. The cop from earlier in the day was long gone. He jumped in the driver's side, and the two of them made small talk on the trip back to his house.

Tarryn started thinking of the lies that he needed to tell next. She thought that he had cats. He couldn't have her running down the street once she discovered that there were no furballs on the property. He also had to decide when to tell her that particular piece of information. Before or after she was inside?

Trying to keep the light shining in Carmen's eyes, he didn't mention Simon or Gus on the drive home. Instead he pointed out the beauty that surrounded them. Women liked pretty things—he had learned from watching reality television shows like *The Bachelor*. He drew her attention to the left to admire a beautiful front yard, then to the right to acknowledge a funny-looking dog out for a walk. "Everywhere," he pointed out, "there is beauty in the world. Including inside this car." *Kiss her, kill her, kiss her, kill her.*

As they pulled into the back-detached garage, he made up his mind. Once inside the confines of the single car space, he would shut the door and shuffle her into the house. He would wait until they were inside before he would tell her some more of the truth. He had a backup plan under the car seat, in the way of a small Taser gun, one of several that he owned, if things got complicated.

The garage door was ten feet from the back door of the house. They entered directly into the kitchen. Tarryn flicked a switch on the wall, and the small kitchen was filled with warm light. He stepped through into the house and held the door open for Carmen.

THIRTY-FIVE

"I BOUGHT THIS PLACE A FEW YEARS AGO. WHEN MY mother died, I stayed in her apartment for a while, just so that I could feel closer to her. Then when I was finished grieving, I needed to get some space from the memories, and I moved in here. It's small, but it's great for me. Wonderful neighbors and a quiet street."

As the door shut behind them, he spoke in a soft tone, "Hey, um, I have something to confess. When I tell you, I want you to understand that I lied to you only because I care about you."

Carmen's face showed all the signs of someone about to bolt. "What? You're some sort of pervert, aren't you? You lured me here, and now you're going to rape me." Her voice got louder with each syllable of speech. She grabbed the door handle and started toward the backyard. "Why should that amaze me? I finally start to trust another human being again, and you're no different than anyone else."

Tarryn jumped toward her. He grabbed her arm just as she twisted the door handle to freedom and turned her body toward his. He realized within seconds that he had forgotten to grab the stun gun from underneath his seat. Tarryn cursed under his breath for the amateurish mistake. There was something about this woman that was messing with his carefully calculated plans. The situation went from bad to worse, as he realized that she had a gun in her hand and was pointing it in his direction. At least he knew what she was hiding in her purse. However, it was the worst case scenario if he had to choose a way to find out that little tidbit of information.

He backed up quickly and raised his hands in the air, his heart beating a million miles a minute. "Slow down. I'm not a pervert. I just wanted to let you know that I don't actually have any cats as pets right now. I used to, but they passed away a while back. I just wanted you to like me. I knew that you were in trouble, and I wanted to help. I didn't want to base our relationship on a lie. I'm coming clean now. Doesn't that mean something?"

Tarryn had come to realized that Carmen wore every single emotion on her sleeve. Luckily for him, it was easy to see her body relax as she digested what he was saying; the gun was shaking in her small hand. "You're no better than my lying-ass husband. I trusted you. Damn it."

"I'm sorry. Really, truly sorry." Tarryn reached toward her, took the gun from her grasp, and placed it on the kitchen counter just out of her reach. "You don't want to kill me. I'm the only one who really cares right now."

"Oh my God. I have no idea what's going on anymore." With that said, she broke down and cried in his arms.

Tarryn whispered in her ear, "It's been a long day. Just trust me. I won't let you down." He held her in his arms for five minutes. She smelled clean, with a touch of honey and cinnamon. Her hair was soft and silky. *Kiss her, kill her, kiss her* ... he was starting to get confused.

Carmen pulled back from him and asked, "Can I use the washroom? After all these tears, I must look horrendous."

"Sure, just down the hall to the right." Tarryn grabbed two glasses from the cupboard and placed them on the counter. He heard her use the facilities, and then presumably wash her hands and face. He moved the small handgun from the counter and deposited the weapon deep within a kitchen drawer.

A few minutes later when she returned, she had added a small amount of mascara and blush. "It's very homey. Did you decorate it yourself? Looks like it's had a woman's touch at some point."

Tarryn let out a little giggle. "Nope, no help from a woman I'm afraid. Apparently the Crate and Barrel catalog served me well." He walked toward the refrigerator to get the chilled wine as Carmen explored the main level of the house. He wasn't worried that she would find anything incriminating; he was a perfectionist when it came to housekeeping.

"Wow, you have a great collection of art. I'm impressed. I didn't know that cab drivers were so cultured."

"Yep, us cab drivers can be surprising sometimes," Tarryn said, as he entered the front room and handed her a glass of white. "I have a media room downstairs where I keep the stereo." He signaled with his hand to the basement stairs. "Shall we?"

Carmen walked down the stairs to the lower level without any hesitation. Tarryn was pleased with her progress. The welts were burning hot, and his heart was racing. *It was finally time*—number thirty-seven had entered his inner sanctum.

THIRTY-SIX

TARRYN TURNED ON A LIGHT ROCK STATION AND SAT facing Carmen at the other end of the couch. He was too far away to touch her, which was the best he could do to take away any anxiety she might be feeling.

"Are you ready to tell me the rest?"

"We've come this far, I guess I have to. I was telling you about Simon's confession. That night, he had me convinced that there wasn't anything immoral about what they were doing. Sure it was illegal, but the girls were in the country of their own free will, and our company was actually doing them a favor. Here they had jobs, here they had a husband, and here they had a life. Deep down I knew that I wasn't getting the entire picture. It felt like there were some pieces of the story that Simon omitted. But like I was saying, I wanted to believe him with all my heart. I guess I was clinging on to the fairy-tale life that I was living—the big house, the car, the bank account, and the husband. I didn't want to go back to the street. Plus Simon was so damn convincing. He knew me too well and knew exactly what buttons to press.

"I backed off and continued to live the privileged life that Simon provided. He was just as attentive and caring as he had been at the beginning. Having the burden of the secret business off his chest really helped our marriage. I avoided the office. I turned a blind eye, which was exactly what Simon wanted. I still needed a change. I shut down the pet store, and I started volunteering at the local animal shelter, which accomplished two things, I was helping others, and it took away any semblance of guilt that I was feeling as a result of Simon's new underground venture. I was happy and content. And Simon and I were trying for a baby again.

"It was about four months after my detective work and Simon's confession that I turned on the television and things took a turn for the worst. The breaking news story was about a bawdy house in New York, which was raided that morning. The women were being kept as modern-day slaves and forced to have sex with strangers to pay off the debt that they had accumulated when they were brought into the US. I was watching the story with Simon as we ate dinner. We chatted between bites of food, discussing the newscaster's account of how awful the poor girls were treated. They were cut off from their families, and at the rate that the debt was getting repaid, they would be in slavery for decades. Their captors were getting rich, and they were getting used up. I remember being shocked that such a thing could happen in a modern city like New York. Then as I glanced up at the television, I saw a woman's face as she was dragged into the back of a police van. It was the woman that I had seen on the paper in Gus's office. The vibrant woman that I saw on that paper was gone, her eyes were dead. One moment later, or earlier, and I wouldn't have seen her at all. Fate playing a part, I suppose." Carmen took a moment to take a sip of wine.

"Simon was the ringleader of the whorehouse? I didn't expect that?" He wanted his hands on her neck … or was it his lips? *Kiss her, kill her, kiss her, kill her.*

"Fortunately, he wasn't, but he was still involved in my mind. I went into another tearful rant about the new business. Simon said that he had no idea that the woman was being used for that type of work. He denied any involvement in the sex-trade end of the business. He merely brought the women over to the States, what happened after that was nobody's business but their own. We fought for a couple of hours, going back and forth on the subject of where we drew the line on his involvement with slavery, and if he had a responsibility to the women that he worked with. I wanted him to get rid of Gus as a partner and shut down the "importing" side of Phototecnics. I wanted him to focus on the investigative work that we founded the business on. The *successful* foundation of our business, I reminded him. I threatened to leave him.

I didn't want to live in fear that the police were going to knock on the door someday and take him, or myself, away for what they were doing. He was upset. He told me that I would never leave him because I had nowhere to go. I felt totally and completely useless. It was one of the lowest points in my life."

"What an asshole … pardon my French," Tarryn said. Her lips were full, and he admired their shape for a moment. *Kiss her.*

"He is an asshole. In fact he's a *fucking* asshole as you are about to find out," Carmen spat the words like venom from her lips.

In that moment, Tarryn saw the girl that worked selling drugs on the streets of LA and stabbed a man's leg as he entered her apartment, as clear as day. The monster inside was hungry to take away her spark of life. *Kill her … now.*

"The constant lies and betrayal were too much to take. I wanted out of the marriage, but as Simon so eloquently stated, I had nowhere to go. I decided to take control of my life, and I knew exactly how to do it. The next day, I backed down and apologized to Simon for my outburst the night before. I hugged him and asked for his forgiveness. He accepted my apology, promised to talk to Gus about doing background checks on their clients, and we went back on our way, living the facade of a happy marriage. That morning, I started to put my plan in motion. I called Ed and told him that I wanted to meet him later that day. I made arrangements with him to stay up in the loft for a few days while I got my life back in order. He wanted the details, but I just told him that I needed some space from Simon. I remember him frowning and asking if I was in an abusive relationship. Was Simon beating me? If he was, Ed was ready to go and kick his ass personally. I didn't want to get him involved in the mess and assured him that everything was going to be okay." Carmen's anger at Simon was replaced with tears of pain as she spoke about Ed.

Tarryn wondered how far Simon went to keep his secret. "Ed sounds like a good man. See, fate had a hand in picking him to come into your life. Not everything that destiny brings us is bad."

On the odd occasion, he had spoken to his mother about spirituality, but he was in no way a religious person. She believed in fate, which some people said was the belief in a higher power. In Tarryn's mind it was a belief that the universe had an energy, which helped to guide people to their proper destination. This morning he had been guided to Carmen—that was proof enough of the theory.

"Ed *was* a good man. He and I agreed that I should go back home, grab some clothes, and tell Simon that I needed a break. On my way back from the café, the road of my life took yet another crazy detour. I was about five miles from home when my car was sideswiped. I didn't see who hit me. In the split second before I hit the ditch and my car rolled, I realized that by going to Ed, I had put my life in jeopardy. I had underestimated my foe. It was the last time that I made that kind of mistake. I woke up in the hospital, with Simon at my bedside, looking white as a ghost. I had no idea how bad my injuries were, but the look on his face told me more than any doctor's charts could have. I had lost my front teeth when my face hit the steering wheel, broke my collarbone in three places, busted an arm, punctured a lung, *and* I had a rather nasty gash on my head, along with a concussion. All of that was minor compared to Simon's final installment of the injury roster—I had lost our baby. That hit me pretty hard, first because I had no idea that I was pregnant, and second because of how desperately I had wanted that child. I was confused and devastated."

"You were pregnant? Did you find out who caused the accident? Did they get charged?" Tarryn was feeling conflicted. He wanted to hear the rest of her story, but the urge to kill was growing stronger by the minute. He didn't know how much longer he could control the animal inside.

"It was a hard road to recovery. Losing a child that I didn't know I even had inside of me was terrible. From the minute that I met Simon, I wanted to have his baby. It was just another part of the fantasy life that turned out to be a lie. The vehicle that ran me off the road turned out to be a car that was stolen earlier that day. The police questioned me, but I wasn't any help; I truly didn't see anything. The case went cold pretty quickly. For the next few months, I was in and out of the hospital. I had to have reconstructive surgery on my arm." Carmen held it out for inspection. "There are three metal pins in it now. My lung took awhile to heal, and I still have trouble breathing sometimes. The collarbone was a long painful four months to heal. And in addition to all of that, I had to have all new teeth implanted in my upper jaw."

"Holy crap, that must have been horrible. Where was Simon during this whole ordeal?" Tarryn asked.

"He was right beside me every step of the way. He bathed me, fed me, and pampered me every day. And when he wasn't there, he had a nurse come in to assist. I needed the help. Funny enough, for those four months during my recovery, I barely thought about Gus and the business. I just buried my head in the sand. I was so depressed about the loss of the baby that my healing time was double that of a normal patient. My doctors were worried about my health, both mental and physical, and asked discretely how they could help. I turned down all of their well-intended gestures. I was dying inside, and my life was out of control. My saving grace was that Simon was there with me. For all of his faults, he was a bright ray of sunshine each and every day. Eventually, when I was able to come home, he surprised me with a new house, the one where you picked me up, and a new pet, Sabre. I had a purpose again. I started to organize our new home. I had a reason to get up in the morning, and that silly cat kept me company all-day long. When I told you he was my best friend, I meant it. He saw me through the next part of my marriage. The dark and final part." Carmen drifted off again, presumably thinking about the cat that she had just left at the animal shelter. As the tears welled up in her eyes, she excused herself to use the washroom.

Tarryn had a moment of his own to reminisce.

THIRTY-SEVEN

AFTER THE ISSUES HE HAD WITH MARKING NUMBER thirteen with a twelve and his corrective action with victim fourteen, the police had started to sniff their piggy noses in his direction. Someone saw a man who matched his description in the vicinity of the fourteenth crime scene. A composite drawing was released to the television and newspapers, and remarkably, it looked a little too similar for Tarryn's liking. His mother had even commented on the resemblance.

He was disappointed with himself. It was a sloppy kill, and he knew it. It was an act of desperation, and he knew from his many years of studies with his mother that desperate killers were the ones that got caught. He gave himself a three-month hiatus of sorts and only looked, but didn't touch, any of the many potential victims that he ran into on a regular basis.

His mother was slowly coming back to reality. She was more affectionate, more attentive and more alive, than she had been since she started the heavy drug use so many years before. They had actual conversations when he got home from driving cab, and on more than one occasion, he found notes that she had made comparing the Numbers Killer to Mr. Bundy. The documentation in his mother's notebook made it very clear, the Numbers Killer was a force to be reckoned with. While his marks for the first few kills were well below Bundy's previous scores, the more recent ones were getting him high marks. And more importantly, she was impressed with the killer's self-control over the past few months.

Tarryn was ready to tell her. He wanted to see the look of joy in her eyes when she found out that her boy, her son, had absorbed her many lessons and was well on his way to being even better than Terrible Ted. He wanted the moment to be special and bought lasagna from the Italian market down the street. He added tiramisu for a sweet ending—it was her favorite. He drove home and took the stairs up to their small apartment, two at a time. It was finally his moment to shine. He had gone back and forth on the subject so many times, not knowing if he should wait until he broke Bundy's record or tell her early in the process so that he could see her pride with every news article and live video feed from the kill sites. The latter had finally won out in his mind. The sheer anguish of keeping the secret was making him too jumpy. Plus he had reason to believe that she might already suspect who he really was. She had asked him twice over the previous two months how he knew that the murder of Hanna Goldman was the first of the Numbers Killer's spree. *She must know*, he reasoned, *she was just looking for confirmation.* It was in the way that she looked at him—or maybe it was just his imagination. Either way, he was about to find out.

He sat her down at the table, having to pull her away from the nightly news and fed her the wonderful meal. She was smiling and shocked that he had gone to such trouble. "Did you get a raise?" she had asked.

"No, it's even better news," he had replied.

Then with the final crumbs of tiramisu licked from her lips and the dishes cleared, he had told her the story of the Numbers Killer. Her reaction was explosive but not in the way that he had originally expected. Tarryn thought of Carmen's words just a few minutes before and knew that they were equally appropriate in his case—it was the "dark and final chapter" of his relationship with his mother.

THIRTY-EIGHT

CARMEN RETURNED TO THE COUCH, HAVING REMOVED the ponytail from her hair. Her shoulder-length locks fell around her face in a wispy madness. She sat facing Tarryn, her hands between her knees. She looked so innocent and beautiful that for a moment, one fleeting moment, he wanted to kiss her more than kill her. The thought passed almost as quickly as it entered his head, and the welts began to itch again. He knew that she was bringing out some strange emotions in his brain and more than anything, he wanted to get his thirty-seventh kill out of the way.

"Simon had been such a wonderfully attentive husband during the time that I was recuperating, and the gift of the new house had really brought us back together. Part of me was just willing to live the lie and pretend that my husband had a normal nine-to-five job, just like the rest of the world. Even Ed commented that things looked like they were patched up. He visited quite a few times when I was in the hospital and brought me home cooking whenever he could get away from the restaurant. Simon was more tolerant of my old friend, but I sometimes thought that I caught Simon looking at him in a funny way. Assuming that my accident had something to do with my revelations about Simon's business ventures, I tried to keep a watchful eye on his interactions with Ed. After a while, I relaxed and life went on. Ed visited less often, and I was back into a daily grind."

"You kind of suggested before that Ed was no longer with us. Did something happen?"

"I'm almost there." Carmen's face scrunched up into a sad grimace. "First I have to tell you about Gus." Carmen brought the wine glass to her lips and took a sip. *Kiss her, kill her, kiss her, kill her.*

"It was about a year after we moved into the new house, and I finally got up the courage to ask Simon about the business. I'm not sure that I actually wanted the truth. I think what I was really looking for was a sugarcoated version of reality. I was hoping that he would tell me that he and Gus had shut down the illegal part of the company and that they were focusing on the original business model again. Or maybe he could have told me that Gus had moved on to start up his own venture and that Simon was going to rebuild our dream. Instead of a sugary lie, Simon did something that totally shocked me, he told me the truth. After all the years of lying, he said he couldn't go on telling me fictitious stories. He wanted to rebuild our relationship on a clean slate. At first I was pleased that he cared enough about our future to spill his guts, but it was far worse than I had imagined. Not long after the conversation, I became a murderer."

"What?" Tarryn interrupted "You're a murderer? I find that extremely hard to believe." His head was reeling. *Did he just hear her right?* He was a murderer, sitting there contemplating killing another murderer? They say that fact is stranger than fiction. This certainly fell into that category.

"Did I actually kill with my two hands? No. But was I to blame for the murder of two people? Absolutely."

Tarryn let out a mental sigh of relief. She wasn't a murderer. And while that would have made an excellent story for his thirty-seventh kill, he didn't want to believe that Carmen could take someone's life. "Okay—back up. I think I need more detail to understand what's going on. That's quite a bomb you just lobbed in my direction," he said.

"Sorry, I know. You'll understand shortly. Simon told me about how he had expanded the business, not dismantled it. He was bringing more and more women into the country to perform 'special duties' for their owners. I read between the lines—they were sex trade workers. Not the streetwalker kind that hang out on the corner. These girls were slaves to the men that bought them. Contrary to what I had originally

133

found out from my pathetic attempt at detective work, these women came here expecting to be wives and mothers and were being kept hidden away from their families back home. They couldn't go to the police because they were here illegally. They had no one to turn to and nowhere to run. He assured me that they weren't kept in whorehouses and used for multiple men; they were just available to the man that had bought them.

"I was stunned—not only was my husband bringing women into the country illegally, now he was a pimp. I know—not a pimp in the traditional sense, with the velvet business suits and big chains around their necks, but still *a pimp*. He held my hand and assured me that they were well-taken care of by their owners ... that term angered me to no end. They were just a commodity being bought a sold like a side of beef. Then amazingly, he told me that he wanted me to help in the business again. The girls needed a friend to get them acquainted with the social nuances of the US. They needed someone to show them the fashions and the proper way to act. He wanted me to be that person. At first, I was totally traumatized by the thought of getting involved, then after a lot of coaxing by Simon, I realized that I would actually be helping these poor women. I had visions of empowering them so that if they ever ran into a bad situation, they could handle it. I wanted to give them self-esteem, so they could hold their own with their "owners." I reasoned with the moral part of my brain that they were going to come here regardless if I was involved or not. I might as well have a say in how they were going to live their lives."

"Let me get this straight, you helped Simon and Gus?" Tarryn was even more confused by this woman. She was constantly surprising him at every turn. *Kill her, kill her, kill her.*

"Yes, I helped. I'm not proud of that fact, but it's the truth. That's one of the reasons that I'm here with you. I look back and know that while I might have given a few of them some strength, they were no match for my husband and his team of skin traders." Another sip of wine whet her palate as she continued, "I had three basic rules that had to be met for me to do the job that Simon wanted—one, I insisted that I had control over what I said to the women; two, I wanted them to have the ability to contact me at any time after they were placed in their new home; and three, I didn't want to have any contact with Gus. Simon agreed to all of my demands.

"The first time I met one of the women I was so nervous that I could barely function. I had no idea what I was going to say or what pearls of US wisdom I was meant to pass on. It was a clumsy encounter at best. I tried to get to know her on a personal level and make her my friend. Her name was Tasha. She was from Yugoslavia, and she was stunningly beautiful. She had a long mane of red hair, petite features and spoke very little English. I spent two days with her to prepare her for life in America. She had some basic questions like what we ate, the weather in New York, how to catch a bus, what was expected when she was out in public, et cetera. They were all straightforward things that I could answer. We went shopping and bought her some essentials—jeans, makeup, hair products.

"I grilled her about why she was here, why she was taking such a big risk with her life. Her story would be told to me by so many women over the next two years—there was no work where she lived, her family was poor, her government was corrupt, and she wanted a better life. She was genuinely excited to meet her new man, and somehow I was excited for her. Her exuberance was catchy. It was the end of the second day that I explained to her the potential dark side of living with a strange man. I gave her my card and told her to call me at any time if she wanted to talk. I was hoping that I would never hear from her again. Not because I didn't like her, but I knew that she would be kept off the radar, being an illegal immigrant, and I wanted her to have a good life. I knew that she would be expected to perform sex at the drop of a hat and that she might not be attracted to the man who paid us twenty thousand to bring her to New York, but I also understood that her life here was probably going to be better than what she came from."

"I didn't realize that women were so desperate in other parts of the world. You hear things on television, but you had the chance to put a real face to the suffering. It must have been hard for you." Tarryn was inquisitive but anxious. *Kill her, kiss her, kill her, kiss her.*

THIRTY-NINE

"AFTER THE FIRST THREE MONTHS AND THIRTY WOMEN, I felt like I was making a difference. I had convinced myself that I was doing a noble deed. I was helping women find their way and get out of poverty. I had almost forgotten that what we were doing was illegal. Simon and I were getting along even better than those first days when he was wooing me to be his wife. I guess you could say I was happy. I suppose it was like living your life with blinders on. I was so focused on the women that the rest of the world didn't matter one iota. Simon and I were going over the revenues, and he was pleased to announce that we had turned a profit of a hundred and fifty grand in the first three months of me being on board. The customers were clamoring to get one of the women that I had coached. The clients loved that they came with an understanding of US culture and a fake ID to boot. I felt like I was making a difference again.

"Simon was pleased with our progress and talked about expanding the business even further. More women each month, maybe up to twenty in each thirty-day period. We could double our profits. We were already shipping women all over the US and Canada. It was risky. I kept telling him that ten a month was plenty of work for me. I was able to spend a few days with each woman. Importing more women would only serve to spread me too thin and to draw attention to our illegal business. He agreed, but I could tell that greed was starting to kick in. Pigs get fat and hogs get slaughtered. I was worried that Simon was working his way up to the slaughterhouse.

"Another couple of months went by, and Simon kept the number of women the same as before. We had agreed to a maximum of ten per month, and that's exactly what we did. The troubling thing for me was that the women started to look younger as the time went on. Originally most of them were in their late twenties or early thirties. Then I noticed that they started to look like they were midtwenties. Maybe an alarm went off in my brain, but if it did, I ignored it. After six months, the revenues were up. We were dealing with the same amount of women, but we were making 50 percent more money and not surprisingly, the girls were now in their early twenties. I was uncomfortable. They were starting to get too young. I felt like we were standing on a very thin line morally." Carmen shook her head and chuffed out a sad laugh. "I can barely believe that I just said that. I was selling women, and I felt like I was walking a moral tightrope. The whole thought is so absurd that it makes me laugh."

"You are an interesting woman, Carmen. I think I need another glass of wine." Tarryn got off the couch and smiled, "Can I get you something to drink?" *Kiss her, kill her, kiss her, kill her.* Tarryn needed a break to gather his thoughts before she continued.

"I think I'm all right for the moment, thanks." Carmen smiled at him in a way that made his heart miss a beat.

FORTY

TARRYN WALKED UP THE SHORT FLIGHT OF STAIRS TO the kitchen. The daylight was almost gone, and the glow of the sun faded into the sky. While he preferred not to drink more than two glasses of wine during any kill, he was about to have another. She was unnerving to his very soul. Part of him wanted to kiss her more than anything. He reasoned that it wouldn't be like the situation with Marnie. It would be different this time.

He had never had real sex with a woman, let alone one that he was about to kill. The thought, though intriguing, was not one that he felt comfortable with. He needed the kill; it would complete almost twenty years' worth of work. He wanted the kill so that he could finally make his mother proud. Wasn't that the main goal? Sex would only complicate the matter. It wasn't worth the tremendous risk, and in addition, he still didn't have experience with the act.

His mind wandered back to the day that his mother had warned him about the pitfalls of women. She was always right. Except for her reaction to the truth about the Numbers Killer, then she was 100 percent wrong.

He looked at the clock on the stove. It was six o'clock. He told himself that even if Carmen had not finished her story, she would be his, one way or the other by nine o'clock. When he walked back down the stairs, with his final glass of wine in hand, he was satisfied that he had made the right choice.

"You ready to tell me the rest?" Tarryn asked as he sat down.

"I was telling you that Simon wanted to step up the volume of girls that we were bringing in to the country. I was reluctant. The women were just too young, and we were sure to hit some kind of INS radar. I asked each one of them how old they were, and they told me twenty-one. I think Simon coached them ahead of time. Simon did increase the volume, I found out later; only these girls weren't brought to me for coaching before they were delivered to their new homes. Phototecnics as I knew it was long gone. The social experimentation arm of the business was defunct, and the new importing arm had taken over in full force. The men that purchased women from us paid us from fictitious company accounts, limiting their payments to under ten thousand to keep us off the government's radar. We paid taxes just like anyone else so the whole thing looked aboveboard. The small payments also made it so that I wasn't suspicious when we were getting a hundred thousand for one girl. The younger the girls, the more the men would pay. But while I was going about my merry way teaching the foreign twentysomethings about life in the US, my husband and Gus were selling children that they smuggled from Mexico and Canada to pedophiles all over the country."

"Holy shit. What kind of mess are you in?" Tarryn's tone was angry, and his eyes were large with disbelief. "You sold children? You were a victim of that yourself. How could you?" *Kill her, kill her, kill her.*

Carmen started to cry again. Full torrents of tears were streaming down her face. "That's the whole point, I didn't know. I crossed the line with the women, but I didn't know about those kids. You have to believe me. That's one of the reasons that I want to die. Can you imagine living with that for the rest of your life? It haunts me every moment of every day. Dammit, I shouldn't have told you or anyone else, I just should have killed myself, and no one would have known." She seemed angry. Tarryn wondered if she was upset with herself for telling him or upset that he had judged her so harshly. He had been so close to bringing her back from suicide, and now they were back at square one.

Tarryn leaned close to her on the couch and grabbed her hand in his. "I'm sorry, that wasn't fair of me. I'm just a little shocked is all. Knowing your past, I should have realized that you wouldn't have anything to do with it. Please forgive me." He brushed the back of his hand across her cheek, moving the hair that was wet from her tears.

FORTY-ONE

CARMEN CALMED SLIGHTLY, "I ONLY FOUND OUT BECAUSE I had given my card to one of the older girls. It turned out that the man who had bought her two years before got word that Simon was marketing a younger product and wanted more. The first girl was kept as a nursemaid of sorts. She called me complaining that we had broken our agreement. She had never wanted to be one of *many* girls in the house. She wanted to be the one and *only*.

"I didn't know what she was talking about, but she explained that Simon had dropped off a ten-year-old girl recently and that the new member of the household was getting all of the attention, which left her to clean up after the man and his new object of affection. I was totally shocked. Once again my husband took his lies and depravity to a new low."

"What did Simon have to say about it?" Tarryn was still shocked that slavery, especially with children, would still be possible in today's world.

"Of course I talked to him. He denied all of the allegations. I screamed, I yelled, I threw stuff. I was out of control. I had never told him about the situation with Ray all those years before, but I didn't see what difference it made. He was lying to me again and again and again. I wanted a divorce, and I wanted it at that exact moment. I packed a bag, put it in the car, and went back to grab Sabre. Simon, knowing that I would never leave without the cat, had picked him up in his arms and was holding him out of my reach. I screamed and yelled some more.

Sabre looked petrified; his eyes were like saucers. I just wanted the cat, and I would walk out of his life forever."

"What an asshole. That must have been terrible for you. Did Simon give you the cat?"

"Not at first. He insisted that I listen to him before he handed Sabre back to me. I was blind-mad, but my best friend who was restrained by his arms was as important as anything to me. I wasn't going to leave without him. Simon talked for ten minutes nonstop, telling me that he had no idea about the underage children. He swore to me that Gus must be behind the whole thing. As far as he knew, every single one of the women was twenty-one or older, and they wanted to come to the US. If Gus was importing children from Canada and Mexico, it was news to him as well. He was angry that Gus would have put our entire operation in jeopardy. He was furious that Gus was putting our marriage at risk. He even cried, telling me that nothing was more important than our relationship. He would break off the partnership with Gus the next day, and we could start over."

"Really. Did you believe him?" Tarryn had been so tied up listening to the story that he had almost forgotten the whole reason that she was in his basement lair. It came back like a slap in the face. *Kill her, kill her, kill her.*

"It was the first time that he agreed to sever his ties with Gus. I guess I believed him. At minimum, I thought he truly loved me. That was something that I didn't think he could fake, even though he had become such an accomplished liar. I grabbed the cat and went upstairs to our room. I wasn't completely convinced, but I told Simon that if I had proof that he had broken it off with Gus that I would consider staying and trying to work it out.

"The next day, Simon went to work at 6:00 am as he usually did. I didn't hear from him all day. I was conflicted. I didn't want to leave. We had been getting along so well, and other than the fact that what we were doing was not a hundred percent legal, it was helping women who had no good options in their homeland. Like I said, I wasn't proud of what we were doing. When I look back, the only time where I felt pride in what I did was when I was working for Ed. It wasn't much of a job, but it was an honest day's work and it felt good to be a productive taxpayer."

"Did Simon follow through? Did he dissolve the partnership with Gus?" Tarryn asked.

"He did but not in the way that you might think. My understanding was that he went to the office and called Gus in for a meeting. Gus showed up at around 4:00 pm. We didn't have any office staff at that point. No one could be trusted outside of the three of us to protect the secrets of the business. Supposedly, Gus showed up, and Simon told him he wanted out of the importing business. Gus was surprised. We were making a ton of money, and our network of people that wanted product was far-reaching. Gus was amazed that Simon would walk away from the cash cow. Simon told Gus that he wanted to start a fresh life with me and maybe start a family. He didn't want to have the dream clouded with the knowledge that he was involved in the child sex trade. According to Simon, that was when Gus lost his mind and starting ranting about how marrying me had been the worst mistake of Simon's life. He apparently called me every name in the book, and Simon retaliated with some profanity of his own. Then as Simon tells it, Gus whispered under his breath that he should have driven my car off a cliff instead of just off the road."

"Gus was behind your accident?" Tarryn was surprised, but somehow he had suspected that might be the case.

"According to the story I heard from Simon, yes. He said that he was furious that Gus had hurt me. Gus swore that he only did it to scare me—he didn't want me sticking my nose into the business anymore. Simon came home that night with a bloody nose and a bruised face. He said that Gus was in equally bad shape and that we wouldn't be hearing from him again. I was relieved that the bad chapter in my life was over."

"But you said that Gus was dead. He didn't kill him, did he?"

Carmen ignored the question and continued on, "I guess to me the whole incident seemed aboveboard at the beginning. I tended to Simon's broken nose and put ice packs on his face. I almost felt proud that he had stood up for me. I was worthwhile after all. I was more important than the business, I was more important than Gus, and most of all, I was more important than his precious money. He was willing to give it all up for me. Of course, it wasn't true. But it took me another long six months to realize how far I could fall."

FORTY-TWO

TARRYN WAS IMMEDIATELY THROWN BACK TO THE PAST with those words "I was worthwhile after all." That was exactly how he had felt when he finally told his mother that he was the Numbers Killer. He had fifteen kills on his list of accomplishments. Now that he had confessed his secret identity, she could help him complete his task, and he would be worthy of her attention.

He had expected her reaction to be first one of shock—her boy was the Numbers Killer? Then he anticipated a short period of time where she would digest the knowledge, and finally a joyful "Congratulations" would be in order. Sure, he wasn't even halfway to Bundy's record, but based on her notebook, he was getting high marks. Maybe she would be able to help him design the next kills—the two of them would surely be a formidable foe if they put their heads together. He would be the brawn, but her expertise would be an invaluable addition to the brains.

The first reaction was exactly as expected—she was shocked. Not the kind of shock where you open a Christmas present to discover the one thing that you thought Santa had forgotten, emitting a high-pitched squeal of delight; more like the kind where your eyes grow large and your mouth drops open, unable to hold itself in place with the weight of the recently revealed news. She had been totally and absolutely taken aback with the thought.

The next part was what he had hoped as well. He watched his mother slowly grasping the words and their meaning. There was perhaps five full minutes of silence as he watched her brain come to the realization that her son was a killer. Not just any killer, but a successful killer. It was when she finally spoke that she deviated from his expected script. He wanted words of praise, words of comfort, and words of approval, but what he got was an unexpected awakening to the depths of his mother's love for Ted Bundy.

"Oh, you stupid, stupid, boy," she hissed. "What were you thinking? Did you really believe that you were as talented and as smart as Teddy? What he did takes passion and guts." She grabbed the manila folder from the couch and threw it open on the coffee table. "Wouldn't it be obvious to you that you could never compete? You botched your first kill and forgot to number it. I assume that there was one ... not that you have any proof at this point. You killed two boys, and you know how I feel about that. You're not a fudge packer, are you?" She didn't wait for an answer before she continued, "You numbered thirteen with a twelve. I suppose you were trying to be clever, but I think it was just sloppy."

Tarryn, disappointed with her hopeless negativity, interrupted her, "I did it all for you. I just wanted you to be proud of me like the old days before the drugs. Before the damn stuff took over your soul. I want you to help me and guide me to get better. You're the expert. Give me a helping hand. Make me better than Ted. Make me into the best there ever was." His eyes were pleading with her as he turned from a man back into a little boy.

"There is no one better than Teddy. You know that, and I know that."

"We used to talk about the small mistakes that he made. Come on, Mom, you know he wasn't perfect."

Her tone was filled with hatred, "Don't speak ill of the dead. He was the best, and he will always remain in my heart. I won't have you speaking poorly of him ever. Do you understand me?"

"I'm sorry. I promise not to do it again. Will you help me? If anyone can make me better, it's you. You not only have Ted Bundy's memories but an entire encyclopedia of knowledge in your brain. You can mold me to be whatever you want." Tarryn waited for her reply. He wasn't sure what the outcome was going to be, but he knew that if it wasn't favorable, it would be the end of the road for the Numbers Killer. He couldn't stand the thought of disappointing her any further.

"I need to think about it. I'll let you know in the next couple of days. In the meantime don't go bumbling around with any more kills." With those words, she turned tail and went into her bedroom to get high.

FORTY-THREE

THE DAMN MEMORIES WERE INTERFERING WITH HIS time with Carmen. It was as plain as the nose on his face, the thoughts of his mother were flooding back because today he would finally do the unthinkable, he would break Bundy's record. She might not be with him in body, as she had been for the first twenty-five kills, but she was with him in spirit.

After his admission that he was the Numbers Killer, his mother shut down physically and emotionally. She spent the majority of her time in her bedroom, which was strictly off-limits, except in case of emergency. Tarryn wondered if the slow, painful death of his soul would be considered an emergency in her eyes and decided that under the circumstances, it would not qualify. He knew she was still alive. The lights in her room went on and off at the appropriate times, and after work he would find a dirty plate or glass in the kitchen. But the pain, the awful, gut-searing pain, was more than he could bear. He wanted to feel her touch, see her smile—anything to let him know that she still cared.

Out of the mixture of total frustration and sadness, the urge to kill again was unbelievably strong. Each and every day he saw women that were perfectly suited to be his next play toy. With every moment outside of the apartment, his back itched with desire, but somehow he managed self-control. He remembered one of his mother's observations,

"Emotions are the enemy of a good killer," so he waited, and waited … and waited.

It had taken three entire heartbreaking weeks after his confession before his mother spoke to him again. By then he was so eager to communicate with her, that as soon as she made eye contact, a torrent of apologies and pleading desperation burst from his mouth. She held him like a child, the same way that she had done for so many years before, and he broke down in tears.

They had collaborated on the next ten kills. Victims sixteen through twenty-five were planned together and were all the more sweet as a result. It was a special time for him. Her endless knowledge and expertise in the area had made him genuinely better at his craft. They would review potential kill sites, methods, and victims beforehand and then evaluate and grade the experience afterward. Just like all those nights when he was young, she graded his work against Bundy's. His scores were getting better and closer to the master with every victim. In her initial journal entries for the Numbers Killer, she gave him three out of ten, four out of ten, and on the infamous thirteenth kill, a two out of ten. Now his grades had improved dramatically. With her guidance Tarryn was now getting eights and nines. They were proud moments for both of them.

Carmen was taking her time with the next leg of her story, and he had missed some of her narrative, daydreaming about the past. His brain reengaged. *Kill her, kill her, kill her.*

"It had been maybe two weeks after the big brawl when the phone calls started at the house. They were hang-ups mostly, but they came at all hours. During the day, I would answer the phone to find a dead line. At night Simon was on phone duty. I called the telephone company and asked them to trace the calls, but each one was from a prepaid cell phone that they couldn't pin down. I suspected that it was Gus, but Simon, while noticeably angered, didn't think that Gus would stoop that low. He kept reminding me that while the two of them had a schoolboy fight, they were adults and able to handle the breakup of the business relationship.

"The phone calls stopped after three weeks, but Simon was visibly upset almost all of the time. I chalked it up to the fact that he was starting over again with the legal part of Phototecnics and was stressed as he tried to reestablish our links with our old corporate customers.

We had turned away so many of them when Simon and Gus expanded into the importing aspect of the company. Simon said that some were pleased that we were able to take on new projects, while others had newly established relationships with private investigators who did much of the same type of work. Of course, they weren't as polished as our team, but they were cheaper and still got to the end result.

"Then Simon came home one night, and things got worse. It was a Thursday. I know that because I was happy that it was almost the weekend, and we would get to spend a couple of days just being us. No pressure from the clients and nowhere to go. We had plans to go to our favorite Greek restaurant for dinner. I was watching the news with Sabre in my lap when the door opened. I was shocked to see not only my husband, but also Gus, standing in the doorway. Simon's face was pale, like all of the blood had been sucked out by a hungry vampire. Gus just stood there, grinning. I demanded to know what was going on and of course, I screamed that I wanted Gus out of the house. Sabre went flying as I jumped up and positioned himself under the couch. Even he didn't like the man. Gus walked in like he owned the place and sat down on the couch. He told Simon to fetch him a drink. I was just mortified that the slime bucket was in my home."

"What the hell was going on? Didn't Simon do anything to stop him?" Tarryn glanced at his watch, 7:30—ninety minutes and counting.

"I had never seen that look on Simon's face before; it was pure fear. That and the look of arrogance on Gus's ugly mug made me sit down and take notice. Whatever was happening, it wasn't good, and Gus was the one with the control." Carmen sipped her half-empty glass of wine. Remarkably she wasn't looking like a woman who was remembering a terrifying experience. On the contrary, she looked to Tarryn like a woman who was strong and agile. *Kiss her, kill her, kiss her, kiss her, kiss her.*

FORTY-FOUR

"SIMON GOT GUS A GLASS OF SCOTCH AND SAT DOWN beside me on the couch. He explained that Gus was not pleased with the change in our business relationship. From what I understood, his contacts overseas were concerned that the two of us might cause problems for the network in the future. Gus recommended that we rejoin him and the overseas operation. I refused, of course, but then Gus pulled a gun out of his pocket and held it on his knee. It was threatening but not pointed directly at either of us. I felt the blood drain out of my face at that moment. I was petrified. All of my worst nightmares were coming true. I cursed Simon for getting me into this mess, I cursed Gus, but most of all I cursed myself. Gus suggested that Simon explain to me the motivation for us to reconnect with him just like he had explained it earlier in the day. Simon recounted that we were being given three choices—one, we got back into the business and kept raking in the cash; two, we could expose Gus and be arrested for the crimes that the three of us had committed; or three, Gus could put a bullet in each of us and eliminate the whole nasty inconvenience that we were becoming.

"Simon and I sat on that couch for what seemed like an hour as Gus sipped on his drink. I was some kind of angry, but I had spent enough time on the street to know that you don't mess with a crazy person who's holding a gun. There was no easy way out; that much was painfully obvious. I did the only thing that I could think of to get us out of immediate danger, and I started to yell at Simon. I blasted him, screaming that I told him we should stay in the business, we had too much invested, I certainly had never intended to piss off the team overseas, and I was fucking mad that Gus was taking *his* stupidity out on me. You could tell by the look on Gus and Simon's faces that it was not the reaction that they had expected. After a stunned moment, Simon figured out what I was doing and played along. At least at the time I thought that was what we were doing—playing a high-stakes game of who could out-act the other one. Simon picked up on my thoughts somehow, and he played his role perfectly. We argued, pretending that Gus wasn't in the room. Simon picked me up off the couch and clawed at my shirt. My shirt ripped open, and my breasts were exposed. I have no idea if Simon planned that part. The main idea was to get Gus off balance. And it turned out, a naked pair of boobs did exactly that. Simon raised his hand to hit me, and with a quick turn of my leg, I did a roundhouse kick and smacked Gus in the head."

"You didn't tell me that you were a martial arts expert as well as all of your other talents." Tarryn was feeling the energy in the air. *Kiss her, kill her, kiss her, kill her.*

"I'm not. I just learnt a few survival tactics being on the street. I told you earlier—I've seen some unspeakable things over the years. I learned how to keep myself out of harm's way as a result. Anyway, Gus was momentarily stunned from the kick. Simon grabbed his gun and pointed it at his head. With the balance of power shifted, the two of us had a moment to think. I grabbed a blanket to cover up my chest and watched as Simon's hands shook holding the gun. I don't think that he had ever held a weapon, let alone shot a pistol before. All of a sudden the gun looked so big, and Gus looked so small and pathetic. I wanted him to be gone from my life forever. Simon wanted the same thing, I suppose. The two of us glanced at each other, and without another word, Gus had a bullet in his brain. Simon didn't even give him a chance to speak. It seemed a bit surreal at the time. Afterward, neither of us said anything. I just went upstairs put on an old T-shirt and started cleaning up the blood.

"It took hours, but I finally got the house back in order. I wasn't the one that actually pulled the trigger, but deep in my heart I wanted Simon to do it. A little piece of my heart *wished* that *I* had done it. I wanted that nasty man out of my life, and even more, I wanted the children to be safe again. He was a bad man, and he deserved to die. It was about survival more than it was about murder."

Tarryn sat quietly, not knowing the correct response to what he had just heard. Part of him wanted desperately to tell her *his* history. After all he was a killer too—they were connected. The more rational part of his brain told him to shut his mouth until the urge to confess his indiscretions passed. He did just that.

Carmen spoke again, "Are you ready to call the police yet? I just told you about a murder. I expect that could be cause for a phone call to 911."

"I don't think that anyone needs to know what you just told me. Though I am starting to get an understanding as to why you were so upset when I first met you this morning. First, you weren't the one who killed Gus, Simon was. And secondly, Simon probably did the world a favor. I don't think that anyone would fault you for not speaking up about it, given the circumstances." Tarryn was a bit disappointed that he had never committed such a noble act during any of his kills. His victims were merely strangers, not necessarily anyone who desperately deserved it. All of a sudden the thirty-six kills felt inadequate.

"I might not have pulled the trigger, but I wanted to kill him. I wish I would have had the guts to do it. Regardless, I still have some more to tell. Unfortunately, it's not quite over. If you want to hear the rest I'll keep going, but I would understand if you want me to leave now." Carmen didn't make eye contact when she asked. To Tarryn she looked so vulnerable—just the way that she made him feel. The way that thinking of his mother made him feel. *Kiss her, kiss her, kiss her.*

"I want to hear," he replied. It was 100 percent truth, whether he liked it or not.

FORTY-FIVE

"MY MOTHER TOLD ME ONCE THAT IF YOU SENSE AN unseen enemy, you should never run. If you do, you might just run right into the mouth of the danger itself." Tarryn wasn't sure why he repeated that particular piece of wisdom, at that particular moment, but it somehow felt appropriate. Carmen nodded at him like she somehow understood the exact message that he was trying to convey.

"She died ten years ago. I don't think I told you that. There isn't a day that goes by that I don't think of her." Tarryn paused. "Do you ever think about that day with Gus? Does it haunt you?" Tarryn still had some victims occasionally come back to visit him at night. They weren't scary, but their spirits were as real as the couch that he was sitting on.

"Haunt me? Everything that I have told you about my life haunts me. It's not just Gus. After he was dead, I barely gave him a second thought. He was insignificant once he was gone. I buried that in the deepest cavities of my mind along with all the rest of the unpleasant items that happened to me over the years."

"So why now? What happened to pull all of that scar tissue to the surface again?" Tarryn was intently curious as to what her answer might be. His back itched for the first time in a half hour, which was becoming more of an inconvenience than a helpful reminder.

"The final chapter of this story started shortly after Gus's body was removed from our house. We weren't experts in the disposal of dead bodies, so we did the only thing that we could think of—we buried him in our backyard under the garden shed. Not a very inventive way to solve our problem, but it worked for our purposes. We spent the weekend cleansing Gus's condo of any crumbs of evidence regarding the business. He had quite a collection of porn, which we left in place. The majority of it was mainstream stuff, but there were a few videos and magazines that focused on some pretty weird fetishes. His computer was chock-full of cryptic e-mails and pictures. The data had to go, but as Simon pointed out, we needed to replace it with something else. Everyone has a computer, Gus couldn't be different; it would set off alarm bells. Simon was a master with technology and built up a history on a new computer with painstaking detail. No one would ever know that the entire system had been built over a weekend. Simon waited until the following Monday night and reported Gus as a missing person. It made sense that Simon, his business partner, would be the first one to notice something out of the ordinary. Gus had no family in the city, and to the best of our knowledge his entire family tree still resided in Hungary."

"Did the police ever find his body?" Tarryn asked.

"Not yet but perhaps they will soon." Tarryn thought that to be a strange response but didn't say anything as she continued, "At the beginning the cops came to the house and questioned Simon and myself. Did Gus have any medical conditions? Could he have gone back to visit family in his homeland? Did he have a woman that he was seeing? What were his regular haunts? Was he a drinker? Did he have a drug or gambling problem? Pretty standard questions. I remember sitting in my living room with two detectives perched across from me on the couch. Just having them in the house was nerve-wracking for me. I had watched the man die at my husband's hand. They were sitting on top of the crime scene. It was terrifying. Every single word out of my mouth was a complete and utter lie. I had practice though. My years of living a double life came in handy. I was always good at telling just enough of the truth that my fabrications were believable."

Tarryn's chest tightened. It felt like Carmen had opened up his mind and could read every physiologically impaired thought that had ever crossed his mind. His brain circuits were overloading. The uncomfortable feeling wasn't passing. *Kill her, kill her, kiss her, kill her.*

"I guess your crazy past had a purpose after all." Tarryn was anxious to make his move. *Strangulation was probably the best bet* ... but the melody of her voice started again, and his perfect plan to end the evening started to unravel.

"Seeing as we were the closest thing to family that Gus had in New York, the police felt it necessary to give us updates on a regular basis. Sometimes they would contact us by phone, and other times they came into our home. No matter how they did it, I felt their accusing eyes on me, and I wanted to confess the whole thing. I can't tell you how many times the words were on my lips. Somehow I just couldn't bring myself to actually say them. Then a strange metamorphosis happened—I started to get cocky. The stupid cops had stood on top of the very spot that Gus had died, and they were none the wiser. I started to get angry with them. Why were they so blind? As you can tell, rational thought hasn't been one of my strong suits. In fact rational *anything* has completely left my life. Eventually, the police came by to tell us that Gus was most likely dead. I cried. I assume that they thought I was upset about losing a friend."

Tarryn thought that he could have given her tips on how to avoid the unpleasant disposal of Gus's body, but as with a lot of things in her life, the wisdom he would impart now would be far too late. "They didn't suspect you or Simon?"

"Funny enough they never looked twice. We had no reason to kill him. We had a successful business together, and we didn't profit from his death. He didn't have a life insurance policy that was in our name. We had no ties to his condo. In fact, as we told the police several times, losing Gus hurt our business. They did, however, start to look closely at the type of work that we did. I explained the nature of our investigations, and they thought it might be a catalyst for murder. We explained that Gus was a figurehead and didn't do on-site work. They even interviewed a few of our more recent customers. That hurt us financially. Like I was telling you before, discretion and privacy were key elements to what we did. Having the law poke around was not something that our customers appreciated."

"When the police started looking into the business, didn't they find the importing piece? What happened to Gus's work computer?

Did they search the office?" There were so many questions whirling in Tarryn's brain.

"We had cleaned up all of the evidence of the illegal side of the operation. It wasn't hard. Most of what Simon and Gus did were cash deals or could be construed as a standard part of the legal investigative business. We were cooperative, not secretive, like you might expect. I always believed that it's easier to hide things in plain sight instead of the dusty corners—that's where people look first. The depression was settling into my head though. I had lost who I was and all of my hopes and dreams." Carmen stared intently at Tarryn when she asked, "What defines you? Is it how you look? The home you live in? The car you drive? Your job? The company you keep? I was intensely upset because I no longer could define who Carmen was. The innocence had been lost long, and all that I was left with was a shell of a woman. I wanted to rebuild myself, reinvent myself into something greater, grander than before."

Tarryn watched as she slipped away again into the abyss that was her past. He took a moment to remember the time in his life when he too had tried a personal transformation.

FORTY-SIX

AFTER HIS CONFESSION TO HIS MOTHER, THEY HAD
planned each kill with meticulous detail. But by the time his twenty-
fifth victim took her last breath, he was starting to feel stifled by the
constant pressure for perfection. His own personal style was gone from
the game, replaced by his mother's need to supervise every single action,
every single moment of the act. She had insisted that number nineteen
had to be a blonde between twenty-five and thirty and had to be
stabbed, number twenty-two had to be a redhead in her forties, number
twenty-three had to come from another part of the city, number twenty-
four had to be a brunette and had to be strangled. It was becoming a
chore.

She was his mentor and he valued her input, but the process of
selection and seduction were no longer left up to his instincts. He
wanted her assistance but at a high level. The thrill and spontaneity that
he felt on his first kills was replaced with a stifling resentment that he
had told her his secret so early. Part of him knew that he should have
waited. He should have only told her when he completed his mission.
But it was too late to go back. Where he had previously seen shelter
and safety in her gaze, he now saw only opinions and attitude. He
desperately wanted to complete a kill on his own. It was a curious feeling
at the time. After ten collaborative and successful outings over a period
of three years, he was free to dabble in his own creative juices again.

Victim twenty-six was a young woman who presented herself as he was walking down the street to buy a coffee one afternoon. The tingling in his back was immediate when he noticed her perched on a park bench, sipping a diet soda. Her shining brown hair was cut into a short bob. While he preferred women to have longer hair, she was alluring. After a half hour of casual conversation, they left together hand in hand. Not only was she stunning, but she was also a pushover to boot. Tarryn was pleased that there were still people who trusted on the earth but knew from personal experience, the only one a person should really trust was themselves.

They wandered down the street, looking for a good place to have lunch. Tarryn suggested a shortcut that would take them between two high-rise buildings. It took all of a few seconds for him to cut her throat and mark her with her number. As he watched her die, he felt guilty for not having included his mother in the event, but in the same sense, he felt a freedom that he had not had in years. It was invigorating and saddening. Feeling emotionally disoriented and ashamed, he had walked the streets for hours, not sure what he was going to say when he got home. He didn't want to face the one woman who understood him inside and out and see that he had let her down.

When he finally walked through the door to their apartment, the kill was already plastered on the news channels. He was angry with himself for the delay in getting back home. He had wanted to intercept his mother to give him a chance to explain. *The urge was too powerful. It had just happened. It wasn't even planned.* He corrected himself—it was planned but just as the opportunity presented itself.

He remembered the look of total loathing on her face. He thought that he saw the origins of evil in her stare. He was expecting her to raise her voice, to tear a strip off each side of him, but instead she just went to her room and shut the door. She didn't slam it like he anticipated. She just gently pulled the door into its frame until the latch gave a quiet click.

Tarryn stood watching her door. He didn't want to disturb her and make the situation worse. He hoped that she would forgive him and that the next time the door opened, she would open her heart to him again.

For twelve hours he waited patiently outside her bedroom, staring at the peeling white paint, his nerves fraying more and more by the second.

The light under her door was on the entire time. He wondered if she had fallen asleep, or if she was still seething over his betrayal.

At 10:00 am he finally gathered the courage to knock. When she didn't answer after several raps and several heartfelt apologies whispered into the wood barrier, he took a chance and walked in. His mother, the one and only person he had ever truly loved, lay dead on her bed with a half-full syringe of heroin still stuck in her arm.

He called 911, held her hand, and stroked her hair while he waited for help to arrive, but it was too late. The paramedic said that the overdose looked like a suicide because in his words, "No junkie would ever try to boost that volume of drugs in one sitting."

FORTY-SEVEN

CARMEN CONTINUED WITH AN HONESTY THAT HE hadn't heard yet in her voice, "I remember sitting down with Simon and having the 'I've lost myself' discussion. He couldn't relate at all to what I was trying to say. He was confused. Wasn't the house big enough? Wasn't my cushy life enough? Wasn't *he* enough for me? I tried to explain that with all of the bullshit that we had gone through in the past couple of years, I just needed some time to regroup. I knew that he needed me to help him rebuild Phototecnics, but I wanted to go back and work a few shifts at the diner. You know, get back to my roots, so to speak."

"I take it he didn't agree?" Tarryn found himself feeling a bit protective of Carmen and wanting to ring Simon's neck for being so cruel to his wife.

"He thought it was degrading for me to work at the café. I was his wife, and we had enough money that I shouldn't have to do 'that kind of work.' He wanted me back on the reception desk at the office. I basically refused to go. I gave him two options, either he let me go and work with Ed or I was going to die a slow mental death at Phototecnics. He reluctantly agreed. I remember the look on his face when I told him that I had already spoken to Ed and my first shift was the following Thursday. He was pissed off that I had gone so far down the path without checking with him first. I knew it was the only way that I was going to be able to pull myself back from the depths of depression."

"I bet Ed was happy to have you back on board? Was Janice—that was her name, right?—was she still working there?" Tarryn was expecting excitement in her voice, but just as he had come to expect from Carmen, her reaction was unexpectedly somber. Every time he thought that he had her figured out, she threw him another curve ball. *Kill her, kiss her, kill her, kiss her.* The battle was still raging.

"Ed was happy to see me, and no, Janice wasn't there anymore. She moved out of state to take care of her ailing mother. I was so far out of touch with them that I didn't have a clue. It was hard to get back into the swing of the busy restaurant. I had forgotten how physically demanding being on your feet all day could be. After the first day I had huge blisters on both feet. I suffered quietly, not wanting to hear the I-told-you-not-to-do-it from Simon. But I was having fun. By the end of the first week, I was back to my old routine, and I was remembering the regulars and what they liked to order. The pay was miniscule, but it was never about money, so I didn't care."

Tarryn needed some blanks filled in before she went on. "Didn't Ed ask you what was going on? Wasn't he curious as to why you were back?"

"Of course. He did the fatherly thing and asked *again* if Simon was abusive and was I happy in my marriage? I assured him that I just wanted to interact with people again, real people, not the corporate stuffed shirts that called Phototecnics. He might have been suspicious, but he never pushed me to tell him more. I wanted to. And in hindsight, I wish I would have. It might have saved his life."

"Huh? How did he die? Don't tell me that Simon had something to do with it."

Carmen continued on the path that she thought was most important. "Simon told me that he was getting back on track with the business—the legitimate business. Our bank account already had a substantial balance, and I saw it staying about the same. Simon took care of the majority of the financial burdens—mortgage, utilities, phones, the gardener, the cleaners. I threw my pittance of a paycheck in the joint account, but a few dollars on top of hundreds of thousands didn't look like much of a contribution. Anyway, he seemed happier and seeing as I was happier, things started to improve in our relationship. We started to forget the whole mess with Gus, and I felt like we were moving in the right direction. It was about six months ago, a year after I started back with Ed part-time, that the bottom fell out for the final time."

Tarryn was pleased. They were into the homestretch. But when he looked over at Carmen, he knew that it was going to be the worst part of the day. Her once beautiful features were wilted, and she looked tired. It was time to do his final gesture of generosity.

"Can I get you one more glass of wine for the final chapter of the story? You've been doing a lot of talking, you must be getting thirsty."

Carmen nodded, but only the slightest corners of her mouth turned up in a forced smile.

FORTY-EIGHT

TARRYN WALKED UP THE STAIRS TO THE KITCHEN AND looked at the clock. Carmen had made it well past his original deadline. It was 9:10. He still couldn't decide if he wanted to have an intimate encounter with her before the final act. He was sure that she would be up to it, if he wanted her in that way. All of a sudden it struck him that he had never had a woman in his bedroom. He bought the house shortly after his mother had passed, but even with all of the privacy that living alone provided, he had never had the urge—until now.

He looked around the house and could feel his mother in each and every corner of the home. At first after her death, he was angry. Angry at himself for branching out on his own on the last kill, angry at himself for telling her about his secret too early, and angry at her for taking her own life. He sat in the apartment mourning the loss of a dream. They had come so close to having a perfect kill—a perfect record. She had taken it all away. *No, he couldn't blame her, after all he was the one that made her upset; he was the one that should shoulder the burden.*

It had been three weeks after the paramedics had taken her away on the gurney with a grey bag zipped over her beautiful face that he decided to clean up her room. It was too painful to look at her unmade bed and her clothes strewn on the stained carpet. She was never going to return—although part of him wanted to believe that the whole thing was just some nasty joke and she would come back to him.

He packed her things into cardboard boxes. Several of them housed her well-worn clothes—they went to the local homeless shelter. The more challenging pieces were her collection of true crime books and her tattered papers, comparing every one of the criminals in the past thirty years to her precious Teddy. Tarryn didn't want to throw them away but couldn't stand to keep them either. He had a few teary-eyed moments as he remembered their time together. All those years when he was a kid spent dissecting the killers' every move, their faults, their strengths, and breathing in the sweet perfume of his mother's hair.

He was flipping through the pages of Bundy's biography when he found something astonishing. Out of the yellowing pages a note fell to the floor. It was in his mother's handwriting, and it was the reason that he could afford the house that he now lived in. She was an amazing woman right up until the very end, and her final words made him wail like a baby. It was dated a year before she died.

Tarryn,

You have been and will always be the light that lifts me up. I can't imagine what my life would have been without you by my side.

You were always a good student, and you have grown into a very strong man. You have accomplished so much, and I am always proud to call you my son.

I know that we have never been able to afford all of the fancy things that I wanted so desperately to give you. The drugs were a speed bump that I never wanted, but it was the hand that I was dealt. Please understand that I did the best I could. There were days when all I wanted was to put all of the money up my nose or in a vein. The drugs have a powerful draw that I hope you never find. But believe it or not, there were other days where something was holding me back. I guess I had some self-control that I wasn't always aware of.

There is a bank account in your name (and your name only—thank God) that I used to deposit extra tips in those years that I worked. I don't imagine it is much, but it's my way of saying that I was always thinking of you, even in those times when I wasn't thinking of myself.

Love,
Mom

The attached bank statement showed a balance of ten thousand dollars, which gave him the down payment on the house. He wished that she would have told him earlier and that they could have shared the home together. It was heartbreaking that he never had a chance to thank her or tell her how important she was in his life.

It was then that he knew the only way to prove his love was to finish the task at hand. At that point, he had completed twenty-six with another eleven to go. Today was that day that he would finally get to thank his mother for all that she was to him. Tarryn wiped a single tear from his cheek, took a deep breath, and took the two wineglasses down to the basement. *Kill her, kill her, kill her.*

FORTY-NINE

"HERE YOU GO, M'LADY," TARRYN SAID AS HE DIPPED INTO a gentleman's bow in front of Carmen. He watched her face light up when he passed her the final glass of wine.

"I can't believe that you haven't called the cops on me yet. Or maybe this is a last glass of wine to keep me in place until they get here?"

"You haven't told me anything yet that requires police," Tarryn replied. "Plus I don't feel like you are a threat to my well-being. I haven't done anything to warrant an attack, have I?"

Carmen smiled just a little. "Just the part where I pulled a gun on you earlier. Other than that, the answer is no. This whole day just seems so absurdly strange. I just met you, and so far I have told you about being molested, doing drugs, dealing drugs, social experiments gone wrong, trafficking women, and murder. I can't say that I expected today to turn out anything like this."

"I told you at the beginning that I was a good listener. I might be just a lowly cab driver, but I still have value in the world. Just like you. You're a good woman, Carmen, and from what I understand to this point, you have been a victim, not a perpetrator of any crime." *Kiss her, kill her, kiss her, kiss her.*

Carmen's physical appearance and stature morphed from one of relaxed comfort to a hellfire bitch in a split second. "Look, let's get this straight right now. I was never a victim. I made conscious choices at every step in my life. I let Ray touch me, I chose to do drugs, I chose

165

to marry Simon, and I chose to look the other way when my fantasy world was crumbling around me. I could have told my parents about Ray, I could have gone to counseling all those years ago, I could have been more practical about my choice of a husband and not such a naive child, I could have exposed Simon at the very beginning, and more importantly, I could have chosen to get out before it was too late. Don't go calling me a victim. A victim is someone who has no control. I have always had control. Haven't you been listening to me at all? I didn't control how I was born, but I will control when and how I die." Carmen slumped back on to the couch as if the tirade had drained the last ounce of her energy.

Tarryn was taken aback by the outburst but fundamentally understood what she was saying. He was no different. No matter what anyone would say about him later in his life, he made the choices that got him to this point. "I'm sorry. I get it. Really." Then his body took over from his brain, and he leaned toward Carmen until his mouth was just an inch from hers. *Kiss her, kiss her, kiss her.*

Carmen look confused by his reaction, but her body responded to him anyway. Their lips touched tenderly, as he closed his eyes. It was nothing that Tarryn had ever experienced before. It sent a bolt of lightning though his body from the top of his head to the very tips of his toes. It was magnificent. He pulled away just as quickly as he could. He wasn't sure what to feel or think. The smell of her skin lingered on his as he retreated to his side of the couch.

"I'm sorry. I … I don't know why I did that," he said with an awkward timbre.

"That's okay. It was nice," she replied but didn't make eye contact. She took another sip of the wine that she was still holding in her hand.

FIFTY

TARRYN, EMBARRASSED BY THE IMPROMPTU KISS, CURSED himself for being so impulsive. *Emotions are the enemy.* "I think you were about to tell me how the bottom fell out."

He thought that Carmen looked relieved to continue with the story rather than having to discuss the kiss. "I was telling you that Simon and I were getting along much better. I was working with Ed again part-time, and things were looking up. Ed was pressing me to explain why I was back working at the café. I felt like he deserved an explanation. He was such a good man and kept taking me back under his wing whenever I needed help. By then I was already a murderer and couldn't stomach telling him the truth. I didn't want to see the disappointment on his face after all he had done for me. So I lied. I told him that Simon and I had been trying to have a baby and that we recently discovered that I was physically unable to have kids. I didn't have to elaborate further—men don't like to talk about that kind of thing, especially men of Ed's age. He held my hand and told me he was sorry to hear such an awful thing. He told me I would make a great mother and suggested that we adopt. I told him that Simon didn't want to. It felt like such an innocent lie, but I suppose that all lies seem innocent at the beginning. I just wanted him off my back. It seemed like a plausible explanation of why I was trying to keep myself busy. I reasoned that the truth would hurt him more than the little lie I had just unloaded."

"You were trying to spare him from reality. I think you did the right thing."

"I went home to Simon and told him the story that I told Ed. I wanted him to be aware, just in case he ran into Ed somewhere. I didn't want him to be caught off guard. He was pissed off that I had talked to anyone at the restaurant about our lives and accused me of having a death wish. Did I know what would happen if I went to jail? Didn't I know that they weren't nice people in there? He said that they were evil and would eat me for lunch. I guess he was afraid. I think more for himself than for me. He didn't want to go to jail and neither did I. I kept explaining that I told the story to Ed to protect our secret, not expose it. He was furious and stormed out of the house. I sat there for hours, afraid of what was coming next. Not knowing who was going to walk through the door—the husband that I loved or a monster of a man that I wouldn't recognize."

Tarryn was only half listening to the story. He was still wrapped up in what had happened a few minutes before. *He had kissed her.* It wasn't like him to deviate from the methodology that had taken so many years to perfect. There had been only one other instance in the past where he had veered off course, and it had ended in total disaster.

Shortly after his mother had died, he had chosen what he thought would be victim twenty-seven. Still feeling drained from the loss of someone so close, he was sloppy with his choice of locations. The anger and sorrow were driving him, and he had chosen to take a woman's life in the alley behind his house. Looking back, he wondered if he wanted to get caught—maybe to end the pain that he was feeling. At a mere eighteen years old, she had looked like she was twenty-five. He was putting the garbage out in the alley late at night, and she was just a block past his house. He grabbed a piece of rope from the ground and stalked her for the length of three houses. He had originally planned on strangulation to end her life, but somehow when he was positioning the thin rope around her neck, she had sprayed Mace in his eyes. She had escaped, but the manhunt was on and his house was one of the targets. With sirens and lights filling the street, the cops had knocked on his door. Did he see anything? Did he hear anything? He told the police officers that he had been watching television in the basement and hadn't heard or seen a thing. He thought that they had believed him, but they came by for a second visit a week later. Did he think of anything that might help them? They told him that she was just a little girl—it was his duty to tell them everything he knew. Tarryn remembered that one moment and played it over and over his brain for an entire month—the middle-aged officer, his balding head peppered with age spots, his critical stare searching for the truth. It was a wake-up call. Another of his mother's sayings popped into his head "Why reinvent the wheel. Stick with what works."

He had made a mistake on number twenty-seven and learned a valuable lesson. But today wasn't just any day, and he was so far off his standard practice that it was scary. Perhaps it was the culmination of so many memories or the fact that he was beginning to feel the tendrils of sleep tugging at his brain. Whatever it was, he had to get back on track and fast. *Kill her, kill her, kill her.*

"Simon showed up at 2:00 am drunk as a skunk, smelling like he had tried to drown every cell of his body with beer. I was just relieved that he wasn't angry anymore. If he needed to get drunk to make himself feel better, I could live with it. I would talk with him in the morning and get things sorted out. I got up at 8:00 and put on a pot of coffee. Simon was still snoring. It gave me time to reflect on my life. I remember thinking about the compromises that we all have to make along the way. Sometimes the easy road might not be as taxing, but it doesn't give you the greatest rewards either. I wanted to stay in the marriage, and I was going to make it work no matter what. Anyway, Simon got up and was in no shape to talk. He looked like a wet rag, crumpled and limp. I made him breakfast and went off to work. It was my last shift of the week, and we would have plenty of time to talk over the weekend." Carmen stopped and tilted her head up to the ceiling. The tears were running down the slides of her cheeks. "Then I found out that the bastard had killed Ed."

"What? He killed Ed in the night? What happened?" Tarryn was amazed at the set of balls on this man. He was a cold-blooded killer with no regard for his personal relationships. That was a line that even Tarryn stayed away from. *Kiss her … that was what she needed.*

"I went on shift just like I always did. It was the first time in the history of the café that Ed wasn't on the premises. No one knew where he was. I went upstairs to the loft apartment, thinking that he might have slept there overnight. I was hoping that I could give him some good-natured ribbing for sleeping in and showing up late for his shift. When I got up there, the door was ajar, and he was lying on the floor in the makeshift kitchen. He didn't deserve to die. He was an honest, caring, loving soul. I wish that I had never gone back. He might still be alive. Worst of all, by talking to you today, I might have put you at risk too." Carmen sobbed, covering her face with her hands.

Tarryn ran upstairs and grabbed an entire roll of toilet paper to mop up the seemingly endless supply of tears. *Just kill her. Get it over with. Put her out of her misery and suffering. Kill her, kill her.* The welts were burning, and Tarryn touched his back. They seemed more prominent than usual. The monster was trying desperately to escape.

FIFTY-ONE

TARRYN TOUCHED THE TOP OF HER HEAD AS HE PLACED the roll in her lap. "I'm so sorry to hear about Ed. I know that he meant the world to you."

Carmen looked up and wiped her face with big swipes of a wad of tissue. "That fucking bastard killed him." The fight had come back into her voice. "The police said that it looked like a heart attack."

"How did you know it was Simon? Maybe it was a heart attack. From what you told me, Ed wasn't the youngest guy on the block."

"The asshole had left me something. No one else would understand—it was a message meant just for me. On the counter in the kitchen, there was a box of Caramellos. Ed was diabetic and would never have bought anything with that much sugar. It was obvious. It was a warning. If I messed with him again, I was going to be the next to die."

"Why didn't you go to the police right then and there? He committed two murders. He killed your friend. There had to be a way to stop him." Tarryn was trying desperately to think of how he would have gotten out of the situation. He soon realized that there were no easy answers, no simple solution to such a complex and convoluted problem.

"I was an emotional wreck. I didn't want to go back home and face the man that killed Ed, let alone sleep in the same bed with him. I had no clue what to do. What was I going to tell the police—Ed had a box of caramel candy on his counter and therefore I knew that my husband had killed him? If I exposed Simon, I exposed myself. There were several points that afternoon where I was willing to go to jail just so that Simon would get what he deserved. I wanted him to feel the pain that I was feeling. I wanted him to know what it felt like to have someone that you love betray your trust. I was desperate to get revenge, but I wasn't stupid. I knew that I had to plan my escape and Simon's payback very carefully."

"I'm confused, you must have gone back home because that's where I picked you up from. You went back to him?" Tarryn asked.

Carmen let out a big sigh and wiped a few stale tears from her eyes. "Yep, I went back, and I pretended like nothing had happened. It was one of the hardest things that I've ever had to do. I was so distraught about Ed and at that point, I had nowhere else to go. Simon had removed all of my options. I went to the funeral the next week with Simon by my side. It was a beautiful memorial with all of the staff and customers that Ed had served over the years."

"Wait a second, you took Simon to the funeral of the man that he had killed? Don't you see a problem with that?" Tarryn clicked his tongue with disapproval. *How could she have been so disrespectful?*

"It was awful, but I didn't want to let on that I knew Simon was involved. It was disgusting holding his hand during the service. It made my skin crawl. I could only hope that Ed was watching over me and could see what was in my heart. That he would understand my true intentions."

"And what were your true intentions?" *Kill her, kill her, kill her.*

"Look, don't judge me for what I did. You can't tell how you are going to react until you get thrown into a situation. Sorry, but I didn't have a lot of experience with a murderous husband who killed my employer. I did the best I could."

Tarryn's mind flashed his mother's letter in his mind, *Please understand that I did the best I could.* Damn it—this woman was fucking with his brain. Was she some kind of psychic witch? His lips didn't make a sound, but his mind was screaming—*Stop it or I'll take your life this second. Fuck your story. I doesn't matter how it ends. I'll tell you how it ends—with my hands around your throat.* The sound of a raving lunatic in his brain stopped him cold. Was this what he had come to? Was this the culmination of twenty years of practice and experience? Could this woman have gotten so far under his skin that he was incapable of rational thought?

Carmen was still telling him about the funeral. "I paid my respects to Ed, and that was all that mattered to me. It felt like the end of another chapter in my life. I was on my own. I didn't have a safety net. No wires to hold me up in case I faltered. But I was strong. I was the Steel Rose. I still had a spark of honesty and goodness left. I was going to make things right no matter how long it took. I wanted revenge. So I started to build a plan. In the beginning, I just fantasized on ways to get back at Simon. I dreamt of doing a Lorena Bobbitt and taking his manhood. I thought about injecting him with HIV so that he could have a long, painful death. I thought of a lot of things, but the logistics were never right. I wondered if I could kill him in his sleep. That one had some merit, but then he would be getting off easy. I really wanted him to suffer. Not just a quick gunshot wound done in 'self-defense.' I wanted him to have time to think about what he had done. Time to let his demons eat away at his brain.

"After Ed's funeral, our relationship had changed back to two strangers living under the same roof. There was no passion, no warmth, no comfort when I was at home. It had become a torture chamber for my mind. I constantly saw images of Gus lying on the floor, of Simon drunk on the couch after he killed Ed. If it wasn't for Sabre, I would have lost my marbles. He was a welcome distraction on the days where the depression felt like a bottomless pit."

Tarryn shook his head in amazement. "That certainly doesn't explain why you are sitting here on my couch. You told me *you* were going to kill yourself." Tarryn wondered how much longer the story would take. It was 9:45.

"I didn't say it was a perfect plan, but it was the only one that I had. By that point I knew that Simon's biggest motivations were money and power. He obviously didn't have any moral fiber and certainly no capacity to have any real connection with the people around him. I played along for months. I was the doting wife. I cooked, I cleaned, and when necessary, I had sex. I loathed every moment—it was disgusting." Carmen said it all so matter-of-factly that she might have been telling a story about someone else.

Tarryn saw the origins of madness in her eyes. She wasn't the woman who was brokenhearted just a few minutes ago. Now she had transformed into a cold-blooded killer. What scared him the most was that even though the sentiment behind her words was eerily familiar, the conviction was nothing that he had ever felt. He had only ever killed to get to the prize—it looked like she had taken blood lust to an entirely new level.

"I started to do research on my husband. Something I should have done well before I married his sorry ass. I had learned a few tricks of the trade while Phototecnics was going strong. I spent hours on the Internet, trying to find anything or anyone that might give me some insight into the man that I lived with. I wanted dirt. There are Internet sites that will give you quite detailed background information on anyone in the country for under a hundred bucks. It was a good place to start. The sites promise to provide all known addresses and places of employment for the past twenty years as well as names of the people that Simon would have lived with. The original thought was that once I found his weak spot, I would start to use it to drive him insane. I paid the money, and twenty-four hours later I had an e-mail. It wasn't at all what I expected. Simon Halder hadn't even existed until ten years ago. The only addresses and jobs were the ones that I already knew of. There was zero information on him prior to the time that I had met him."

Tarryn's back was writhing like a pit full of earthworms; he wanted to kill, needed to kill. But things were starting to get interesting again, and he calmed himself with relaxation techniques. Long deep breaths, in through the nose, out through the mouth, visualize a happy place. After a minute, he was under control again and able to focus back on the story.

"His parents, the ones that I met at our wedding, they didn't exist either. There was no documentation of two people with the surname Halder that had ever been in Spain, let alone living there for any period of time. Maybe he hired them to play the part of the doting parents. In hindsight, I never called them—it was always them that contacted us—they could have been anyone. We had been so focused on the business for the past ten years that we hadn't seen any of his old co-workers for eons. I didn't want to set off alarm bells and get word back to Simon that I was snooping, so I chose to work on what I had. All I knew for sure was that Simon Halder was just another fabrication in the web of my life."

"Simon isn't Simon? Then who is he?"

"He is Simon legally, I suppose, or he got a fake ID somewhere. We got a marriage license so the name was registered at some point. He has a driver's license and credit cards. For all intents and purposes, Simon *is* Simon. What I wanted to know was who he *used* to be before I met him. I was at a bit of a dead end. His parents weren't real, and I had no idea what his former name was. There was no record of him changing his name in New York so it had to be done out of state. Then I started to think about the only person who Simon had been close to over the years, the person who probably knew him better than I did—Gus. I ran the same search on Gus and didn't get a single hit. According to the investigation site, Gus never had a US address or social security number. He was untraceable. Believe it or not, that only made me more determined to find the truth. I wanted … no … I deserved to know. Almost ten years of my life were a lie. It was disturbing.

"I put the happy wife mask back on during the evenings, but during the day I turned into Carmen Super Sleuth. Double life again. I know, it's a trend, don't say it. For weeks, I went through every desk drawer in Simon's office but found nothing. I went through our personal papers but found nothing. I looked through every inch of his closet but found nothing. I was frustrated. Then I thought of Gus and the time I spent under his desk. I went back to Simon's office and looked underneath the desk drawers. I finally found what I was looking for. He had taped an envelope to the underside of the drawer. The tape was yellowed with age. It had obviously been there for a while. We had that desk when we lived in the condo. The truth had been right under my nose all along. I probably sat staring at it for a good ten minutes before I dared to look inside. I thought about the days when I first met Simon and how much in love I had been. I remembered our honeymoon, how he nursed me back to health after the accident. I knew that once I looked in the envelope there was no going back. No matter what secrets it revealed, I would have to deal with yet another bump in the road. I was sure that whatever it was, it was going to set me free. I guess it did to an extent but not in the way that I had expected."

"How much worse can this guy get? Looks like he's been an asshole for quite a long time." *Tick, tick, tick. Kill her, kill her, kill her.*

"Well, let me start by saying that the envelope just gave me the starting point. At least I found out his real name. The entire contents of the envelope were just two pieces of paper, a birth certificate for Sandor Horvath and a photograph of Simon and another boy looking like they might be about ten. The birth certificate was from Hungary and didn't list the names of any parents. The black-and-white photo was grainy and old, but I thought that the other boy had a resemblance to Gus. The smile was the same—that slimy reptilian smile. They were standing in front of a brick building—no name, no street signs. I thought it looked like a school. I later found out that it was a convent. Anyway, I took copies of the paper and the photo and stuck the envelope back to the bottom of the desk drawer. Simon walked through the door about a half hour later. I was sure that he would be able to see the guilt that was written all over my face. I was so afraid that I would do something that would tip him off. That somehow, I would expose the fact that I was investigating him, and lo and behold, I was on to something. Of course, I didn't know what it was. But I just knew somehow that what I found was important."

Tarryn knew that particular emotion all too well. In the early days of the hunt, he felt invincible—above the law. After his mother's passing, he was noticing a touch of paranoia just around the edges of his consciousness. It was a change that he didn't like one bit. *Emotion equals errors. Paranoia equals prison.* Recently, he was aware of cops around him more often. Where in the past, he didn't even consider them in the equation until he had targeted a victim; now he saw them everywhere. The times when he was in close quarters with anyone of authority, he couldn't make eye contact. He was afraid that the guilt was obvious, that it was written in big letters on his forehead—*I am the Numbers Killer.* He was feeling sympathy for Carmen. She was him, and he was her. *Kiss her, kiss her, keep focused—kill her.* Tarryn thought he looked sufficiently intrigued and nodded for her to continue.

"I moved my research from New York to Hungary. This is where it got a bit tricky. I had zero contacts in that country. I needed someone that I could trust who could gather information for me, four thousand miles away. So I did what all good thirty somethings do, and I googled investigative firms in Budapest."

"Aah, good thinking. The Internet is a wondrous tool. I wish they had it when I was in grade school. It would have made research for reports a whole lot easier," Tarryn said. He felt like he should say something to encourage her.

"Yeah, we had the good old *World Book Encyclopedia* too. I found a company that I thought would do the job for me. Their rates were reasonable, but I still had one problem. If I put it on my credit card, Simon was sure to see it on the statement at the end of the month. I didn't have enough cash to wire the money, so I got creative again. I sold my SUV."

"Didn't Simon notice that you were missing a vehicle? I would think that it would be pretty hard to hide."

"I had to concoct a whole story. Like I said before, I'm not a victim. I can be pretty resourceful when I need to be. I told him that the engine blew up and that I had it towed to the shop. I even had it towed so that there would be a charge on the credit card. Then after it was towed, I just drove it away and sold it. Realize that I had to find out the truth but I also had to be smart. If Simon found out what I was doing, he would probably kill me just like he killed Ed. I needed time. I figured that I could keep the blown engine story intact for maximum a month. I wired ten thousand dollars to Budapest, took a taxi home, and waited."

Tarryn was amazed at how complex she had made her hoax. Down to the last detail, everything was perfect. Simon had obviously messed with the wrong woman. It still didn't explain why she had wanted to cut her own life short. He looked at his watch—ten o'clock. He calculated the next chain of events in his head—listen to the rest of the story, kill Carmen, move the body, branding, a shower, a few hours of sleep—he was never going to make it for his midnight shift driving cab. He would have to remember to call in sick once he had Carmen secured.

"How long did it take for them to get back to you? You were saying earlier that some of your investigations took months. And the more important question—what did they find?"

"I gave them a deadline. They had three weeks to tell me everything that they could about Sandor Horvath aka Simon. It was the longest three weeks of my life. Number one—I was housebound without a car, and number two—I was on pins and needles wanting to know who I had shared my bed with for the last ten years. I researched Hungary during the day and tried not to upset the delicate balance in the house at night."

"He didn't suspect anything? Even with the SUV missing for so long?"

"No. I gave him regular updates pretending to phone the service shop once a week. I got him to drive me to the grocery store a couple of times to keep up appearances. I was getting impatient and nervous near the end of week two. That's when I realized my biggest mistake—once I had the information, how was I going to get my truck back? I had sold the SUV for forty thousand to a dealer, but now I only had thirty thousand and no vehicle. I was so desperate to get information, that I had forgotten to plan for step two. That was my downfall. That one little error ..." Carmen drifted off, presumably going through the mistake in her mind, wishing that she had thought things over a little more thoroughly. *Kill her, kill her, kill her.*

FIFTY-TWO

TARRYN WATCHED CARMEN, INTENTLY STUDYING HER from head to toe. She was simple yet complex, wholesome but malicious, soft and beautiful but unyielding. She had morals but was immoral. Her eyes were guarded, but she wore her heart on her sleeve. She was the most confusing and tantalizing specimen of the human race that he had even encountered. He had spent so many years calling the devil his friend, that it was becoming harder and harder to identify with regular people. He felt like his life had been spent looking out of a picture window instead of living in the world outside. He thought that Carmen might feel the same way if he told her his analogy.

"By the time the third week rolled around, I was in the throes of a full-on panic attack. Every time I saw Simon I could barely breathe. I had screwed up. Even if the investigator gave me some juicy tidbits of information, I would have a week—tops—to act on them. Seeing as I didn't have any details on what I was dealing with, it was hard to start the wheels in motion. I had no idea what direction the report would take me in. The investigator finally phoned me—day twenty-one—to say that the report was ready. I remember thinking that he sounded somber. I told him to e-mail the information. I had set up a free Internet mail account just for the occasion. I sat in front of the screen hitting Send/Receive every thirty seconds until the email came in an hour later. When it showed up in my inbox, I was afraid to open it. I realized that I had probably risked my life to get this information. What if there wasn't anything concrete that I could use? What if Simon was just a man that had changed his name and moved to America? How was I going to explain that I sold my truck? It was terrifying."

"Don't keep me in suspense. What did the report say?" Tarryn noted that his voice was showing signs of anxious energy, but he didn't care. It was a valid tone given the conversation.

"Simon—Sandor Horvath—was abandoned in an orphanage just outside Budapest. His mother just showed up one day after giving birth and left him and his brother on the doorstep. There's no record of who she might have been or who his father was. From what I understand, the orphanages are not as nice as the ones in the US. They are cold, stark, antiseptic rooms filled with row upon row of cribs. There are few staff, and the babies are left alone for long stretches. They have very limited human contact. Simon's brother was two when they were abandoned but was in much the same situation. Hungary is a poor country, and the majority of orphans don't get adopted. With next to no physical and mental stimulation, they were basically left to fend for themselves at a very young age. Simon's brother was one of the lucky ones. He found a home when he was ten, but the family that took him wasn't willing to take on two children—Simon was left behind. He stayed in the orphanage until he was fifteen. The investigator spoke to a few of the staff that were still working in the building. They described Sandor as a sad child who was smart but cold. The investigator said that no one really had much detail, as they spent so little time with each of their wards.

"Simon disappeared off the radar until he was seventeen. He was caught stealing from a street merchant. He was released with a slap on the wrist and went MIA for another two years. At nineteen he showed up again when he got a legal job in a grocery store. The store was long gone by the time my investigator started looking, so it was a dead end. However, when my Budapest contact did some digging, he found the owner of the store. The man remembered Sandor quite well and told a story that I hope will be Simon's ultimate downfall."

"You actually found some dirt on him. Holy shit." Tarryn wanted to hug her as a congratulations. *Kiss her, kill her, kiss her, kiss her.*

"The owner of the grocery store, Mr. Toth, was somehow sucked in by Sandor. He felt sorry for the boy—who he described as a broken shell. He had spent two years in an orphanage himself and knew the hardships that the children had to endure. He gave Sandor a job stocking shelves and eventually allowed him to do purchasing of product. That's where Simon got his computer experience. Toth taught him the basics so that he could do his job but encouraged Sandor to learn more about the computer so that he could get a good job one day. Sandor spent hours teaching himself the intricacies of computers. It was in Toth's best interest that he learn and climb the corporate ladder, after all Sandor had started to take a shine to his sixteen-year-old daughter." Carmen scowled but continued, "Toth told the investigator that Sandor and Eva were inseparable during the first year. He apparently doted on her day and night. She would come to visit him every chance that she had and spent her evenings in the cold grocery warehouse, doing her schoolwork, just so that she could be close to him. Toth was happy. He liked Sandor and was pleased that his daughter was spending time with such a motivated and respectful boy."

"I take there is more to this than meets the eye." Tarryn's started to feel the tug of sleep at the corner of his mind.

"Of course, Simon has yet to disappoint me with the depths of his evil—this time was no different. The investigator's report was very detailed. He did an excellent job considering that I only paid him ten thousand dollars. He had recorded the conversation with Toth and had the transcript word for word. He even put notes as to when the man started crying. Eva was a good, honest girl, and her father had warned her about having sexual relations with boys before she was married. Like all fathers, he wanted her to stay pure as long as possible. He even had a conversation with Sandor to make sure that his wishes were understood. Sandor could date Eva, but if he wanted to move forward with a physical relationship, there would have to be a wedding ring involved. He would not tolerate his daughter's reputation being soiled by an unwanted pregnancy. Sandor lived by the rules for another six months. But one night things got out of hand when heavy petting wasn't going to satisfy his lust. I understand that she fought back, not wanting to disappoint her father. Sandor, the man I called Simon, beat her and raped her. I guess he didn't have any respect for women back then either."

"Sandor ... Simon ... whoever he is, deserves to suffer. Did her dad call the police? Was she okay?"

"Eva's father found her the next day lying in a pool of her own blood in the grocery store warehouse. He had been frantically looking for her all night and finally decided to check the store at five the next morning. Sandor was nowhere to be found. At first he couldn't fathom that the well-mannered boy was involved. He thought that maybe Eva was a victim in a robbery and perhaps Sandor had been hurt as well. Just like me, he wanted to believe, and just like me, Simon had played him. Eva was in the hospital for a week while she recovered. The bruising was apparently quite extensive, and she had a broken jaw. When she could speak, she told her father the whole story. Toth contacted the police, and the search was on for Sandor. The trail ended there. Sandor simply ceased to exist in Hungary. The police never found him, and to this day, Toth is still looking to get his revenge."

"But we know that Sandor is Simon. Can't we do anything?" Tarryn realized that by saying "we" he had just taken ownership of the problem. He cursed himself for becoming emotionally involved. He heard his mother's voice, *Emotion equal errors.*

"*I* knew that Sandor was Simon, but I had no proof."

"What about DNA evidence? Couldn't you compare Simon's DNA to Sandor's DNA from the crime scene?"

"I thought about that. Don't forget this was many years ago. DNA wasn't readily used back then, and Hungary isn't known for its world-class police investigations. I still needed to track down how Simon came to the US. I needed paperwork so that I could take the next step. I was three weeks in to the investigation, and at best I had a week left until Simon was going to start calling the mechanic himself, looking for our missing SUV. I contacted the investigator again and asked him to do one more thing for me. I wired him another five thousand dollars and asked him to track down Sandor's brother. I figured that if I could find his brother, I might be able to find out how Simon changed his name and made it into the country. It was a long shot, but I was running out of time and options. I gave the investigator three days to get me a name and contact information. It only took him two."

"Did he give you what you needed?" Tarryn's third, or fourth, wind took hold and he was back to his fully alert self again—this was too interesting to pass out from exhaustion.

Carmen's face was pale as she downed the final few drops of wine from her glass. "This part is one of the strangest, I suppose. Sandor's brother was a boy named Gazsi. Like I told you he was adopted when he was ten by a family who had three other children, all girls. The boy was quite a handful and talked constantly about his brother that was left behind. He never forgot Sandor and was increasingly abusive to his adopted siblings. He left home to try and find his long-lost brother when he was eighteen. Sandor was sixteen at the time. The family had no contact with him for over ten years. However, one of his childhood playmates told the investigator that Gazsi had changed his name and moved to the US over a decade ago. Gazsi had changed his name to Gustov."

"Gus was Simon's brother?"

"I think so. Again, I don't have proof, but it makes sense. The photo that I found was of Simon and another boy that I thought looked like Gus. It was probably the last picture that was taken of the two of them before Gus was adopted."

The seriousness of the situation was starting to gel. Simon had killed his brother.

FIFTY-THREE

"DID SIMON KNOW? THAT MEANS THAT HE DIDN'T JUST kill two men, he killed a member of his family—the long-lost brother that had been searching for him."

"I think he knew. He told me that Gus was an old friend from school when we first met, but I never heard any schoolyard stories. I suppose that he didn't want to tell me that Gus was his brother, or the rest of his past might come to light as well. It was a sobering thought—if he was capable of murdering a family member ..." Carmen's voice trailed off. "I was afraid. All of a sudden he was an unpredictable force."

"Did he threaten you?" Tarryn had a hundred-word, profanity riddled, tirade go through his head.

"Not until he found out about the SUV three weeks ago, but that's almost the end. Let me finish filling in the blanks. So I had the information about Simon's past and what I thought was information about his brother Gus. I still didn't have enough information that I could go to the Budapest police to get him arrested for Eva's rape and beating. I just wanted to connect the dots. I was so close. I reasoned that if I could get the charges from the past resurrected, Simon would go to jail and I wouldn't have to expose the other areas of his life that tied back to me. He would have no idea that I had crafted the entire thing. He would just believe that his past had finally caught up with him. I researched the prison system in Hungary—their jails are worse than ours. He would get to suffer. Just like I wanted. But I only had a couple of days before the truck was supposed to be ready. My brain was totally fried. I was barely sleeping. Every moment was critical time that I couldn't afford to waste.

"I still had twenty-five thousand remaining from the sale of the SUV, but I certainly couldn't buy anything close to the same quality for that kind of money. I searched the Internet and found what I thought would be a perfect cover. I spent the rest of the money on an older Corvette. I paid cash so the dealer gave me a good deal. He looked at me suspiciously when I pulled out a wad of hundreds, but when I showed him my driver's license with my Bellview Heights address on it, he stopped worrying and took the money. Before you ask—Simon was furious. I told him that I was tired of waiting for the SUV and I had traded it in on the 'Vette. I told him that I was bored of looking like a soccer mom and wanted something a bit sportier. He kept yelling, telling me what a shitty negotiator I was and how I had no business buying a new car without consulting him first. I was back to being a worthless street urchin again. That pissed me off." Carmen's brows were set into an angry lump of skin.

"I can see that. Did you remind him that he was a worthless sack of shit and that you didn't think he would have negotiated any better?" Tarryn used his most outraged tone.

"I didn't want to press my luck. I was already walking a pretty thin line at that point. There were a lot of things that I wanted to say. Instead, to keep the peace, I pretended to feel regret and had sex with him. He was rougher than normal. I think he was struggling to keep the anger inside him under control. I went to the bathroom and cried afterward. I just kept reminding myself that it wouldn't be much longer. Once I could connect the puzzle pieces, it would all be worth it. I wasn't just exacting revenge for myself, it was for the women that he bought and sold, it was for Ed, for Eva, and I suppose it was even for Gus."

"Gus doesn't deserve your sympathy. He tried to kill you once, remember?"

"I remember. But last week the final part of my life began, and I realized that Simon had manipulated Gus just as much as he had manipulated me." Carmen stopped and looked at her watch for the first time. "Oh my God. I can't believe that it's so late. I'm sorry. I should have left a long time ago." She said the words and squirmed a little in her seat, but her body made no effort to get up.

"We're not going to start that again, are we? You're almost finished now. Tell me the rest and between the two of us we'll figure out what to do next. I'm already thinking of ways to help you." *Kill her, kill her, kiss her, kill her ... strangulation, stabbing ...*

"For the first week after I got the car, every night that Simon came home and saw that Corvette, his blood pressure skyrocketed. I could see it the pulsing veins in his temples. He was beyond furious with me. I was equally upset, but I was smarter than he was about controlling my emotions. I felt superior—I was in the process of taking him down, and he had no idea how close he was to a filthy Hungarian jail. I was still trying to figure out an endgame strategy. I had started doing online searches in every state for people that had changed their name to Simon Halder. Nothing was coming up. I knew that the missing link had to be there somewhere. Then last Monday, Simon blew his top. The argument started over the car. He was ranting again about how he wore the pants in the family and how I shouldn't be so disrespectful to the breadwinner of the house. After all, he reminded me, I wasn't even bringing in the pocket change I had called a salary from the café anymore. After Ed passed away, I couldn't bear to go in the door. It sickened me to hear him talking about Ed. I lost it and threw a lamp across the room. It missed him by a mile, but it took his anger up to a whole new level."

"Too bad you didn't hit him," Tarryn mumbled.

"It was too big and too heavy—it didn't fly all that well. He started yelling about how hard he had worked to make a good life for me and how I didn't appreciate or understand the sacrifices that he had made along the way. Then he started spewing all sorts of information. Things that I don't think he even knew were going to come from his lips. I finally had the truth and it's not pretty. Simon and Gus started marketing women almost immediately after we started Phototecnics. I think the story about the Houston oil executive was a cover. I don't think he ever existed. When I put together the information from my guy in Budapest along with Simon's angry outburst, I think that Gus was selling women in Hungary for years. Initially, I think that he was the equivalent of a wholesale pimp. He sold girls to other pimps who would put them on the street or keep them hostage in hotel rooms where they would service up to sixty men a week. The problem with that was the lack of money that he had coming in. There are so many girls in Hungary that are for sale that the market price was quite low. They could only get a small percentage of the money that Americans were willing to pay.

"Gus wanted to expand the business into the US and cater to a particular clientele. I think that's when he got a hold of Simon and came to New York. It was probably right around the time that Simon and I were getting married. I think that he truly loved me then. I don't believe that it was a premeditated path that he chose. But I do believe that the money and power took control. Back then I thought that my love was going to be enough for him, but it never was, nor will it ever be. Even his relationship with Gus, his own brother, wasn't enough. I feel so guilty that I didn't make better choices. How many people's lives have been changed because of my apathy?"

"Don't blame yourself. It doesn't sound like you could have done anything to change the course of Simon's life. He had tendencies that you just weren't aware of at the beginning. He didn't show his real self until it suited him." Tarryn wondered if he wasn't giving her a last warning about his own motives. Or maybe he was trying to convince himself that he didn't have a choice. She had to die—the wheels were already set in motion.

"He admitted to me that the women were never brought over to be housekeepers and nannies. All of them, every last one was brought into the country to be a sexual partner for the customers. The men had certain needs that American women didn't want to fulfill. He justified it by saying that they wanted a better life and he gave it to them. All they had to do was allow the customer to use their bodies. How many times had he told me that—he was giving them a better life?" Carmen shook her head and continued, "He reminded me that they were fed and watered ... that was his exact term ... and that in their own country they would have starved. It was disturbing how little he cared about them. He even bragged that some of the clients were so happy with our product that they had even placed repeat orders once they were finished with their first purchase. I asked what happened to the first girls that the men had purchased. He said that he had another buyer who recycled the women. Recycled ... do you believe it ... like an old soda can. At that point, I couldn't even scream anymore. I was numb. Not only was he a monster, a rapist, and a murderer, but he was also the lowest human being I had ever met. And to top it all off, I was his partner—physically, emotionally, and oh yeah, in business. I had taken those innocent women who only wanted more for their families and themselves, and I had delivered them over to the devil."

"You didn't know. How could you have known? It's not your fault. It's certainly not worth dying over. We can figure this out together," Tarryn pleaded with her, his back itching like he had fallen into a patch of stinging nettle.

The waterworks turned on again. Carmen buried her face in her hands. "He never shut down the business once during our marriage. He admitted that he just toned it down for a while, but he never stopped what he was doing."

"I'm confused. Then why did Gus threaten to kill the two of you? Why did he come to your house the day that Simon shot him?"

"I didn't figure that out until later. I believe that the day when Simon came back to the house with Gus, it was all *his* idea. I think that he wanted Gus to scare me into returning to the business. Maybe I really was the intended target, but once Simon saw a chance to kill Gus, he saw an opportunity to increase his share of the profit. Simon was still ranting about how I was no better than the women that he bought and sold. His anger was escalating at an alarming rate. I kept thinking that he was capable of anything. He had killed his own brother. All I wanted to do was get out of the house in one piece. I didn't say a word. I just grabbed the car keys, the cat, and started toward the door. He stopped ranting and watched me. I think he finally realized that I was going to leave. I wasn't going to take any more of his bullshit. By the time I realized that he was starting toward me, it was too late. I'm still amazed that he got across the room that fast. I woke up the next day with a goose egg on my head. I could barely move."

"That bastard. Where was he when you woke up?"

"He was at my bedside. He smiled at me and told me everything was going to be okay, that I had hit my head during our argument. He said he was sorry, that he didn't want to fight anymore. He just wanted me to feel better. I had such a massive head ache. I just lay there trying to put together the pieces of the night before. It came back pretty quickly, and I tried to get up out of bed. I was too weak. He was feeding me a pretty heavy dose of painkillers, which kept me knocked out for most of the day. When he did allow me to regain consciousness, he pleaded with me to stay. Knowing that the only way to get him to stop medicating me was to agree with him, I promised that I would never leave his side. That was four days ago. I lay in that bed for another twenty-four hours and let him tend to me, bring me food. I think he could smell the fear, but of course, he and I both knew that I couldn't go to the police. He had control. That's when I decided on my plan."

"That you were going to kill yourself."

Carmen looked toward the floor. "Yep that's part of it. I just can't take it anymore. I have no idea where to run to—I have nowhere to go. I don't have a single close friend in the entire world. Other than Sabre, I'm alone."

"Isn't there anyone that you that you trust? Someone that can help you get out of this mess?" Tarryn asked, feeling emotionally exhausted from the conversation. The question was somewhat asked out of curiosity but also to see how much at risk he was if he took her life. It had already taken so long to get to this phase in the plan that every moment was jeopardizing a clean kill.

"Not really. My lifestyle hasn't allowed me to have a lot of friends outside of the ones that I have with Simon. When you're involved in illegal activities, it's best not to have too many close friends." Carmen drifted off into her own thoughts. "You're probably going to laugh but there was one person that comes to mind every time I dreamt of a knight in shining armor. Constantin Eugene Georgopoulos was the headwaiter at The Parthenon, my favorite Greek restaurant. He had dark hair, a larger-than-life smile, and was always upbeat. I was always faithful, as a wife should be, but I often wondered if I was single, would Constantin be one of my potential suitors? He had a ridiculous mouthful of a name, but I had a schoolgirl crush. He was the kind of man that I thought Simon was going to be—successful, loyal, family oriented, and honest. He moved to Florida a couple of years ago, so there was never anything more than standard pleasantries and menu discussions. So to answer your question, was he someone that I could turn to in times of trouble? Not likely."

She really was alone. Tarryn liked that fact and hated it. "If Simon is watching you so carefully, how did you get out today? Where is he now?"

"I did my best to convince him that I was sorry for the fight. I told him he was right, I shouldn't have bought the car without telling him. I told him that I would be a better wife, that I would be more appreciative of how hard he works to give me a nice life."

"And he believed you?" Tarryn wasn't sure if he believed that Carmen was the best actress on the earth or that Simon was one of the most gullible men.

"I'll let you in on a little secret, known by women all over the world—sex is a great motivator for men. Most of them equate sex to love. Sorry to be crude, but if you can stomach having sex with someone, and you do it well, the control shifts a little. Simon might still have the bulk of the power, but he believes that I am his loving wife—after all, I gave him my body. He thinks that we have some issues to work out but that we can get though them."

Tarryn remembered his mother's warning about women so many years before. He was shocked that Carmen would give herself to Simon after all of the terrible things that he had done but in the same sense, felt that she was only doing it to save herself. *Kiss her, kill her, kiss her, kill her.* "How were you going to do it ... you know ... the suicide?"

"You probably thought that I was going to use that gun that I pulled on you earlier. Sorry about that, by the way. I've never even fired a pistol, and I certainly don't know how to aim one. I have other plans. I want you to understand that I don't want to kill myself to take the easy way out. I want to take Simon down with me. That's the plan anyway."

"I'm not sure what you mean. How does taking your own life get revenge on Simon? That seems a bit like cutting of your nose to spite your face."

"I have no proof that Sandor and Simon are the same man. I realize that I don't have enough information to go to the Budapest police to get him arrested for Eva's rape. I also don't have access to any financial resources after the Corvette incident, so I can't hire anyone to continue the investigation. If I tell the police about Gus—I'm going to jail. If I tell the police about the dark side of the business—I'm going to jail. And finally, I don't have any proof that Simon killed Ed. There is no easy way to solve the problem. But I can't let him go on like this. I know that if

I continue to live in that house, he will take my life. It's not a matter of *if*, it's a matter of *when*. His touch disgusts me. I can't stand looking at his face. Every time I look around my house, I see the hands of evil. And worst of all, when I look in the mirror, I see my face. I used to like how I looked. Now all I notice are my perfectly white, straight teeth. I got in the car accident because of Simon, and his dirty money paid to fix my teeth. They're like a shining beacon, constantly reminding me of everything horrible that I have become."

Tarryn interrupted her, "You haven't answered the question."

"Tonight, I'm going to check in to a hotel with my last few dollars. I'm going to call Mr. Toth in Budapest and give him Simon's address. I'm going to write all of the detail down, everything I know. All of it—the rape, the murders, the women. Every single sordid fragment of information. I'm going to leave all of it on the bed, and I'm going to draw myself a bath. I have some pills, and I have a razor blade. Between the two of them, it should do the job. I'm not going to give him the satisfaction of dumping me in the backyard like he did to Gus. I want control of how I die."

"I hate to tell you, but it's a lousy plan. Without evidence to validate your allegations, the police won't arrest Simon. He might get hauled in for questioning, but I doubt that anything will ever come of it. After all, it would come down to his word against the word of a dead woman."

"I have Sandor's birth certificate, details about Gus's murder that no one else knows, the bloodstains in the carpet, a body in the backyard, information about the sex trade ring, and the detective's report from Budapest. I'll write it all down—every single horrible word of it. It will have to be enough. Someone will believe it—they have to." Carmen added, "You said you wanted to help, you can tell the cops what I've told you. I'll be dead so you won't have to worry about me going to jail."

"Why not go to the police yourself and see if they will give you immunity if you testify against Simon?"

"I thought about that but they'll let him out pending trial, he will hunt me down and kill me. I won't give him the satisfaction. Plus my conscience won't let me rest. For the rest of my life I will have to live with the pain of what I have done. It's just too much."

Tarryn got pissed off. He was tired of her self-pity. Everyone does things that they aren't proud of. Everyone. Sometimes good people do bad things and yet other times, bad people do good things. "Damn it Carmen. You're not the monster. Simon … Sandor, he's the monster. Quit feeling sorry for yourself. You hooked up with a bad man, we all make mistakes. I had the opportunity to change my life several times, I didn't." Tarryn thought back on his life and knew that this moment was another one of those opportunities and wondered which road he would choose. He still hadn't decided. *Kiss her, kill her, kiss her, kill her.*

"Haven't you been listening to me at all today? I'm out of options. I can't stand to look in the mirror anymore. Simon will kill me if I go back, he'll hunt me down if I run away, and I don't want to pretend to be happy, not for one more minute. I have basically no job skills, and I don't want to go to jail. I don't want to live with the memories. They haunt me—every moment of every stinking day."

"Of course, I was listening. That's what this whole day has been about. I want to help you, I really do. I don't have the answers right now, but you've just dumped an entire lifetime of shit in my lap. It's going to take time to sort through it and make some sense of how to solve the problem." Tarryn moved toward her and lifted her face up to his. "I don't think you really want to die. I think that what you really want is help."

Carmen put her head on his shoulder and cried in great wracking sobs. "I don't want to die. I just don't know what else to do."

She finally admitted it. Tarryn was ecstatic. He had brought her back from the edge—another boost for his ego. *He was a master.* This morning she had her toes hanging over the boundary between life and death, and now she had taken two steps back. It was almost over.

FIFTY-FOUR

TARRYN HELD HER IN HIS ARMS AND STROKED HER HAIR, breathing in the fresh scent of her skin. It was five minutes before she pulled back from his embrace. "I don't want you to die either," he whispered.

"Oh God, what am I going to do? I can't believe that you are still sitting here with me after all that I've told you. I never imagined that I would tell my life story to a stranger. And I didn't think that anyone could convince me that there might be another way out. I have no clue where to go next. I want this miserable life to end. But I don't want to die."

Tarryn thought that he had never seen someone so exposed. He had ended so many lives, and every single person looked helpless and defenseless in their last moments. This was different, she was scared, but she wasn't weak. In this case, his victim was impervious to pain, having already felt the full spectrum. She was an anomaly—he couldn't inflict anything more on her. By killing her, he would be alleviating all of her suffering. It might be the only time in his life that he would be doing a valiant gesture.

Then it struck him, today was an opportunity to give meaning to a kill—to use death as a tool for good. Today he would not only beat Bundy's record, but he would also be an instrument of change.

"I wish that we would have met earlier. You know, before all of complications with Simon. I would have liked to have been there for you—to help you through the bad stuff." Tarryn meant every word. Perhaps if he had met Carmen way back when, his life might have turned out differently. Maybe he wouldn't have killed so many or maybe he wouldn't have killed at all. Regardless, he knew that he was a man who, like Carmen, had chosen every single step that he had taken.

There were no excuses for either of them. Sometimes life takes you down a path that you never thought you would travel. And after a while, you realize that with all of the forks in the road, you can't even see the point where you started anymore—even if you wanted to back track and try to start over.

It was time to move on the final phase of his plan for Carmen. His back was telling him that a kill was overdue. The welts seemed to be more prominent, more raised up, and hell, they were itching. It was now or never. If he didn't act soon, he might lose his mind.

"You want anything else to drink? A coffee maybe?"

Carmen nodded. "Black please. It's been a long day." She looked up at him and smiled.

The vulnerability that he saw earlier was still there, but now Carmen was vibrant once again. Her eyes had a glimmer of hope, and he felt an unbelievable urge to hold her. He thought that in that moment, she was perfect imperfection. She was worthy of the honor he was about to bestow. She was his crowning glory.

Carmen watched as he rose off the couch and added, "I just want you to know, Tarryn, I'm happy that I met you. I can't believe that you put up with me the entire day. I'm sure you had better things to do than listen to me for hours on end. I started out as a blubbering idiot, and somehow you have transformed me back into a strong woman—back to the Steel Rose. I don't know how to thank you. Not only did you give me back my sanity, you may have given me back my life."

"Believe it not," he replied quietly, "I should be thanking you. I can't explain it to you, but you have given me something equally as valuable." Tarryn turned and walked upstairs with a bounce in his step that he hadn't had in such a long time. Any traces of fatigue disappeared into the night.

STEP 4—BETRAYAL
11:00 PM

FIFTY-FIVE

AFTER HOURS OF LISTENING AND TORTUROUS WAITING, it was finally time. Tarryn bounded up the stairs, ecstatic about the choice of victim he had made for this momentous occasion. He was finally going to surpass Bundy's body count. His mother might not be here to see it, but he knew that she was watching from somewhere up above and that she would be proud on so many levels. He desperately needed to sleep, but as the saying goes, there would be time for sleep when he was dead; now was time for action.

He wondered what the press would have to say about the Numbers Killer tomorrow. Would they report the fact that he had exceeded the number of victims that Bundy had taken? Would they crown him the number one selective killer in America? *No, of course not.* They would call him a *serial* killer. Maybe he would leave a note somewhere that would specify the correct term.

He knew that this would be his final kill. The conversation with Carmen had changed him somehow. It wasn't a tangible modification. It seemed like the mere act of remembering his life had shown him that he had accomplished so much. More that he had expected when he started, more than Bundy, and more than his mother could have ever wanted. With kill number thirty-seven, he would find himself at another crossroads, and this time, he planned on taking the path less traveled.

Tarryn was tempted to walk away from the kill. Carmen was a special woman. He had never felt such an overwhelming urge to protect someone. Could they become a couple? Would it be possible to have a real relationship with her? He twirled the thoughts around in his mind, searching for an angle that he hadn't already explored. There were too many complications. He had no idea how to connect long term with another human being. Maybe it was like Carmen said earlier—men had a way of confusing sex with love. He knew it was more than sex. He wanted to hold her and be held by her. But then again, she had no idea who he really was. If he stopped now, she would never have to know how close she had come to being number thirty-seven.

His thoughts were interrupted by sputtering coffeemaker as it spewed the final dark liquid into the pot. He was letting emotion cloud his judgment. He could never have a relationship with Carmen—no matter how badly the carefully constructed veneer of the Good Tarryn wanted it to be possible. She deserved more than what he could ever offer. He had a job to do. He had betrayed his mother's love so long ago, and now it was time to finish a task that was twenty years in the making. It was time to end Carmen's misery.

He poured Carmen's final cup of coffee and grabbed a small handheld Taser gun from his kitchen drawer. It fit neatly into the belt of his pants and didn't make a discernable lump. It was very effective at immobilizing his victims long enough that he could bind them to a chair. That was all he needed—just a few moments to get her into position.

He walked slowly back down to the basement, trying to keep his hands from shaking, and careful not to spill the hot liquid. His heart was pounding with anticipation when he turned the corner and saw her resting on the couch, one knee tucked up underneath her body. She was deep in thought, but her face was regaining its color.

"Here you go," he said, the charm meter on full tilt. He leaned in to pass her the cup but instead kissed her gently on the mouth. Her lips were warm and inviting. It wasn't as electrifying as their first kiss. This one was more intimate. It was the closest thing to love that he had felt since the early days with his mother. "You really are a special woman," he whispered in to her ear. *Kiss her, kill her, kiss her, kill her.*

Carmen's entire face was lit up with happiness as he pulled away to look at her. Moments later, as the volts of electricity went through her body, she had the wide-eyed look that he had longed to see the entire day.

FIFTY-SIX

THE PAIN OF BEING HIT BY A TASER GUN IS EXCRUCIATING. Tarryn had accidentally felt the awesome power of the tool when a victim had grabbed his arm, just as he hit her with the gun. The electricity had transferred through both of their bodies and knocked the two of them to the ground. He had learned a lesson with number twenty-nine and was much more cautious when he used the gun since then. Twenty-nine had paid the price for the pain that he felt—she was the only one that he had tortured before he put an end to her life.

With Carmen temporarily incapacitated, he quickly grabbed some handcuffs. He moved her to the special chair on the other side of the room. First he cuffed her hands to the back of the chair. He then slapped on some specially modified leg irons that attached to the metal chair base. The chair was a special addition when he did his renovations to the basement and was cemented into the subfloor. It also had a special reinforced steel back to eliminate the cuffs being torn from the seat. With his extensive experience, Carmen was secured in under thirty seconds. He reached into the drawer of the stereo cabinet and grabbed a gag and duct tape. He filled her mouth with the gag and secured it to her face with the silver tape. There was no way for her to move the gag to scream and no possible way for her to remove herself from the chair. She was perfectly situated for the next part of his plan. *Kiss her, kill her, kiss her, kill her* … his damn brain just wouldn't shut up. He looked upward for some sort of sign. It only took a moment for his decision to be made.

Happy with his handiwork, Tarryn did something that he had never done in the past. He pushed the couch forward so that it sat immediately in front of his victim's chair. He sat facing Carmen, watching as she came to, and the magnitude of the situation started to register on her face. He didn't need to speak just yet. He wanted to be sure that she was able to comprehend what he was about to tell her.

When the tears started streaming down her face he began. "As you just figured out, I lied about more than just the cats. You don't know the man that you've been confessing to all day. The man before you right now is your worst nightmare. I am everything that your mother warned you about and more. I *am* the Numbers Killer." He waited for that tidbit of information to sink in before he continued. When the realization came and her eyes were as wide as saucepans, he knew that the message had hit the mark.

"Some of what I told you is true. My mother was a drug addict, the stories about our neighbor Betty were true, growing up in New York is true, being a roofer … true, when I started driving cab, also true—the main point that I missed is quite obvious … the killing streak. But I also missed out a couple of other key messages along the way. I'd like to tell them to you. You confessed your darkest secrets to me, and I will return the favor. Tit for tat, so to speak."

Carmen's face showed the extreme fright in the core of her being. He had committed what he had set out to do earlier in the day—he had brought her back from the dead, and now she was in a position of no return. He could have her at any time now. He could kill her in any way that his heart desired. Part of him wanted to slit her throat right then, but he had bigger plans for Carmen. Part of him wished that he had found other suicidal victims earlier in his career. The power was surging through his body—his back itching and pulsing. But before he could finish the task at hand, he needed to finish his story.

"You see, my mother was a wonderful person. She taught me everything I know about killing. She was infatuated with the act. As far as I know she never took a life, except for her own. I can tell you that part later on. She never killed, but you could tell that she always wanted to. I think it was a secret fantasy of hers. She loved all the true crime tales, but Ted Bundy was her hero. He was one messed-up kid, let me tell you. His unwed mother pretended to be his sister when he was growing up and his grandparents raised him. He was scorned by a potential lover early on. He was charismatic, smart, and good-looking. He was everything that my mom valued. They say that no one showed him any love and that's why he started killing. I think it was just in his genes, the same way it's been in mine my whole life. My mother saw that glimmer of success in me and nurtured my gift. She didn't know it, of course. I didn't want to tell her that I was the Numbers Killer until I knew it would make her proud. Bundy killed thirty-six women, and today I will reach thirty-seven." Tarryn watched Carmen to see if she showed any signs of being impressed. He saw none.

"I'm a bit disappointed. Today marks the end of my journey, and my mother won't be here to celebrate with me. With us, actually. See if I hadn't met you this morning, I would never have reached this goal today. I was telling the truth when I said that you were a special woman. Had we met when I was a young boy, I think I would have fallen in love. It's too late for that, but back then … well, let's just say that things might have been different.

"I'm going to tell you everything, every detail of the kills. As much as I can remember anyway. Some were so long ago that the specifics have slipped my mind. Some of them you might remember from the news. The police have the gory details, but I have the memories." Tarryn turned and lifted his shirt to expose the permanent brands on his back. It was almost covered from the tops of his shoulders, to the waistline of his pants.

"Thirty-six scars, each and every one represents a life that I have taken. Each one is the initials of the person and the month and year that they helped me achieve my goal." Tarryn heard Carmen whimper behind the gag. He didn't turn around. He didn't want to see the disgust on her face. He wanted her to see the proof but not the pain.

FIFTY-SEVEN

WHEN HE HAD GATHERED HIS COMPOSURE AGAIN, TARRYN pulled his shirt down, turned to face her, and sat down on the couch. "I'll start with my first kill. Her name was Hanna Goldman. I stabbed her to death on a beach. I might have started out trying to impress my mother, to get her attention, but it turned out that I enjoyed the kill and wanted more. I was good at it. I wanted to be better, smarter, more sparkling than Bundy. My second victim was a boy named Grant Hallan. I beat him to death in a park. My third was Chad Bellows. His death was nasty. I decapitated him and burned the rest of his body. I left the head beside his charred corpse to make sure that the police knew that it was my handiwork." Tarryn noted the anger and disgust as it registered on her face and wondered if he could go on. He knew that he had to. As he had told her earlier, confession was good for the soul.

"I started moving locations after my third kill. It was what my mother recommended. I have killed in four states and twice in Canada. Bundy only killed in three states and never crossed the border. Number four, Charmaine Porter, was strangled. Number five, Susan Holt, was poisoned. I stabbed number six. Her name was Brenda Farmer. Number seven was Lisa Smithson. She was beaten with a rather heavy rock. Number eight, Kathy Ruiz, was strangled. Number nine, Norma Collens, was also strangled. I like to watch as the life leaves their eyes. Number ten, Jill Baker was stabbed ..." The stories went on for what seemed like forever. His memory was getting bad on some of the victims in the middle years. The earlier ones were easier to remember, as were the most recent. He didn't want to have to look in a mirror to remember each girl's name; his mother would not have been impressed by that.

He had stopped looking at Carmen after number ten. It was hard to tell another human being the atrocities that he had committed. It needed to happen, so he looked past her at the abstract painting depicting a woman in bondage. He had strategically placed it over top of the special metal chair as a way of warning his victims. No one had figured it out. After recalling each victim's name and method of death, he felt quite proud. He thought that perhaps he had messed up the order of twenty-five, twenty-six, and twenty-seven, but it was of no consequence at this late stage of the game.

"I'm like Bundy in a lot of ways. He was lonely and sad. I guess that until I met you, I was lonely as well. I don't think I saw that in myself until now. You have been the reason for a lot of self-reflection today. Bundy was smart and charismatic. I think I fit the bill on that front. That's where the similarities end. He didn't have the love of his mother. I always felt loved, and I was never wanting in the parenting department. I have been able to forge some decent friendships over the years. The fabricated Tarryn, the one that you spent the day with, is able to make friends easily. When my mother was slipping deeper and deeper into the quagmire of drug use, I wanted her back by any means. That's where it all started for me. I just wanted to regain her love. She was the only woman, up until today, that I really felt connected to. I can see similarities between the two of you. She was a strong woman as well. Before the drugs took control, I would have described her as self-assured, confident, and loving. Afterward, she was broken and lost. I wanted to save her back then, and I wanted to save your life for the same reasons today. I think this morning when I met you, I felt that if I failed you, I failed her.

"Thank you for redeeming my soul today. I brought you back from the brink of suicide so that I could make you the most special victim of all. My last. I have been so excited all day. With you, I would finally achieve the unachievable task of thirty-seven kills." Tarryn looked deep into her eyes, took a deep breath, and explained the details of what he would be doing next. Carmen closed her eyes as he spoke, the tears wetting her designer T-shirt.

Tarryn left Carmen secured to the bondage chair to prepare for the final step in his rather lengthy career as a selective killer. He wasn't sure what would happen once he had his final kill under his belt. Would he be able to put the past behind him? Would he be able to return to a regular life, like the rest of society? Killing was his passion and had consumed his every thought for so many years. What would become of Tarryn the monster after today? Would the façade that he had perfected after all of these years be able to hold up as a whole person? Unbelievably, it wasn't something that he had ever considered. He just wanted to have some peace. After kill number thirty-seven, would he finally be able to find the inner calm that he wanted so badly? Without his mother around to witness, would the final moments be as sweet? There were so many questions.

Tarryn picked up his more powerful Taser gun from the kitchen cupboard and told himself that those were all questions that could only be answered once his final challenge was completed. He was ready. His body was strong, and his mind was sound. There was no better time.

He walked out the front door and got in the Mustang. He just had to pick up one final prop before he could continue.

FIFTY-EIGHT

SIMON WAS PACING THE FLOOR, FURIOUS WITH THE NOTE
that Carmen had left him. Her cell phone was lying next to the paper
and her Corvette was in the garage. She had walked out on him without
so much as a conversation. What kind of woman walks out on her
husband like that? He wondered how far she could have gotten in the
short time he was gone. Was she having an affair and someone picked
her up? Did she hoof it? He calmed himself and called the neighbors
to see if anyone had seen her today. Cheryl and Chris next door had
been at work and hadn't spoken with her for almost two weeks. Todd
and Patty, on the other side, were on vacation in Thailand and weren't
reachable, according to their housekeeper. *Where the fuck is she?* He had
checked her closet, and her clothes and makeup were still there. Her
goddamn orange furball of a cat was missing too.

The note was some rambling scribbles about how she couldn't live
with the lies any longer and how he had deceived her. *Where did she
come up with that bullshit?* She was nothing before she met him. She
was a waitress for fuck's sake. He gave her everything she wanted—a
house, a nice car, and a considerable bank account. What more did she
want? Sure, he was prone to getting a little angry every once in a while,
but that was only when she was unmanageable. She had to be taught
that you make sacrifices along the way to get what you want out of life.
Nothing good comes easy or cheap.

Carmen was just too much of a bleeding heart. The women that he had bought and sold over the years were just as guilty as he was. They were looking to move up in the world, and he gave them what they wanted. *Boo-hoo, I have such a tough life in Yugoslavia. I want to live in America where I can have nice clothes and a big house.* They got what they deserved—the money-hungry bitches. They had to make compromises just like everyone else.

Carmen, he realized now, was not that different from them. She wanted the grandiose lifestyle but without surrendering her lofty morals. Every single time he made the arrangements for a girl to move to the US, he did it for her. He did it so that she could have the perfect Barbie-doll life that she always dreamed of. All that work to make their lives better, and the bitch repaid him with a Dear John note left on the kitchen counter.

Simon grabbed the single sheet of paper and tore it in to pieces. His rage was overwhelming. He couldn't wait until he found Carmen. He would show her what kind of sacrifices people made when they loved someone. He would teach her a lesson that she would never forget. He went to the refrigerator and threw open the door, almost tearing it off its hinges. He wanted a beer to calm his nerves. If Gus was still around, he would be spitting bullets right now. After all, Gus was the one that told him to get rid of Carmen years ago. He always said she was just trouble with some tits and ass. To Gus, love was forged between his legs and nowhere else.

Right or wrong, he had a soft spot for Carmen since the day that he saw her. She was beautiful back then—every little gesture that he did lit up her face—and best of all, she made him feel like a stud in the sac. She seemed to have an old soul even in her younger years. He was attracted to her strength but found the subtle frailty equally appealing. Carmen finally finding some balls was never part of the plan. Simon liked her much better when he had her under his thumb. He should have kept her drugged up for a while longer. She played on his good nature. She had taken away his control today, and someone was going to have to pay for the mistake.

FIFTY-NINE

TARRYN DROVE THE FOUR BLOCKS TO THE LOCAL convenience store on autopilot. His mind was reeling with the knowledge of what he was about to do. It was perfect in every aspect. The smooth chocolaty feel of the brain waves were almost intoxicating. He felt light headed and euphoric. Funny how things had changed so dramatically since 8:00 am. This morning he was searching for his next victim, and now he was planning his retirement.

Somehow everything was falling perfectly into place. He wondered if his mother's spirit was guiding him. Was she telling him that thirty-seven was enough? It seemed like a strange coincidence that all of the pieces of the puzzle could have possibly come together so quickly and without conscious thought. If it was fate, or his mother's intervention, it didn't matter. All that concerned him now was fulfilling his destiny.

Tarryn strolled through the aisles in the store for a few minutes picking up some beef jerky, soda, and potato chips for the road. He knew that he would be hungry later on. He laid the items in front of the cashier and had to hold back a laugh. The young man behind the counter had fluorescent yellow hair, was covered in tattoos, and was sporting a black skull shirt over his khakis. Tarryn found it hard not to smirk at the kid's pathetic attempt to be cool. Lenny Kravitz and Bono were cool—this guy just looked like an idiot.

Stifling his laughter, he purchased a prepaid cell phone with a ten-dollar limit. It would only be used for one phone call. As the teenager behind the counter tried to upsell him, he thought about telling him how ridiculous the canary-colored hair looked but then thought better of it. It didn't matter how long the kid took with his sales pitch, he knew that Carmen wasn't going anywhere. Tarryn tuned the kid out and observed the total tranquility that he was experiencing. He was never anxious before a kill, but today was the first time that he had left a victim alone in his house. He would have expected some sort of stress reaction, but there was none.

After the kid behind the counter had exhausted his many canned sales routines, Tarryn left the store and got back into the Mustang. It was still dark in the city, but he knew that by the time the sun rose above the horizon, the Numbers Killer would be the top news story—everyone would know his name and would recognize his face. The canary haired kid would have a story to tell his friends tomorrow—assuming he had any.

SIXTY

SIMON WAS STILL PACING BACK AND FORTH IN THE kitchen. His anger was building by the second and increased substantially with each beer that he hurried down his throat. He ripped the toaster out of the socket and smashed it in to the wall. The drywall buckled under the pressure. The next projectile was the coffeemaker, then the knife block, and finally the pot rack that hung above the kitchen island. The pot rack made the most racket and was more satisfying to his ears. With each thud, crash, and clatter of the destruction, he imagined that Carmen was the target. She was a major liability right now. She knew everything, and he knew that the little bitch wouldn't keep her mouth shut.

He raced through the possibilities in his mind. If she had gone to the police, they would be here by now. Ed was long gone, another liability that he was forced to take care of. She had no friends outside of the neighbors. She would come home. She had no choice. She was nothing without him. His head was spinning with thoughts of rage and revenge when he heard a voice from behind him.

"Simon, I presume?" the voice asked.

Simon turned to face the stranger that occupied the space in the kitchen directly behind him. The man was five-foot-nine and about a hundred and ninety pounds. He looked familiar somehow, maybe like a movie star. Before he could ask the obvious question that had already formed in his brain, "Who the fuck are y—?" he hit the ground with a massive thump.

Tarryn wasn't expecting Simon to be quite as big as he was. He expected a man of average height and maybe a hundred and seventy pounds. The man on the floor in front of him was about five-foot-eleven and probably weighed closer to two hundred and twenty. He hoped that he had brought enough of the drug with him. He pulled a syringe out of his pocket, pushed the needle into Simon's arm, and pressed the plunger. He would have to work quickly if he was going to relocate Simon before the effects of the drug wore off.

The muscle relaxant was similar to the ones used during surgery and based on Simon's size he would only have about an hour to get Simon into the trunk of the car, do the forty-minute drive back to his house, and get him secured next to Carmen in the basement. It would be touch and go if he could make it or if Simon would be ready for a fight when he opened the trunk back at home.

He looked around the house, taking in the sights, sounds, and smells of Carmen's home. With the clock ticking away at his success, he was limited to a few quick glances before he had to snap back into action.

He quickly retrieved the furniture dolly that he had left outside the back door and dragged Simon's body onto the cart. It was a long way from the kitchen, and he was a dead weight. Tarryn, pumped full of adrenaline, wasn't struggling with the load too much, but was feeling the pressure of the clock. He had parked at the side of the house, on a narrow driveway that led to the gardener's shed. It was secluded and dark—perfect for the movement of a body after the sun had gone down.

Standing outside the Mustang, Tarryn found that the more challenging part of moving Simon, was positioning him into the trunk. The trunk of the Mustang had proven itself worthy for smaller women, but a large man was never going to fit. Tarryn's muscles groaned and complained as he maneuvered the massive man into the passenger seat of the car. The whole thing took about ten minutes longer than he had anticipated, and Tarryn was starting to lose his composure. Wishing that he had brought an extra syringe with him, he regretted his loosely woven plan for the first time. Simon's size was a fly in the ointment that might screw up the entire arrangement. It wasn't optimal, but in for a penny, in for a pound. It was too late to turn back.

As Tarryn drove back to his house, he was disappointed that he didn't have more time to explore Carmen's home. The palatial home was well decorated from the limited amount he had seen. She has chosen a palate of neutral colors, lush fabrics, and textures. Nothing was ornate or overdone. It was simple elegance. Tarryn thought it reflected her personality perfectly. He would have liked to have seen her bedroom and her closet. He wanted to know her even better than he did now. He wanted to be intimate with every nuance of the woman who had changed his life.

He glanced at the clock in the car—1:00 am. He had injected Simon about twenty minutes ago. He was forty minutes from home. He started to sweat. Any tiny mistake at this point would result in disaster.

SIXTY-ONE

TARRYN GLANCED OVER AT THE PASSENGER SEAT AND looked at the crumpled man to his right. He didn't fit. His large frame filled the entire space, and his body was twisted at an unnatural angle. He looked drunk, and based on the acrid scent of beer wafting off him, he could very well be. From looking at him, you would never have guessed the evil that coursed through his veins. He was relatively well dressed, had short brown hair, and other than the fact that he was scrunched in a ball, could have passed for a decent-looking man. Tarryn was about to do the world a favor. Simon was incapacitated for now, and he was pleased. He wanted this to work out—it was a doubly good final kill.

Tarryn tried to calm his nerves. Driving too fast would get him pulled over; driving too slow would waste precious time that he didn't have. It was a balancing act just like the rest of his life had been. His eyes darted back and forth between the road and the clock.

Knowing that his final moments as the Numbers Killer were closing in, he reflected on his life and the two men that he had become. He liked both for different reasons. The selective killer was strong, virile, and cunning. That portion of his psyche was the most dominant by far but also the most fragile. The killer was there to serve a purpose, and his role was almost complete. The publicly perfected Tarryn was friendly, charming and had the kind of personality that shone brightly. He was the submissive but more centered side.

Tarryn knew that he was going to have to learn to be more assertive and self-assured as the tamer man worked his way deeper into his mind. Meeting Carmen had somehow melded the two together. He would always be Tarryn the animal, but perhaps now he could manage to be a kinder, gentler beast.

Looking at the clock again, Tarryn started to worry. If he was lucky, he would have twenty more minutes—tops. He started to speed up on the freeway. He needed to make up an extra ten minutes.

It hadn't been more than two minutes, at seventy miles per hour in a fifty-five zone that the red and blue lights from the police car shone in his mirrors.

He pulled over to the side of the road, wishing that he had planned this differently. He grabbed his driver's license and registration as he waited for the cop to run his plates. They wouldn't find any issues, not a single traffic ticket. His record was sparkling clean. Still, there were two concerns—a limp body in the passenger seat and the constant ticking of the clock.

SIXTY-TWO

"DRIVER'S LICENSE AND REGISTRATION," THE COP demanded. He shone his flashlight in the window at Tarryn and frowned. "Have you had anything to drink tonight, sir?"

Tarryn passed the documents through the window to the man, who was now shining his flashlight into the passenger side of the car. He had to think fast. "No, but my buddy here had his fill as you can see."

The cop looked curiously at the lump of a man crushed into the space. "You weren't drinking with him?" he asked with a raised eyebrow.

"No, sir. I just got the call from his wife asking me to pick him up. She didn't want to deal with him. Sorry, I guess I was speeding. I just don't want him puking in my car. I'm trying to get him home as quickly as possible. He's a good friend but not so good that I want to smell him for the next month." Tarryn turned on the charm meter just enough to seem sincere.

The cop looked Tarryn in the eyes, determining if any of what he had just heard was the truth. "Just wait here for a minute." He walked away, back to the flashing car.

Tarryn watched in his mirror as the cop retreated. Two options ran through his mind—take off and risk a car chase or wait it out and pray that the drugs were enough to keep Simon under control—hitting him with the Taser again was sure to attract attention. Knowing that the first option would probably lead to even more issues, he sat waiting on the side of the road, watching the precious time tick away.

It was five agonizing minutes before the cop returned to the open window on the Mustang. He shone the light into the passenger seat once again and handed Tarryn his licenses and registration. "Keep your speed down. I won't be as nice if I see you again." The cop cracked what looked like a smile, but Tarryn couldn't be sure. He wasn't going to wait around to figure it out.

"Thank you, sir. I'll keep my eye on that." Tarryn looked at the clock again—1:25. Damn it, he was in trouble.

Tarryn pulled away from the curb in a most organized fashion and pulled back on the freeway. The cop was directly behind him for the next five minutes. He watched with relief as the police car finally took an exit.

The clock read 1:32. Simon stirred in the passenger seat. Time was up.

SIXTY-THREE

FOR THE FIRST TIME IN A KILL SITUATION, TARRYN started to panic. At first his pulse quickened, just a little, then a few beats faster, and faster, until he thought his heart was going to jump right out of his chest. He peeked at himself in the rearview mirror and didn't like what he saw. He looked like a madman, drenched in sweat, wide eyed, and jittery.

He hit the gas pedal a little harder. He was still ten minutes from his house, and Simon would have to be transported inside. He needed fifteen. Minimum. Knowing that he couldn't watch the body in the passenger seat and drive safely at the same time, Tarryn exited the freeway and pulled the Mustang on to a side street. At the rate things were progressing, he still had the luxury of a few more minutes to get Simon back under control.

Tarryn walked to the back of the car and popped the trunk. He hoped that he still had the rope and duct tape in tow. Luckily both were lying there, ready for use. He always kept special items handy, just in case a kill presented itself at the last minute. He was always prepared. Tonight being the exception on all other fronts.

It didn't take long to tie Simon up and get a swath of tape covering his mouth. The sailor's knots that he learned on the Internet wouldn't hold that size of man for long but hopefully just long enough to get the big galloot of a man to his garage. The final few feet could be handled with a combination of the stun gun to keep Simon quiet for a couple of minutes and another syringe of muscle relaxant, kept safely in the kitchen.

Tarryn put the car into gear and continued through the backstreets to his house. Simon was coming around and struggling at his tethers. Tarryn was never so grateful for the small seats in the Mustang as he was now. Simon didn't have any room to maneuver, which hindered his ability to get out of the rope prison. When they finally reached the front of his house, Tarryn's back started to burn once again.

Safely in the privacy of his garage, Tarryn was able to get his breathing and rapid heartbeat under control. He opened the side door of the car and looked down at Simon. He looked confused but oddly, not afraid. He should have been worried about his fate, but all his face showed was anger. Tarryn was impressed by his bravado and pissed off that he wasn't showing the proper amount of respect. Was Simon that cocky that he thought he could get away? Tarryn hit him with the Taser one more time.

He hurried to the kitchen and grabbed another syringe of drugs—the same dose as the last one. It was overkill for moving Simon downstairs, but he didn't want any more mistakes. After all, this was his swan song.

It was only fifty seconds later when he returned to the garage but Simon was already recovering from the voltage of the stun gun and working at freeing himself from the rope. Tarryn watched with curiosity for a moment as he wriggled and writhed in the minuscule seat. It made him nervous. It was his last syringe of drugs. He had to get it into Simon and couldn't afford for the needle to break. With great pleasure, he hit Simon with the stun gun again and moments later injected him with the relaxant. Seconds later, he was still.

Getting Simon into the Mustang had been a chore, and getting him out turned out to be equally difficult. Tarryn moved the passenger seat as far back as he could for easier access, but the space behind was so small and Simon was so large that it was like trying to remove a fat lady from a pair of tight shorts. He tugged on Simon's legs and got them through, but his upper body was stuck. It took what seemed like an hour, but was probably only fifteen minutes, of pulling and twisting before Simon was free of the car. Tarryn grabbed him under his arms and dragged the body through the kitchen to the top of the stairs. He thought about just giving him a good push and letting him tumble to the bottom but didn't want Carmen to think that Simon was dead when she saw him. He had been working on a much better plan.

SIXTY-FOUR

TARRYN DRAGGED SIMON DOWN THE STAIRS, shoulders first, to the basement and laid him on the floor. He scanned the keypad and opened the door. He looked inside to see exactly what he expected, Carmen was still in the bondage chair, but her expression had changed. Tarryn knew that if you gave a person enough time to contemplate death, they were usually able to come to terms with it. He imagined that this was what had happened to Carmen since he had left. She somehow looked at peace with the idea. Tarryn was pleased.

Dragging Simon's heavy frame was starting to hurt his back, but Tarryn knew that it would only be a few minutes until he would have time to rest. He just had to secure the man. He dropped the body in front of Carmen and disappeared in to his storage room. His first task was to lay out a large plastic tarp in the middle of the basement floor. The thick plastic was the foundation for everything that he did in the space, and he had several new sheets on hand. Next, he grabbed a specially designed bed and rolled the wooden plank into the main media room.

The bed was a modified ambulance gurney. He placed it beside Simon's body and lowered the base. With the bed only eight inches above the ground, hoisting Simon on top was a breeze. He had enhanced the flat part of the gurney, making it larger and had bolted metal restraints to the base for both hands and feet. Once battened down in a spread-eagle position, it was virtually impossible to escape. Simon was quite a bit taller than his usual victims, but luckily the bed worked.

With Simon secured, Tarryn positioned him at a forty-five-degree angle to Carmen's chair. He expected that it would take another twenty minutes before Simon would be 100 percent conscious and coherent. He wanted Carmen to be the first person that he saw.

Tarryn walked over to Carmen and touched her hair. "He was bigger than I thought he would be. He was a pain in the ass to move. I need to clean up. I'll be back shortly."

Carmen whimpered something, but Tarryn couldn't decipher it because of the tape over her mouth. He imagined that it might be words of thanks to him, for finally ending her painful life.

SIXTY-FIVE

TARRYN WALKED UPSTAIRS TO HIS SMALL BUT functional bathroom and turned on the water in the sink. While the hot water made its way from the basement up to the second-floor spigot, he took some time to examine himself in the mirror. At thirty-five, he felt that his body was at its prime, and his mind was equally as strong. He had watched as so many people let themselves deteriorate once they hit a certain age. With obesity at an all-time high, he was pleased that he was in such good shape. He moved his hair back from his forehead and investigated his hairline. It too had weathered the tides of time. So far.

The years had taken their toll however. The constant yearning to meet his goal was starting to show. He observed the lines around his eyes that were becoming more prominent with each passing year. Thirty-five would be considered juvenile for some professions, but as in pro sports, killing was a job best left for the virility of youth. He turned and faced his back toward the mirror as the steam from the sink started to encroach on his view. His entire story was branded on those couple of square feet of flesh. He touched the area where his final two brands would be placed. He watched until the steam enveloped the entire mirror and then he splashed the hot water on his face. It felt good and gave him the energy to continue.

By the time that Tarryn returned to the basement, he was feeling much better. The sweat washed from his pores, he felt rejuvenated and alive. He changed his clothes and put on a T-shirt and a black nylon tracksuit. While he knew what he was going to do with Carmen, he hadn't totally settled on Simon's fate. He wasn't sure if it was going to get messy, so the tracksuit was the best attire—just in case.

Simon was still tethered to the gurney but was awake. Carmen was slumped in the bondage chair, her eyes focused sharply on Simon. Tarryn noticed a mixture of pity and contempt as she looked at her husband. Simon wasn't sharing her glances as he struggled to release himself from confinement.

Tarryn wondered if she was going to enjoy watching as he killed Simon. Would she avert her gaze or would she stare intently? Would she relish the moment that he took his final breath or would she cry for him? He didn't know how those final minutes would unfold, but he knew that the next few hours were going to be the most painful that Simon had ever experienced.

Tarryn walked into his storage room and started to gather the tools of the trade. It took five trips with armloads of equipment before he finally had all of the items that he wanted. With the last trip, he realized that he had basically cleaned out the entire storage room. Everything was going to be close at hand—mise-en-place as the French would say.

The first trip consisted of electrical devices that were powered by the generator he had turned on earlier. In hindsight, he was ecstatic that he had thought to get the juice flowing so many hours ago—it was going to come in very handy for the high-wattage devices. He could chose from tools that were designed to send electrical current through any part of the human anatomy—head, arms, chest, back, stomach, legs, feet, a probe for the sphincter and of course, genitals.

The second and third trips to the storage area were simply to bring out cutting devices. He had an electric handsaw and Dremel, as well as all manner of manual cutting blades. His collection had grown dramatically over the years. In the beginning he had permanently disposed of all knives used during a kill. However, as he grew more confident, there were certain blades that were more effective than others, and he started to store them for future use. The collection of over forty pieces was now laid out strategically in Simon's line of sight.

Tarryn's favorites included a samurai-type sword and a serrated foot-long knife that had never been used. The man at the outdoor megastore had told him it was intended for gutting large tuna and shark. It was perfect—not too large that it was cumbersome but not too small that it wasn't effective. He noticed that some of the razor-sharp implements still had blood on them from other victims. Tarryn scolded himself for his lack of housekeeping activities but didn't think that Simon would know the difference.

The two final trips to the back garnered his drilling devices—electric drills, an ice pick, and hole saws. As well, he gathered what he liked to refer to as skin devices—acid and gasoline. With all of his paraphernalia gathered around the room, Tarryn finally saw what he wanted from Simon—fear. His veins were popping, his eyes were bugging out of his skull, and his body was drenched with sweat. Tarryn didn't even turn toward Carmen for a fleeting glimpse into her mental state. His focus was strictly on his prey. With his back on fire, he looked Simon squarely in the eyes and stared for a full minute before he spoke.

"You're a bad man, Simon. Your wife explained to me how you like to treat women—using them for your entertainment. I myself have hurt a lot of women but never, ever, solely for the entertainment value. I think it's time for you to keep me amused for a while." Tarryn the killer was taking over. The sadistic monster was stronger than he had ever been. He was ready to show the world that he was more than just a selective killer; he could be cruel and torturous too, when it was required.

SIXTY-SIX

TARRYN PICKED UP ONE OF THE SMALLER KNIVES AND cut away Simon's clothes to expose his chest, legs, and penis. Simon winced as Tarryn attached the electrical probes to his nipples and toes. He wouldn't turn the power on quite yet but wanted Simon to know what was in store. Anticipation surged through his veins.

He had thought about torturing a human being before. By design, there had been a few victims along the way that didn't die quite as quickly as others. Sometimes, a distant rage reared its head and took over on the kill. Afterward, Tarryn felt remorse and a subtle regret. He wasn't in the business of cruelty; he was in the business of murder. There was a big difference in his mind between the two. Killing was a means to an end. Torture just prolonged the waiting of being able to put one more tick on his list of accomplishments.

Today was different. Today was all about unleashing the sadistic thoughts in his brain, and he liked it. This kill was not only for the glory, but it was also in honor of his mother. He wondered if she would mind a little extra violence thrown in for Carmen's sake. He decided, that in this case, his mother would approve.

Simon was still trying to wriggle himself free from the gurney as the first wave of pain registered in his flesh. Tarryn used the serrated blade to cut small fissures in his legs. Each cut was then filled with acid that blistered the skin and muscle below. Trickles of beet-red blood ran down Simon's calves and thighs. When the initial sting had subsided,

Tarryn took his Dremel from the table beside him and jammed the rough stone into Simon's ears and nose, ripping the flesh out in jagged chunks. More acid was applied to the fresh wounds.

Simon's body tensed into a solid mass of tissue as the acid ate into the lesions. His screams were muffled by the gag in his mouth, but Tarryn heard the fear and anguish, and it fueled him on. The blood felt like it was rocketing through his veins. With his adrenaline high, he hit his thirty-seventh victim with the first jolt of electricity through his body. Just a little taste. Simon passed out.

Tarryn checked to make sure that Simon still had a pulse. Happily, his heart was pumping away as usual. Having Simon die within the first few minutes was not going to satisfy the hunger. This needed to last. And last. And last.

With a few minutes to spare until Simon regained consciousness, Tarryn took some time to plan the next attack. Maybe he would inflict another smattering of acid, along with a few amputated fingers. Perhaps he would scalp him and hang the head of hair on Simon's foot for optimal viewing. He wanted to keep him alive and able to see what was coming next. No work on the eyes yet. No sight equaled no fear. The eyes had to stay, at least for the time being.

His mind wouldn't allow his body to turn in Carmen's direction. He could feel her presence and smell her sweat. That was all he needed. The monster was loose, but the man that had spent the day with her, still had *some* control. For now.

It was two minutes later when Simon awoke to the buzzing of the jigsaw. Tarryn grinned at Simon as he spoke.

"You have strong hands, Simon. How many times did you touch your wife in anger with them?" He paused, knowing that the answer was never going to come. "You're a big burly man, huh? I think I need to fix that."

Simon clenched his fingers in to tight fists, but he was weakened from the pain in the other parts of his anatomy. Tarryn smiled as he straightened each hand out and removed both the right and left thumbs. More acid in the wounds, a minute break, another dose of electricity, and another five-minute break. Simon passed out for the second time.

The next wave brought more cuts and abrasions, a half-inch hole drilled through the base of each foot, more acid and more electricity.

Simon didn't pass out this time, which was disappointing. Tarryn decided to move the two contact points from his playmate's feet to his scrotum. Simon's nose flared, and his breathing became more intense.

Tarryn stood over top of the gurney and watched Simon's face. "Don't hyperventilate, Simon, or you'll pass out again. I'll just wait until you wake up to continue. I have all night you know. Or option number two is that I have to find a more creative way to wake you up myself. That might hurt worse. Hey, it's up to you." Tarryn shrugged his shoulders.

Simon's body was starting to lose its vitality and strength. His mind was still strong, but Tarryn wanted more time to exact his control over the large man. Time for a break. "I'm going to give you a little rest, Simon. Today is a first on so many fronts that maybe I'll even make an exception with my plans for you. Rest up, my boy. I'll be right back."

Tarryn walked up the stairs to his kitchen to grab a bite to eat.

SIXTY-SEVEN

THE DIGITAL CLOCK ON THE STOVE SHONE BRIGHTLY IN the dark of the kitchen. Five o'clock in the morning had come so quickly. So much had happened, but the entire day had flown by in a heartbeat. As Tarryn turned on a light and opened the refrigerator, the killer was tucked neatly into a safe corner of his brain. He washed his hands of Simon's blood and made himself a ham sandwich. He wanted to have enough energy to finish the job. His shift had started at midnight the day before, and he had gotten out of bed at ten. Unbelievably, he was officially thirty-one hours without sleep. His brain was firing on all cylinders, but his body was starting to ache and show signs of fatigue.

While he ate, Tarryn grabbed a spool of wire and started to fashion his two final brands—SH 07/09 and CH 07/09. He placed his plate and cutlery in the dishwasher and wiped down the kitchen counter. He was always afraid of ants coming in the house and had become a bit of a clean freak over the years. No crumb would be left unattended, even now. His mother had been a clean fanatic too. An image of her face shone in his mind. Today was for her. Today was everything that she had ever wanted for him and more.

He examined the wire brands that would soon become his crowning glory. Simon would perhaps be equally famous. After all, he was officially number thirty-seven. He needed to finish off the job. The clock said 5:20 am. He wanted to have both of the bodies in the basement taken care of by 6:00 am at the latest. It was time to take Simon's pain to the next level. As Tarryn turned toward the basement stairs, the killer took control once again.

By 5:45 am Simon only had one finger remaining on his right hand—Tarryn had left the middle one as a mocking gesture to the police who would eventually find the body. He had three gaping wounds from the hole saw—one for the left nipple, one for the right, and another where his belly button used to reside. In addition, his scalp was burnt to a crisp, and he was covered in raw crimson cuts and angry acid burns. Tarryn immediately regretted the scalp part due to the stench of burning hair that now dominated the room. Simon had received three additional jolts of electricity, all through his scrotum, and Tarryn looked over the gurgling pile of flesh with great satisfaction. Simon had paid his debt to society and to Carmen. It was finally time to finish the job.

Tarryn's first instinct was to cut his throat and watch him bleed out. Option number two was strangulation, but the logistics were difficult due to Simon's position on the modified hospital bed. Settling on the next best thing, Tarryn began the final installment of pain.

"I think you've learned your lesson, Simon, so I'm going to stop the gratuitous torture. I've been trying to think of the best way to finish you off, and I'm a pretty creative guy. There's a bunch of different options open to me. Most of the time I like to keep things simple, so today will be no different. However, I'm going to let Carmen decide your fate. After all, you've been controlling her for so long—it's only fair that she gets her turn to be the big dog." Tarryn turned to face Carmen for the first time since he had started to work on Simon. She wasn't struggling to escape anymore, but she looked exhausted. It had been a full day for both of them.

He investigated the length of her body to see what she was feeling. Her face gave little away, but he thought that he saw a glimmer of the dark side of her—the same one that he had seen when he first picked her up. He stared at her for several minutes, trying to figure out if he was correct in his evaluation of her psyche. His mother's face flashed itself over Carmen's momentarily. He shook his head from side to side to clear the image. So many hours without sleep—he was starting to lose track of who was in the chair.

"You get to chose how he dies. Blink once if you want me to electrocute Simon through his penis, or blink twice if you want me to cut through his heart with the jigsaw." Unable to move her head, Carmen shifted her gaze to the floor.

Tarryn glanced over at Simon who was watching his wife's eyes carefully. With her vision focused on the ground for a minute more, she finally raised her eyes to meet Simon's. She stared at him for what seemed like forever before turning her stare toward Tarryn. He wondered if she was going to be able to make the decision, or if he would have to make it for her.

Simon whimpered behind his gag, and a lone tear fell across his scarred cheek. Tarryn watched as Carmen looked back at her husband, perhaps to catch a glimpse of the man that she had fallen in love with so many years before. Simon glared back with a mixture of fire and terror.

Carmen stared directly into Tarryn's eyes and blinked twice, slowly and deliberately. He was pleased—she understood. "Good choice," Tarryn whispered.

In the final moments of Simon's life, Tarryn cut through his chest with the jigsaw. It was a small handheld device, and it couldn't make it through the man's thick chest in one pass. It took several left to right movements to finish the job. Simon probably only felt the first two, but the pain he did feel was excruciating, based on the look in his eyes.

SIXTY-EIGHT

TARRYN STUDIED THE MANGLED CORPSE OF VICTIM
number thirty-seven. It was a masterpiece, if he did say so himself. The
vision was a testament to all that he had strived for over the past twenty
years. He found it arousing but not in a sexual way. Simon was a bad,
bad man, and Tarryn had killed him to avenge the pain that Carmen's
husband had inflicted not only on her, but also on the hundreds of other
women over the years. He was a fitting victim for the all-important
number thirty-seven spot. His only disappointment was that thirty-
seven was a man. He hoped that his mother would understand. To make
it official there were two more details that needed to be taken care of.

Tarryn took a black marker and wrote a three and a seven on his
victim. The top of Simon's head was charred from the earlier bout with
the blowtorch, but he found a place a little closer to the eyebrows that
was suitable. He then took the blowtorch and heated the wire that he
had fashioned in to a brand earlier in the evening, until it was white
hot. He felt along his lower back, close to his belt line until he found
an empty space on the canvas. The pain felt satisfying as the searing
hot metal hit his back. It marked a true master—a man who had
accomplished his goals. Tarryn knew he was a man of power, cunning,
intelligence, and pride.

He looked up to the ceiling, blood spatter on his face and clothes,
and imagined his mother smiling down on him from her heavenly perch

up above. He grinned so wide that his mouth might crack and spoke to her, "I did it. You can rest in peace now, Mom."

He had all but forgotten about Carmen, as his eyes filled with tears. He turned to walk upstairs and jumped a little with the shock of seeing her in the chair. Tarryn wiped the tears from his face and stared in wonder at the woman he had met just shy of twenty-four hours before. He thought back to the early morning call on the radio and how much his life had changed since that moment. It was unfathomable that one woman and her screaming feline could have made such a difference in the direction that his life would take. Originally, he thought that twenty-four hours with him would have changed her life—it turned out that *her* life had changed the course of his twenty-four hours. It was an irony that didn't go unnoticed.

Tarryn moved in closer to the chair and stroked Carmen's hair as he spoke softly, "You're a remarkable woman, Carmen. Don't you forget it. I fulfilled my destiny and in the process, removed a festering pimple of a man from the face of the earth. This morning, I would have sworn that number thirty-seven would be you. It would have been an honor to have your initials permanently part of my body. She would be proud of me ... my mother. I told you earlier that I wanted to save you, so that somehow, I could save her. It would be easy to kill you right now. I could hook up that electrical circuit or simply cut your throat with the jigsaw that I used on your husband." Tarryn drifted off, momentarily fantasizing about what might have been. "I could do that, but I won't. Mother would want you to live. You can move on and be all the things ... do all the things that I dreamt for her life. With Simon gone, there's nothing stopping you."

Tarryn leaned in, kissed her gently on the forehead, and whispered a final message in her ear. He took a step back and looked deeply into her eyes. Her body was relaxed and her face calm and serene. He wanted to kiss her on the lips one more time but knew that the gag had to remain in place. He walked toward the stairs, turning for a final glimpse of her before disappearing to the upper level of the house.

Once upstairs, Tarryn showered quickly and donned a fresh pair of jeans and a heavy T-shirt. This time he didn't need to clean up the basement floor or dispose of his soiled clothing—he just left them in a bloody mess lying on his unmade bed. Tarryn felt somewhat liberated by the lack of housekeeping that was required. He looked up at the clock as he walked in to the kitchen. It was 6:30 am. He gathered the few items that he had purchased earlier at the convenience store and walked toward the garage.

Tarryn drove the Mustang down his street for the last time. It had been a good neighborhood, with friendly people who kept to themselves for the most part. He wondered what they would have to say about him when the news finally broke. The news about his real job. The media circus would begin within the next hour. It was going to be a crazy day. Everyone and their dog would have some kind of insight into the mind of the Numbers Killer. Everyone that lived on his block would have their fifteen minutes of fame.

After driving for two miles, Tarryn pulled over to the side of the road and pulled the prepaid cell phone out of the bag. He knew the number to call, as did everyone else in the free world.

"Emergency. What is the nature of your call?" a strong female voice spoke to him.

He tried to sound panicked as he told the woman about blood-curdling screams that were coming from the house next door. He gave the woman the address, hit the end button on the phone, rolled down the passenger window, and tossed it out of the car into the ditch.

SIXTY-NINE

TARRYN WATCHED THE BREAKING NEWS STORY FROM the comfort of the twenty-four-hour truck stop, situated twenty miles outside of the city limits. It was simply decorated, like you might expect for the road warriors, but it smelled wonderfully like deep fryer grease and hairspray. The laminate tables were clean, and the coffee cups were full. They had live television, and that was all that really mattered. For the first time, Tarryn didn't care if the patrons noticed him. He sat prominently at the breakfast counter and ordered coffee, a grilled cheese sandwich, and tomato soup from the young waitress. It reminded him of Betty the babysitter and his youth.

It was 7:35 when the first newscaster broke the story. He watched as the live video feed of his home was broadcast over network television. The man on the screen was in his midforties and was wearing a black overcoat. An early-morning wind was blowing his once perfect hair across his face. Tarryn giggled to himself, wondering if the television personality knew how ridiculous the comb-over looked in the wind. It was a nice mental break. The box underneath the man's picture stated that his name was Darren Wallace.

"I am standing in front of a home that could be in your neighborhood. It's a nondescript home on a quiet, working-class street. It's a house that anyone would walk by without a second thought as to who might live inside. Channel Five has just been informed that this quiet suburban residence has hidden a dark secret. Tonight the police received an anonymous phone call complaining of screams inside. What they found, when they showed up just over an hour ago, was unbelievable. Inside police found the Numbers Killer's thirty-seventh victim and remarkably, a woman, bound and gagged but still alive. Police have not released the name of the thirty-seventh victim or the woman who escaped being number thirty-eight." The reporter paused for effect— anticipating the collective gasp of the viewers who were watching the show from the comfort of their kitchens. "As you can see, the police have secured the area and are releasing very few details at this time. However, Channel Five has discovered that the home belongs to Tarryn Cooper Love, a thirty-five-year-old cab driver. No one is saying what his involvement is in this gruesome scene, but a confidential police source spoke with us a few minutes ago and said that Mr. Love is a person of interest in the investigation. The police officer that we spoke to expressed an immediate concern with Mr. Love and noted that he could be armed and dangerous. We will report back regularly as we gather more information at the scene." The live feed was cut, and a feed of the newsroom came back into focus.

Tarryn watched as the on air newscaster recapped the breaking story and then moved on to the local traffic report. He felt relieved and disappointed at the same time. His name had been spoken on the television, which was good, but the context was all wrong. He wondered how much Carmen would remember to tell them. He wanted it to be very clear that he was number one—the most prolific selective killer in the history of the United States. He leaned back in his chair and signaled for another coffee. He wondered how long it would take until Darren Wallace would be able to explain the full extent of the damage.

The breaking news was updated every fifteen minutes. It wasn't until eight o'clock that someone managed to get a hold of his driver's license picture and plaster it up on the screen. It was a bad picture, as they all were, but it was recent enough that someone would be able to recognize his face. His hair was an inch longer in the photo, and his eyes were brighter, but it was easy to see the resemblance. It wouldn't take long now—his quest was nearing its end.

He smiled at the waitress, leaving his coffee on the counter, and walked to the men's room. He deliberately tripped on the carpet that flanked the doorway to the washrooms and cursed loudly. He turned back toward the other patrons and shrugged his shoulders in apology, allowing them to get a good long look at his face. When he returned to finish his coffee, he noticed that the mood in the diner had changed. It was exactly what he wanted. He touched the gun that he had confiscated from Carmen's purse, feeling the cold steel against his warm hand. It was still there and easily accessible. He fingered the safety latch. Tarryn wasn't sure that it would be required in the final phase of his plan, but he felt more secure with it close at hand.

Tarryn could feel the hot stares on his back. It felt like the other patrons had X-ray vision—that they could see the welts and were reading each and every one. His back was starting to burn with the intense focus. He needed to remain calm. He thought of his mother and of Carmen. None of the footage had shown Carmen's face—he wished that they would include her in some way. He wanted to see her one last time. He wondered if it wasn't better that he remembered her the way she was in the final moments. Any pictures of her now would be of the police rushing her from his house. She would be scared.

He waited patiently at the counter, sipping his coffee and reminiscing about his time with Carmen until eight thirty. It was at that point that he noticed that he was the only one left in the busy truck stop—even the waitress and cook, who were always visible, had gone missing. The time had finally come. It was his moment to shine.

Tarryn turned in his seat and got up from the counter. His hand went to the weapon in his pocket. His eyes scanned every inch of the diner, looking for the telltale signs of the ambush. He caught a glimpse of something shiny at the entrance of the building and pulled the gun from his pocket, releasing the safety as he positioned it beside his thigh.

The next three minutes seemed like they were moving as slow as New York traffic in rush hour. He heard a man on a bullhorn, who identified himself as Officer something or other, demanding that he come out of the restaurant with his hands in the air. Tarryn took a step toward the door and stopped. He looked around the diner, not for an escape route, but merely for the comforting warmth. It was dingy, but it reminded him of his childhood—it was just like the place where his mother had worked for so many years. It was home. He felt the warmth of the grilled cheese and tomato soup digesting in his belly. And images of his mother and Betty danced in his brain. Carmen was there too. Only now she was smiling at him with love in her eyes.

The sound of the bullhorn dissipated into the air. Carmen must have told them who he was. The police weren't in the business of taking "persons of interest" by force. He hoped that she would remember all of the details that he told her. He hoped that she would do exactly as he had instructed.

He took one final look at the diner and walked toward the front door. His hands were still at his sides, the gun in his right. The street was filled with the swirling red and blue lights of twenty or more police cars. They were everywhere and reminded him of jelly beans. He stood for a moment at the glass entryway, seeing the red dots of the sniper's rifles dancing on his chest. The officer with the bullhorn was yelling something, but Tarryn's ears no longer wanted to hear. He focused his vision past the barricade of cop cars looking for the cameras. He didn't see any but hoped that someone had picked up the takedown on a police scanner and were somewhere in the background filming the event. It would have been the perfect ending.

Tarryn looked up to the heavens and shut his eyes. A tear trickled down his cheek as he dropped the gun on the floor and raised his hands into the bright, sunlit sky. He wasn't going to put up a fight—preserving the canvas on his back was critical. He couldn't let them put any holes through his masterpiece.

STEP 5—BRANDING
July 14

SEVENTY

AFTER A BRIEF VISIT TO EMERGENCY FOR TREATMENT of dehydration and stress, Carmen spent the next three days explaining the details of her detainment to the police. She tried to be as accurate as possible. She told them about meeting Tarryn in his cab, being upset about giving her cat to the shelter, how kind he was at the beginning, how he took her for lunch. She told them most, but not all, of the story. Maybe 80 percent.

She omitted a few facts. She didn't tell them that she was suicidal. It seemed like a moot point, now that she no longer felt that way. She didn't tell them the specifics about her husband's business. She said that she didn't know why Tarryn had gone to get her husband or why she had been left unscathed. She told them it was a miracle.

She didn't give out all of the details of Tarryn's life. She told them about his mother's sick obsession and her drug habits, which was enough to validate her story. She didn't tell them Tarryn's final words to her and his requests. She did, however, tell them about the brands, in hope that with Tarryn's incarceration, the victims' families would finally have some peace.

She told the cops that she was sickened by what Tarryn had done. All of those people killed in the most horrendous ways. It was mind-blowing. The part that she omitted was that, although she would never be able to justify the trail of blood that he had left behind, she somehow felt sympathy for him. He never had a chance. Killing was all he ever knew. She thought of a line from a Gowan song, "A criminal mind is all I've ever had. Ask one who's known me, if I'm really so bad … I am …" Tarryn had been a monster, but she had seen something that no one else would ever see—his heart. It was as black as night and as hard as titanium, but it had a soft, caring core buried deep inside. She was living proof.

When the police were satisfied that the countless hours of questioning had given them what they wanted, Carmen was free to start living her life again. Her first stop was the shelter. They had a ten-day isolation policy before any surrendered animals could be put up for adoption. Sabre was still being observed for signs of feline distemper and upper respiratory virus. He was back in her arms within an hour, and she had completed one of the things that Tarryn had asked her to do. The other two would come later.

The media circus was unrelenting. The story was still front-page news two weeks later, as more details of Tarryn's killing spree were discovered. There was a constant lineup of reporters at Carmen's door, and her voice mail was full every day. It seemed that the public just couldn't get enough of the horror, devouring every scrap of information with a ravenous gluttony. The major networks were calling for interviews, including the queen of the small screen, Oprah. There were publishers looking to cash in on the action, offering her book deals. And to top it off, there were old co-workers of Simon's who wanted to comfort her in her time of need.

She had recognized immediately that Simon was going to need a funeral. She wasn't sure who would bother to show up. She expected the next-door neighbors and maybe a few business associates from the days when there was a legitimate business. The funeral was held a week later, after she had Simon's remains cremated. She dressed in black and mourned openly during the thirty-minute service. She wasn't sure that she was capable of tears over Simon anymore, but they had come in torrents. They might have been tears of sorrow, that it was her last good-bye to Simon, or they might have been tears of joy, that he was finally gone. Either way, it was what the media and the other attendees expected to see.

SEVENTY-ONE

AFTER THE FUNERAL, CARMEN CLOSED DOWN THE office. She hadn't been in the space for over two years. It hadn't changed, not that she expected it would. The hairs on her arms went up, just being in the four walls. She looked at the reception desk, which had been empty for so long. For an instant she returned to the days so many years before when she occupied that space and Simon would stand behind her and kiss her on the head, so proud of what they had accomplished together. Back then, she felt like the world was hers for the taking. Now she felt like the world had taken more than it had given.

She went through the door into Simon's office, grabbing files and hard drives. She did the same with the space that Gus had once called his own. Touching the files made her feel greasy and dirty. It took six trips down to her car before she had cleansed the office of its past. When she got home the files were burned, the hard drives were smashed, and Sandor's birth certificate went up in flames. She watched as the paperwork turned to embers and the last ten years of her life went up in smoke. She could finally start anew.

The house went up for sale the next day. The oh-so-caring neighbors didn't want her to leave but understood that the house held too many memories of Simon and his tragic end. A week later, with a signed offer of four million dollars on the table, she organized a trucking company to take all of her furniture and other belongings to one of the more sparsely funded women's shelters. They were extremely grateful. Simon's

Escalade was donated to the Cancer Society, and his clothing went to a local homeless shelter. The rest went into a dumpster.

With the final puzzle pieces put in place, her life in New York was over. There was nothing here for her anymore. There were no friends, no family, and no life. She wanted to go back to the only place she had ever felt safe. The bulk of the media attention was in the US and she still had citizenship in the frozen north. She wanted to go back to Canada.

Four million would buy her a nice ranch where she would get a few horses and Sabre would have a big yard where he could catch mice to his heart's content. The proceeds from the house and Simon's one–million-dollar life insurance policy would give her enough of a cushion to get her by until she could start up her own diner. As she drove the Corvette to Alberta, she was already planning the menu and the décor.

EPILOGUE

CARMEN WALKED INTO THE DINER AND WAS GREETED by a raucous cheer. The staff had decorated the walls with colorful streamers and banners that screamed "Congratulations" in foot-high, multicolored letters. Her regular customers stood and applauded along with the waitresses, cooks, and dishwashers. It was a shock but a nice surprise. Everyone came over and shook her hand vigorously, grins on their faces, and champagne on their lips.

Pam, the head waitress was the first to speak. "Well, boss, congratulations. Not only do you have a successful restaurant, but your book hit the *New York Times* best-seller list today. We couldn't be prouder of you."

The crowd cheered again and raised their glasses for a toast. As the glasses clinked and bubbles were sipped, Carmen felt the happiest she had felt in years. Her newly adopted family was all in the room. None of them were blood relatives, but as she looked at the familiar faces surrounding her, she felt like they were more than just friends. She scanned the crowd and saw Pete, the somewhat ancient rancher who drove in every morning for coffee, eggs, and bacon; Harold, the owner of the dry cleaner next door; May, her hairstylist; Linda, a new mom and regular patron; and of course, Pam, her ever loyal waitress and confidant. The list of friends was endless, as was the gratitude that she felt toward Pam for throwing the party.

Pam was a true friend in every sense of the word. When Carmen returned to High River, she was the first one to try and make her feel welcome. She owned a little postage stamp of land next to the acreage that Carmen had purchased and was a wonderful neighbor. They had instantly hit it off, and Pam was the only one who knew all of the details of her former life.

Keeping promise number two to Tarryn had been difficult. Juggling the restaurant and writing his story had been a challenge. Pam started working at the diner to help out and prodded Carmen on a regular basis, telling her to get it all in writing before she forgot anything. Carmen knew that everything was permanently etched into her brain but agreed that it was better to start and get it complete. The book, *Tarryn's Tale: For a Mother's Love*, was written over a six-month period. Once it was started, Carmen found it hard to stop. The emotional baggage came flying out onto the page. The four-hundred-and-fifty-page novel told the story of Tarryn's life and how he became the Numbers Killer. It was the truth, as she knew it—well, at least 80 percent of it. Simon's business ventures were kept out of it, as were her own skeletons. The rest was factual, raw, and real.

When the rumors got around that she had written a book, the entire community had jumped on board. When they realized that it was not a fictional account, they gathered around her and embraced her even more. After the initial shock wore off, it was business as usual—one of the many benefits to small-town living.

Three publishers had a bidding war over the novel, and she had finally settled on a five-hundred-thousand-dollar advance. The highly anticipated book had hit the best seller's list in the first week. Not wanting to profit over Tarryn's crimes, all proceeds from the book went to women's shelters across North America.

The book was Tarryn's legacy, but the diner was her dream. It was, at least in her estimation, the perfect mix of homey and sophistication. The warm glow of the small town radiated in every corner of the restaurant. Ed's picture hung proudly behind the counter as did one of her parents. Their images gave her comfort and a sense of pride. Her parents would have liked the diner, and Ed would have loved the patrons.

After the party, Carmen thanked everyone for coming and gave Pam a big hug. "Thanks for everything. I have to go now. I still have one more promise to keep."

Pam smiled at her and walked her to the door. She knew that today was the end of another chapter in Carmen's life. "Do you want me to come and help?" she asked.

"No, I have to do this on my own. But thanks. You're a really good friend." They embraced again, Pam hugging a little tighter than before.

Carmen turned on the lights in her ranch-style house and was greeted by Sabre's tail wrapping around her leg. She leaned down to stroke his soft fur before walking into the kitchen. She was afraid of what was going to happen next. She didn't know what to expect. She hoped that it wasn't going to be as bad as her imagination had conjured up.

She thought back to Tarryn's final words to her, and a chill went down her spine. She had completed two of the three tasks. In a few moments number three would be finished and she would have repaid him for giving her back her life. She felt his warm breath on her ear once again as she remembered his whispers, "I'm saving your life today, but there are a few things that I want you to do for me in return. Number one—go get your cat and live your life. Never look back. Go and do whatever makes you happy. Number two—tell the world who I am. Remind them how successful I was and tell the story of how much I loved my mother. And number three—remember me—not the killer but the man, and know that I love you."

Carmen had already fashioned the wire into the symbol that she wanted. It was simple TCL 07/09—his initials and the date that he gave her back her life. She heated the homemade branding iron with a blowtorch, just as she had seen Tarryn do two years before. She looked up to the heavens and said the only thing she could think of, "Thank you, Tarryn Cooper Love. I will never forget."

She screamed in agony as the hot metal ate into the top of her arm. The pain was blinding, and she had to focus to stop herself from passing out. It was everything that her imagination had come up with—times ten. The smell of burning flesh made her gag as she removed the brand from her arm. Her skin tore back and continued to burn for a few more seconds on the wire. She collapsed on the floor and cried.

Tarryn Cooper Love pled guilty to thirty-seven murders and was sentenced by the state of New York to be put to death in the electric chair. His execution is scheduled for September 24, 2012. He has told the media that he has already chosen his final words—they will be the same as Ted Bundy's—"I'd like you to give my love to my family and friends." If his mother were still alive, she would be proud.

ACKNOWLEDGMENTS

A big thank you to my family and friends who have supported me over the years and helped to shape this novel (while on their couches, in their beds, and in one case, on a train): my Mom and Marty; Tania and Jerry; Stacy and Lin; Ekim (Mike); Pete and Joan; Mary C.; Don H.; and finally, Bob and Kathy.

And a particularly big high five to Steve for the fantastic cover graphics.